# It's a

# Mad, Mad

# Murder

# It's a
# Mad, Mad
# Murder

## A Maddie Montgomery
## Mystery

# Cindy Vincent

**Whodunit Press**

Houston

It's a Mad, Mad Murder

A Maddie Montgomery Mystery

Published by Whodunit Press

A Division of Mysteries by Vincent, LLC

For information, please contact:

CustomerCare@mysteriesbyvincent.com

ISBN: 978-1-932169-57-7

Printed in the United States of America

# Dedication

*To Rob, my wonderful husband,*
*expert encourager, constant cheerleader, ready reader,*
*and a guy who really knows his way around the kitchen.*
*Yes, those kitchen appliances really are "power tools!"*
*I couldn't do this without you.*

# Chapter One

"Blaze needed a weapon and she needed one fast. The crash of shattering glass from the floor above had already alerted her to the incoming danger. Yet before she went in search of some implement of self-defense, she took a protective glance at the chocolate soufflé rising nicely in the oven. Of all the rude, inconsiderate times for a mass murderer to break into her home . . . why did he have to do it while she was filming a chocolate chip cookie and chocolate soufflé segment for her ever popular blog? It was bad enough that he was breaking in to kill her. But breaking in while she was recording one of her cooking videos? Well, that was just bad manners.

Annoyed, she flung her copper-colored hair over her shoulder and quickly grabbed her chef's knife. It was long enough and sharp enough to cut off a man's head.

'Cliché,' she muttered aloud as she returned the knife to the rack. 'I used a knife last week when I solved yet another murder and caught yet another killer. No, sometimes a girl just needs to mix it up a little.'

With that, she smiled and grabbed a handheld mixer. 'Now this has possibilities . . . and so does this,' she added as she picked up a cellophane-wrapped roll of chocolate chip *cookie dough that she'd just pulled from the freezer, having made it the night before.*

*But she'd barely spoken the words when Count McMatton, the man responsible for the town's latest crime wave, came thumping down the stairs to her kitchen. He held a gun in one hand and pointed it right at her.*

*Blaze rolled her green eyes. 'How did you ever manage to commit so many murders with all that stomping around? Clearly, stealth is not your strong suit.'*

*Count McMatton flashed his most charming smile. 'Most of the women told me they got tingles when they recognized the sound of my very masculine footsteps. Of course, that was right before they realized our courtship had technically come to an end, considering I was there to kill them. Imagine their surprise.' His thickly accented voice boomed across the kitchen.*

*Blaze glared at him and put an index finger to her lips. 'Shush! Mind keeping it down, your eminence? I've got a soufflé cooking here.'*

*Which only made him laugh. Uproariously.*

*And in the split second that he closed his eyes, tilted his head back, and let out a laugh that emanated from the depths of his washboard belly, Blaze got him right between the eyes—with the rock-hard roll of frozen-solid cookie dough. She'd thrown it in a spiral worthy of any college quarterback.*

*Then she pounced on him with the handheld mixer, hitting him with the whirring beaters in a left hook that knocked him out cold. No doubt, he'd stay that way for a while—at least until the police arrived to collect him and his confession that she'd just unwittingly filmed.*

*'Never forget,' she announced to his inert form on the floor. 'Every good kitchen is loaded with lethal weapons!'*

*Naturally, he didn't respond, considering he was unconscious. And of course, that also meant he didn't notice when she tied him up with cooking twine. When she had finished, she glanced again at the oven and at her perfect soufflé that was still standing. Soon she would be serving it to the man of her dreams, who, according to her oven clock, should be showing up at any moment.*

*She sighed with satisfaction. 'When Detective Steele sees that I've got the killer trussed up like my herb-butter-infused Thanksgiving turkey, and when he takes a bite of my chocolate soufflé, I just know he's going to say . . . whir . . . whir . . . hum . . .'"*

"Whir, whir, hum?" I, Maddie Montgomery, repeated as I stared at my computer. "Wait a minute . . . Detective Steele would never say 'whir, whir, hum.' Where did that come from?"

I blinked a few times and shook my head before I realized the source of those words. Or rather, those *sounds.* It was coming from right outside the bay window of my second-story home office. I turned to eyeball the object that had broken my writer's trance and jarred me out of the world of Blaze McClane, the culinary crime solver in my best-selling mystery series. At that moment, I was probably just as annoyed as Blaze had been when Count McMatton had interrupted her work. Not only was I a mere chapter shy of typing my two most favorite words in the English language—"The End"—but I was also just pages away from hitting a major milestone. Yes, finishing this newest title, *Soufflés and Assassinations,* meant I would have written my thirtieth book.

And hit my deadline.

Still, there was no ignoring the hovering craft just outside my window. Especially when it blinked its little lights at me a few times, most likely to make sure it had my attention.

Truth be told, I thought it was kind of cute. "You again, Evinrude?" I said to the marvel of modern engineering that reminded me of a firefly. A big, metallic firefly.

Also known as a drone.

And one that was carrying my mail in its clutches. Exactly like it had on so many other days when the mailman didn't bother with pesky little things like putting the right mail in the right box. As near as I could tell, he figured it was good enough to randomly toss the envelopes and flyers into the various boxes of our cluster mailbox at the end of our cul-de-sac. After that, he left it up to the neighbors to sort things out.

Which is exactly what we did.

Now I simply waited for the inevitable phone call that always accompanied Evinrude's visit. And sure enough, while my sleek black cat, Agatha, and my longhaired orange cat, Ellery, jumped onto the window seat, hoping to make mincemeat of that drone, my phone started to play my ringtone—the theme song from Peter Gunn. Normally, I kept my phone turned off while I was working, but since I was going to a funeral later today, I left it on, in case someone needed a ride. The display showed "Unknown Caller."

Which meant this caller was actually pretty "well-known" to me.

It was my almost-elderly neighbor, Spencer Poe. "Good morning, Mrs. Montgomery," came his gravelly voice when I answered.

"Good morning to you, too, Spencer. You know you can call me Maddie." I pried myself out of my desk chair and stretched joints that were stiff from sitting too long.

"Thank you, but I would never show such disrespect to your late husband, the Colonel. And please do accept my apologies if I am interrupting your work. But this, I fear, could not wait. I thought it best that you receive this news prior to attending the funeral."

"News?" I joined Agatha and Ellery at the window and watched the drone circle around and down toward the front walkway.

"Starting with your mail, I am afraid."

I scratched the kitties behind their ears. "Thank you for sending it over again. Though you don't have to deliver it by drone. I'd be happy to send my son over to pick it up. Or you could swing by, since you only live a couple of doors down and across the street."

"You can never be too careful, Mrs. Montgomery," came his usual reply. "The postal service is run by the U.S. government. And I do not find it coincidental that they perpetually deliver your mail to me, hence trying to force me to come out of my house and bring it to you. It is all the time they need to secretly search my home and plant a few bugs. No, it is much safer to deliver it by drone."

"But Spencer . . . I thought you used to work for the government." I turned from the window and took a quick visual survey of my office, at the wide array of trophies, award plaques, mementoes, and photographs that were sitting on every available surface or hanging on the walls. Though not on the wall behind my desk, which only displayed framed covers of every one of my novels.

"All the more reason to take extra precautions," Spencer went on.

As always, my first inclination was to ask him for specifics about his government work, but I'd learned long ago not to bother. He was a pro when it came to dodging the details of his past, details that were sketchy at best.

But, quite frankly, that was *his* business and none of mine.

"Well, I appreciate your bringing my mail to me. No matter how it gets here." Phone in hand, I moved across the hardwood floors to the hallway, and then to the Juliet balcony above my curved staircase.

He sighed. "You may not appreciate it so much when you read the letters on top."

His words caused a twinge at my temple, and I quickly raced down the stairs, my bare toes digging into the carpet runner of the steps. "Spencer, surely you didn't read my mail."

I trotted across the front entryway and opened the oversized front door made from heavy, Brazilian hardwood. I got there in time to see the drone hovering about a foot off the ground before it maneuvered gracefully to the brick-outlined walkway and dropped my mail. Then I waited until the tiny craft had returned to an altitude of about seven feet, about fourteen inches above my head, before I stepped outside. Leaning down, I retrieved the various letters and flyers and such.

"I did not *open* anything, of course," he went on. "But naturally I had everything x-rayed and scanned. To make sure there were no microdots or toxins inside the envelopes. For your safety as well as mine. As a result, I did end up reading the contents of the two letters. Inadvertently."

"Umm . . . okay . . ." I started to say, not completely sure what the proper response was to someone doing a full-scale inspection of my mail.

"The first letter is from the HOA," he went on. "They are citing you for a trashcan violation. They claim it is visible from the street."

My jaw dropped. "That trashcan has been in the same spot for years—hidden behind a thick evergreen hedge. It's certainly not visible!" I walked back inside my house and shut the door, probably a little harder than necessary.

"Not without an infrared camera anyway," Spencer informed me. "And even then, it is hardly distinguishable."

"Huh? You've got a . . .?" I started to ask and then thought better of it. "What's the second letter?"

"It is from your agent, Mrs. Montgomery. I regret to inform you, but your publisher has folded and closed their doors. Permanently, it appears. And your agent is terminating your relationship."

My heart skipped a beat or two. "Paumpass House Publishing has gone belly-up? How can that be? Besides, I've got a contract . . ." I stepped into my ornate dining room and dropped the mail onto the table.

Then I picked up the letter from my agent, ripped it open, and used my speed-reading skills to digest the whole thing. And sure enough, Spencer had been right.

"I am terribly sorry, Mrs. Montgomery."

By now my head was starting to spin, and my neighbor's voice sounded like it was coming from far away. How could this be happening? It must be some huge mistake. Or maybe I was in the middle of a dream. Last I knew, my publisher was doing well, and so were my book sales. So why had they suddenly gone out of business? And why was my agent letting me go, too? I was, after all, a best-selling author. None of it made any sense.

Though one thing was for sure, I needed to get to the bottom of this. Mostly because writing books was how I made my living. And the idea of starting over in a new career at age forty-eight sent my blood pressure soaring.

"Spencer, I've got to go now," I managed to breathe. "I need to make some phone calls."

"Not so fast, if you please," he said. "I have an even more pressing matter that I need to discuss with you."

*More pressing than losing my livelihood?*

"Well, okay . . . " I glanced out one of the floor-to-ceiling windows in my dining room and watched the drone gain altitude.

Just as my seventeen-year-old son, Parker, came from the kitchen to see Evinrude buzz toward the street. "Mr. Poe has the coolest drone. I wonder if he'd let me borrow it sometime."

I covered the mouthpiece of my phone. "Maybe you could ask him. *Later*."

Parker responded by pointing to the replica Paddington Station clock on the wall in my front entryway. "'Later' is good, Mom. Because we're gonna be late for Mr. Rathburn's funeral."

He raised dark eyebrows above dark eyes, which looked even darker thanks to the black suit he had on. He'd inherited both his suit and his good looks from his father. He'd also inherited his father's military punctuality.

I gave him a quick nod and made a beeline for my bedroom, which was decorated in all the calm colors of a Bermuda bay—blue, white, and seafoam, with just a hint of pink. Though thoughts of such a serene setting escaped me at the moment, and I felt more like I was sitting on a beach with a hurricane headed straight for me.

Even so, the fact that my life had suddenly taken a nosedive was no excuse to be late for a funeral honoring someone *else's* life. After all, June Rathburn and her husband, Randall, were the sweetest neighbors a person could ever ask for. Randall's death had come as a shock to us all. June had been hoping that he'd retire in the next few years, and she'd been looking forward to traveling and just spending time together.

Now that time would never come.

And the very least I could do was be there *on time* to support her. As a widow myself, I knew exactly what she was going through, and how much friends and family could ease the pain of grieving when it came to the loss of a beloved spouse.

So I put Spencer on speakerphone, ran to my closet, and pulled out a black dress.

"I have a favor to ask of you, Mrs. Montgomery," Spencer went on, getting to the point.

"Sure," I murmured as I wriggled into the dress. "Anything." I grabbed my go-to black pumps.

"I would like you to look into Randall's murder," he said so matter-of-factly that it was almost like someone talking about the weather. "Investigate, if you would."

I gasped and dropped the shoes. "Randall's . . . what? Murder? Did you say murder?"

Agatha and Ellery materialized from out of nowhere and gave my shoes a good sniffing over. Almost like they were already on the case and hunting for clues.

"Yes, Mrs. Montgomery. That is exactly what I said," he assured me.

"But Randall wasn't murdered. He had a heart attack while he was driving. And he ran off the road and into a light pole." I petted the kitties and slipped my feet into the taller-than-I'd-remembered black pumps.

"Of course, that is how the killer staged it. To look like a tragic accident. But mark my words—Randall was murdered. And if the killer is not brought to justice, I assure you, there will be more and more murders. Right here in Abbott Cove, Texas."

My heart started to gallop as I hurried into my marble-accented bathroom and ran a brush through my not-so-naturally blonde hair. "Have you called the police?"

Spencer sighed. "Yes, but they refused to listen to me with any sort of seriousness."

Okay, I guess I wasn't terribly surprised by this. I had a pretty good idea that Spencer may have been one of their regular callers, so to speak. Probably to report whatever his conspiracy du jour happened to be. Though no doubt, he would have used an alias and a blocked number. If not a rerouted call. And much as I appreciated my thoughtful neighbor who always made sure I got my mail, well, his view of what went on in the world was most likely a world away from what was really going on.

Not that I had room to talk, considering *I* made up stories for a living. But now I really had to wonder about Spencer's idea that Randall's death had been no accident.

I glanced in the mirror and swiped a red lipstick across my lips. "Spencer, even if Randall was murdered, I'm not sure I could help."

"Of course you could, Mrs. Montgomery. After all, you are a mystery writer."

"As of today, I'm a *former* mystery writer," I sort of sputtered, fighting back tears.

"Now, now," he said in the voice of a calming parent. "Your current situation is simply a setback. Perhaps independent publishing is a viable option for you. I have heard it is the wave of the future."

The mere thought of publishing on my own made me feel like I'd been dunked into ice-cold water. For decades, I'd basked in the shelter of a literary agent and a big publisher who'd handled almost all the aspects of the industry for me. Which freed me up to focus solely on writing my books. I had no doubt that going "Indie,"—and taking care of everything from the editing to the printing—probably came with a mountainous learning curve that I didn't exactly want to scale at this point in my life.

"You have spent years researching and learning investigative techniques," Spencer went on. "And no doubt, you also understand the psychology of suspects. So who better to solve a real-life mystery than you, Mrs. Montgomery? And because the police have refused to delve into this case, you will not have to worry about jurisdictional issues. You will have free reign to investigate. So do not underestimate yourself. You are perfect for solving this crime."

*If there was a crime . . .*

"Maybe we could talk about this later," I told him. "After the funeral? Because I'm going to be late if I don't hurry up. In the meantime, I promise you I'll give it some thought."

Which was probably the understatement of the year. After all, I have been blessed with an imagination that is like twelve different jets taking off in twelve different directions at the same time.

All at top speed.

The same speed that the rest of my life was apparently careening out of control.

I heard a buzzing sound through the phone, and I knew the drone had returned home. "Mark my words, Mrs. Montgomery," Spencer said firmly. "Randall was murdered. And we owe it to him to bring his killer to justice. So when you go to the funeral today, I ask that you use your keen observational skills and your writer's mindset. See if you don't pick up on any suspicious undertones."

Suspicious undertones. Words that were catnip to any mystery writer's ears.

That meant, like it or not, I was now on the lookout for a murderer.

# Chapter Two

Much as I hate to admit it, I wasted valuable seconds just standing there in a daze, right after I got off the phone with my neighbor, Spencer Poe. I wasn't sure what fazed me more—the concept that one of my neighbors had been murdered, or the sudden news that my writing career was now kaput. To top it off, I couldn't wrap my head around the idea of actually investigating a murder.

For *real*.

That's because I only *wrote* about murder, and in a fictitious sense at that. Though it was funny how many readers believed that mystery writers also solved crimes on the side. As a hobby. You know, something to kill time between all those black-tie parties and private-jet trips to Bermuda.

If only that were true.

Though I thought Spencer would have known better, and getting a request from him to solve a murder mystery seemed pretty unusual. Even for him. Sure, he may have been eccentric, but he also had a military background and he'd worked for the government in some capacity. So he understood that I wasn't a real investigator.

And that brought me back to another point: Was there even anything to investigate?

As far as I knew, Randall's death was pretty black-and-white. Open-and-shut. Cut-and-dried. And I really had to wonder why Spencer thought otherwise.

In fact, I couldn't *stop* wondering about it when I joined Parker in my navy blue SUV and backed out of the driveway. A layer of yellow dust blanketed the sidewalks and cars on this bright March afternoon, since it was the time of year in the greater Houston area known as "pollen season." And with trees of every genus and species imaginable either leafing out or adding another layer of needles, pollen was in the air.

And everywhere else.

But on the plus side, the vivid green of the fresh new leaves brought an intense beauty to the tree-lined streets and parks and yards of Abbott Cove. Especially since azaleas—in hues of white, pink, red, and purple—had made their annual spring appearance.

Yet I hardly even noticed all that glory on the fifteen-minute trip to the church. While the small city of Abbott Cove was a bedroom community of Houston, the white-knuckle traffic of the major metropolitan area didn't usually affect our neck of the woods. Except when commuters left early in the morning and returned in the evening. Which, generally speaking, wasn't a wonderful time to be on the road.

And it was a good thing we didn't have an abundance of traffic this afternoon, because I didn't even realize I was driving on autopilot until my son touched my arm. "Umm . . . Mom . . . you just went twenty feet past the church parking lot. Now thirty . . . Now forty . . ."

"Oh." A quick glance over my shoulder told me he was right. Sure enough, thanks to all the issues vying for the top spot in my brain, I had missed the lot to the church. Despite the fact that we attended this church nearly every Sunday.

So I pulled into a driveway a few doors down, backed out, and got headed in the right direction again. Minutes later, Parker and I raced into the large building with huge cathedral ceilings. We scooted into the middle of a pew about ten rows from the back. Just in the nick of time.

I glanced at my son who was sitting soldier straight and not displaying an ounce of emotion—something that wasn't exactly normal for Parker.

I gave him a little nudge. "Are you okay?"

He shrugged. "Yeah, Mom. It's not like it's my first funeral. Are you okay?"

"Dandy," I told him, a word that never failed to elicit his usual goofy grin.

And I was glad to see that grin. Because I'd really been concerned about how Parker might feel today, with us going to the funeral of a neighbor. Especially since it had barely been two years since he'd attended his own father's funeral. Of course, I was mostly worried about how my son would react when he saw the teary-eyed members of Randall's family, including June. I was afraid that being so "up close and personal" might bring back painful memories for Parker.

At the same time, I also knew the importance of rituals like funerals. They gave family and friends some comfort and a sense of closure. So in the end—no pun intended—I decided it was better for my son to come with me, to formally say goodbye to the man who had lived two doors down from us.

But now that we were here, Parker hardly seemed daunted by it at all, and as I glanced around the church, I could see why. For a moment or two, I wasn't even sure we were at a funeral. Silk flowers and wide ribbons were tied to the ends of the pews, and scented candles filled the windowsills. Then there were the huge bunches of real hydrangeas that cascaded from silver stands at the entrance to the sanctuary and at the altar. The whole place was but a couple of steps away on the color wheel from the wedding we'd attended in this very church less than a week ago.

The wedding of June and Randall's only child, Tiffany.

On that day, the decorations had been in pink and pearl, while today's ceremony sported varying shades of blue and purple.

Which included the high-dollar gown of the former mother of the bride. In fact, I drew in a surprised breath when I spotted June coming down the aisle in a stunning, ombré-dyed chiffon gown, one that started out a deep navy at the hemline and gradually turned to a rich purple by the time it reached the plunging neckline. I'm guessing she had the modern marvel of foundation undergarments to thank for making her ample, voluptuous figure look positively svelte. To top it off, her normally silver hair had been dyed blue with purple highlights, in keeping with the color scheme of the funeral.

Personally, I'd barely been able to function during my early days of widowhood. Yet June had managed to coordinate a ceremony so elaborate that the only thing missing was a horse-drawn hearse.

And for all I knew, it had pulled up outside shortly after we'd entered the church.

I had to say, I was truly in awe of the way she'd put an event like this together in such a short time. Not exactly the easiest thing to do, especially when a person was operating under the heavy weight of grief.

I watched as the new widow took the hands of a woman a few pews back. "Darlin', how are you?" June drawled before she flashed a bright smile. "Thank you for coming. My goodness, we didn't even see you at the wedding! If I'd've known it was going to take a funeral to get you to the church, why, I would've bumped off Randall years ago."

This was followed by a stunned silence from the woman who seemed to be racking her brain for whatever words could be considered an appropriate response to June's comment. Finally, the poor woman managed to stammer, "I'm . . . I'm . . . so sorry . . . for your loss."

Whereby June blinked a few times and moved on to another attendee. "You look fabulous!" she said to the next woman. "Have you lost weight? Don't forget Bunco in a couple of weeks."

And on it went.

Eventually, she spotted me as she moved up the aisle. "Maddie, darlin'! So glad you could make it. I'm giving Randall a pretty good send-off, don't you think?" She looked right at me.

And right through me.

That's when I knew—her doctor had probably given her something to ease the pain. The emotional pain, that is. Though apparently, the medication had the side effect of turning someone into a cross between Martha Stewart and Coco Chanel.

A medication I might want to ask my doctor about.

June turned her glassy-eyed gaze up the aisle and moved on to another "guest," as it were, smiling and giggling as she went. She was followed by a very surly and recently turned redhead Tiffany, who clearly had *not* been given the same medication as her mother. Tiffany grabbed huge handfuls of purple petals from a basket that she carried in the crook of her arm. Then she threw those petals to the ground with such force that I feared they might become permanently fused to the carpet. I'd seen flower bearers at a funeral before—solemn young women who carried flowers to the altar ahead of the casket—but I'd never actually seen a funerary flower girl, of sorts. And clearly Tiffany was not pleased with her role. It didn't help that she was petite and had a Shirley Temple-like quality to her, making her appear childlike.

Especially when she stood next to her tall husband, Aiden, who seemed completely oblivious as he wandered along behind the two women. He kept his head down, with his silky, shoulder-length brown hair tucked behind his ears and his thumbs moving furiously atop his cell phone. In fact, his thumbs were almost a blur. If he'd been playing a musical instrument I would have thought him a virtuoso. He was so intent on his phone that he even overshot the front pew when June and Tiffany took their seats. But Tiffany quickly hissed at her new better half, and he managed to glance up for a second before he plopped in beside her.

With the family seated, next came the musical intro from the church's enormous pipe organ, and I figured that was our cue to stand. Though I wasn't entirely sure after I recognized the song that was now being pounded out. And I had to admit, hearing the Bee Gees' tune, *Stayin' Alive*, ringing through the rafters was another funerary first for me.

I glanced to the back of the room and spotted a couple of large men who had started to roll a mahogany casket up the aisle. Or maybe I should say, men who were *trying* to roll the casket up the aisle. Unfortunately, the wheels of their trolley kept slipping and sliding across the huge mounds of purple petals on the floor. And before long, one of the front wheels sort of sucked up a cluster of those petals, and the trolley dragged along like the cart I always seemed to get at the grocery store. You know, the one where a front wheel goes renegade and refuses to cooperate with the other three?

Parker stirred beside me. "Mom, they've got their center of gravity way off. And the front wheel hasn't got enough torque. That casket is going down."

With those words, my tall son leaped out of the pew and ran for the end zone, so to speak. And not a second too soon. Because the men wheeling the casket made a major miscalculation and nearly sent it soaring straight into a pew. From where I stood, I could see the sheer terror on the faces of the octogenarians sitting in that row as they nearly got crushed by the huge mahogany box aimed right at them. In fact, the entire congregation saw it and all gasped at once, adding an odd effect to the Bee Gees' number being cranked out by the organist. Thankfully, Parker arrived in time to avert what probably would have been a major news story on every Houston TV channel that night.

*Dead Man Critically Injures Five, film at 11:00.*

After Parker helped to fix the "center of gravity" problem, he leaned over and pulled the petals from the wheel, all the while lecturing the funeral home men about basic physics. And having been on a National Science Fair winning team, my son knew what he was talking about.

Once the wheel was rolling freely, Parker came back to join me while the men got the casket headed in the right direction again. But they were forced to put on the brakes just seconds later, after being cut off by a tall woman with three kids in tow and a camera hanging from her neck. A camera with a very large lens, I might add. I immediately recognized the woman as my neighbor from the other side of our cul-de-sac, Betty Kraukpott. She and her bunch thumped and stumbled and banged their way into the pew in front of us. The other occupants in the row quickly vacated their spots, scooting out the side aisle and scurrying closer to the front to find seats.

Betty had barely landed when she put the camera to her face, slipped off the lens cap, and began to get her money's worth from the camera's high-speed shutter. Apparently, this was my day for funeral firsts, since I'd never witnessed someone actually taking photos at a funeral before. Was it possible she planned to use them for one of her blogs?

Having read a few of Betty's do-it-yourself blog posts, I could just imagine the write-up to go along with those pictures. It would probably be along the same lines as her post about dyeing your own hair with whatever bottles happened to be in the bargain bin. Regardless of the hair colors inside those very bottles.

As if on cue, she swung her long, blonde-brown-red-black-pink-and-blue hair over her shoulder and tipped her head toward me. "Have you heard the latest? Rumor has it that Randall had a heart attack after he got the bill for Tiffany's wedding. Everyone knew he had a bad heart," she said in a stage whisper.

Just as Randall's high-gloss, high-dollar casket squeaked on by.

Well, if he wasn't happy with the cost of the wedding, he probably wouldn't have been happy with the cost of his funeral.

Without waiting for me to respond, Betty turned her attention back to her brood who were all under ten and all wearing "repurposed" clothing of every color imaginable. They had gone into a game of "Mom, he's touching me," and kept it up until the casket finally arrived at the altar.

Then two more large men jumped in to help position the casket beneath a huge disco ball and between a couple of gigantic flower arrangements. And directly in front of the big-screen-TV-size photo of a very young Randall. The picture showed him in his disco years, wearing a polyester leisure suit and plenty of gold chains. All while striking a perfect John Travolta pose.

I leaned over to Parker. "One day when I die, make sure you use my author's headshot at my funeral."

"Seriously, Mom? That picture's like a hundred years old."

"A hundred?" I repeated a lot louder than I'd intended to, just as elderly, white-haired Pastor Livingston took his place next to a flower arrangement and turned to face the crowd.

"Dearly beloved," he started, only seconds before he let out an explosive sneeze. Then he dabbed at watery eyes, blinked at his prayer book, and went on. "We are gathered here together in the sight of almighty God to witness the union of . . ." He sneezed again and glanced at the casket, whereby recognition dawned on his face. "Oh, I'm so terribly sorry. That was last week's ceremony," he mumbled as he quickly flipped to another page in his book.

I heard a cough from somewhere behind me, and I turned to see an odd-looking gentleman with long, gray hair sitting a few rows back on the other side. His sunglasses, baseball cap, and ratty sweatshirt seemed strangely out of place for a ceremony like this, and I wondered if he was one of Randall's old buddies. But then the man lowered his glasses and peered out at me, raising his brows. Just enough for me to recognize him, despite his crazy disguise.

Spencer Poe.

I had to say, I was pretty surprised to see that my normally groomed-to-military-perfection neighbor had left his house, given his fear that the government might jump at the chance to bug his place. Then again, I also knew that he and Randall had been pals, and, "unusual" as Spencer might seem at times, I knew he'd never disrespect a friend by missing his funeral.

Spencer was seated directly behind one of our other neighbors, Gia Delvecchio, a recent transplant from Trenton. New Jersey, that is, not Texas. Gia had successfully stuffed herself into a leopard-print wrap dress that was clearly testing the fabric's spandex content by stretching it beyond its likely intended capacity. Though her wildly wavy, chestnut hair—which almost seemed to be a life-form in and of itself—hid lots of her upper body and some of her face. Unfortunately, it didn't hide the flask that she was trying to conceal in her cleavage.

Gia smiled and gave me a little wave, and I returned the gesture with a smile and a wave of my own. Then I caught a barely perceptible nod from Spencer, before he tilted his head toward the front of the church in what I could only guess was a motion meant for my benefit.

Pastor Livingston glanced out to the farthest corners of the nave. "While Randall's death is a terrible loss for us all, just know that he is at peace now. He has gone on home, on to Heaven. How do I know this? From the final words that he spoke before he passed from this life. Words that were later relayed by a Good Samaritan who tended to him after his accident. Yes, as he was leaving his earthly body, he uttered two important phrases. First, he said, 'It's yellow.' That's right, our dear Randall was a law-abiding citizen to the very end. He did *not* run a red light when he drove through that intersection. No, he passed through on a perfectly legal, *yellow* light." Here the pastor paused and made eye contact with Tiffany, as though trying to drive home a point about the habits of good driving.

Once she had sufficiently scowled at him, he continued on. "And Randall's last words as he passed from this world to the next were, 'It's snowing.' Those of us who knew Randall knew that he loved the snow, having grown up in Montana. Though he moved to Texas as a young lad, he always remembered the beauty of winter. Yes, his final words demonstrate just that—that he has gone on to that winter wonderland in the sky, and it should bring us all nothing but comfort."

His words made me do a double take. Winter wonderland in the sky? Wasn't that essentially . . . a blizzard? While I appreciated the pastor's attempts to add imagery to his sermons, sometimes I had trouble with the literal meaning of his descriptions.

But there was something else about what he'd said that bothered me. Something I couldn't quite put my finger on. Something significant.

Pastor Livingston continued on with, "Randall's widow has requested a special musical tribute from our choir." With those words, he glanced at the huge flower arrangement beside him and sneezed with the force of Hurricane Harvey roaring into the Gulf.

He sneezed a second time as organ music practically burst forth from the back of the church, and the members of the choir got to their feet. And while they belted out Gloria Gaynor's *I Will Survive* from the late 70s, and the disco ball began to turn, Pastor Livingston's words rolled over and over in my mind.

Or more specifically, Randall's last words. "It's yellow," and, "It's snowing."

Somehow those phrases seemed familiar to me. But why?

And then it finally dawned on me. I'd been a mystery writer long enough to know plenty about poisons and overdoses and such. In fact, it was my business to know about these things. At least, it *had* been my business. Whatever the case, I knew that people who took a medication called Digoxin—or rather, people who had too much Digoxin in their system, resulting in Digoxin toxicity—often experienced visual hallucinations, and they sometimes described the world as looking yellow. To top it off, plenty of them claimed to see snow as well.

Could Randall have died from a Digoxin overdose? And if so, was it possible that he'd been given that dosage without his knowledge?

In other words, had Randall been poisoned?

My pulse started to race as I glanced back at Spencer Poe. While Gia sipped from her flask and danced in the row in front of him, obviously overtaken by the music, Spencer glanced my way, his mouth set in a firm line. If he had wanted me to look for "suspicious undertones" today, well, this was one funeral that was a virtual winter wonderland in the sky full of them.

# Chapter Three

All of a sudden, my heart started to pound like I was running the last mile of a marathon. Not that I'd ever *actually* run a marathon, but I'm sure you get my drift. Of course, I instantly thought of what my neighbor, Betty, had said right before she took her seat—everyone knew that Randall had a bad heart. And since Digoxin is a common heart medication, I wondered if Randall's doctor had prescribed it for him.

Even so, there was a big difference between taking a prescribed dose of Digoxin and taking too much of it. If Randall *had* been on the medication, it was possible that he'd accidentally ingested an extra dose. Maybe he forgot that he'd already taken a pill and took another one by mistake.

But it was also possible that someone had *given* him an additional dose. Or doses. Secretly. With Randall being none the wiser. Meaning, someone might have known about his prescription and used his own pills to poison him. And since death by Digoxin appeared to be nothing more than a heart attack, no one would have been too suspicious if a person with a bad heart died of . . . oh, yes, that's right . . . a heart attack.

No one except for my already overly suspicious neighbor, Spencer Poe. Which made me think of a variation on the old adage about being paranoid. In Spencer's case, just because he was suspicious about *everything* didn't mean he wasn't right about *some* things.

Yet if someone wanted to murder Randall, where would they have gotten the idea to use Digoxin? It probably wasn't something the average Joe or Josephine even knew about.

Or did they?

That's when it dawned on me—I didn't need to look any farther than my own home library for the answer. In fact, any avid mystery reader would know about the drug. I had chosen Digoxin poisoning as the cause of death for one of my own books, *A Heart for Homicide*. And both Agatha Christie and Dorothy Sayers had used a similar drug, Digitalis, in murder mysteries long before I was born. Not to mention, the countless TV mysteries and assorted novels where those very meds had been slipped to some unsuspecting victim, hence sending them to their maker way ahead of schedule. So if someone had been intent on bumping off poor Randall, they could've easily figured out that doubling the dose of his own medication was a simple way to do the dirty deed.

Naturally, all these revelations led me to my next questions: If Randall had been murdered, who would want to kill him? And why?

And those questions kept on rattling around in my brain as Pastor Livingston wrapped up the service, and the casket was wheeled back down the aisle, this time without incident. A very jovial June and her scowling daughter followed, with Aiden bringing up the rear. He had yet to take a break from his cell phone, and I wasn't sure he even knew where he was, judging by the way he tripped and stumbled along while the organ now played Donna Summer's *Last Dance*.

Parker crinkled his brow and turned to me. "Mom, is it just me . . . or . . .?"

I was already shaking my head. "Nope, it's not you."

"That's a relief."

Well, he could say that again.

We waited our turn as the guests began to file out of their pews and into the aisle.

Betty leaned back to me while her children climbed the pews in front of them like boot-camp marines going over a wall. "June should've taken the advice from my blog post last week," she said with a *tsk-tsk*. "She could've saved so much money if she'd just gone shopping at a thrift store. Those places are always loaded with fake flowers. They have everything you need, as long as you don't mind whether stuff matches or not."

Something I had a hunch that June would mind *a lot*, judging by her complete color coordination of today's event.

I glanced at Betty's camera, and I suddenly became aware of her looking at me looking at it. "So . . ." I started, not sure what to say. "You brought a camera . . . Did you get some good pictures?"

She groaned. "Not a single one that I can use for my best blog, *Scrapyard Chic*. I sure wish June had used *some* repurposed stuff. Then I could've had a field day with this."

"Well, funerals are very personal," I said gently. "And everyone has their own taste."

Betty shrugged. "I guess. Maybe the next funeral I go to will be more upcycled."

Despite myself, I couldn't help but choke, and I had to pound my chest a couple of times to get under control. If I didn't know better—and for that matter, maybe I didn't—I got the impression that Betty was just counting the days until someone else died. In hopes they might host a service that used some of her blog suggestions.

Talk about your suspicious undertones.

A cold chill ran right through me, no doubt a reaction to Betty's comment. That, or a breeze was coming in through the doors that had just been opened at the entrance to the church. I glanced back in time to see Randall's casket being loaded onto a flower-adorned hearse. Standing before it were Tiffany and Aiden, taking a series of selfies. That's when Parker and I saw an opening in the line of mourners, and we jumped into the aisle.

I caught a glimpse of Spencer Poe, who momentarily removed his sunglasses and gave me a sidelong glance. Then he put his head down and made a beeline for a side exit. I guessed I'd probably see him at the reception. Though I only hoped he'd leave his disguise and his subterfuge at home.

Parker tugged at my sleeve as we inched along in the receiving line. "Mom, those flowers aren't going to stay on that hearse. They're only attached with tape. The flowers will create drag, and the wind resistance will rip them right off."

And sure enough, he was right. The hearse drove away seconds later, and flowers went flying and tumbling through the air like glitter in a snow globe. At least the streamers and tin cans tied to the bumper stayed on, along with the sign that read "Just (About to Be) Buried."

Tiffany frowned at the mangled flowers that now littered the church driveway, and I wondered if that decorating touch had been her idea. If nothing else, at least she returned to stand by her mother in the receiving line, which only consisted of the two of them and Pastor Livingston, a man who was clearly affected by today's pollen count.

While he continued to dab at watery eyes, June didn't even blink when I finally stood in front of her. In fact, she just kept on staring blankly at some nonexistent spot on the far wall.

I took her hands in mine. "I am so sorry, June. I know how close you and Randall were. And I know what it's like to lose a husband." I did my best to make direct eye contact and break through the haze in her mind, so to speak.

She responded with a giggle. "I hope you and Parker will join us for the reception at my house. We're going to have a grand time. Everyone is bringing something."

"Of course we'll be there. We wouldn't miss it," I told her, though I wasn't entirely sure she heard me. "I'm bringing your favorite—my bacon-wrapped shrimp with honey-garlic sauce."

For a moment, I thought I saw a flicker of recognition in her eyes, maybe with the memory of the scrumptious finger food that she and Randall had scarfed down at my house on more than one occasion. "Oh, that sounds lovely," she murmured before she giggled again and let go of my hands.

So I moved on to Tiffany and shook her very limp hand. "I know this must be really difficult for you, honey. It's hard to lose your dad when you're still so young."

She frowned. "Aiden and I had to come back from our honeymoon early. Now, every year on our anniversary, this is all we'll think about. It's ruined everything."

"Maybe for a year or two," I told her. "But in time you'll feel better, and then you'll just remember the good times."

She let out a loud sigh and pulled her hand away. Then she turned to Parker and gave him a silent nod.

I glanced around for Aiden, so I could offer him my condolences, too, but he was nowhere to be seen.

And with that, we left the church and walked out into the parking lot with the other mourners who silently returned to their vehicles.

"Mom, you looked a little zoned out. Maybe you'd better let me drive," Parker insisted.

For once, I let him do just that. Mostly because there seemed to be a tug-of-war going on inside my head, with so many things fighting to be front and center of my attention. But the overwhelming curiosity about whether Randall had been on Digoxin or not seemed to be winning the battle. And I knew the reception would be the perfect place to get some answers. Though I didn't normally snoop in my neighbors' drawers and closets—and I had a real pet peeve about people who did—I decided today was the day when I would break my own rule and look inside the Rathburns' medicine cabinet. If I found a prescription bottle of Digoxin with Randall's name on it, well, at least that would answer one very big question.

Yet it would probably bring up a whole bunch more.

And much as I was dying to check it out, there was something else I needed to take care of first. So the second we got home, I set my oven to preheat and then raced up the stairs to my home office.

Without missing a beat, I went straight to my computer, pulled up my latest book contract, and phoned my agent. A young woman pushing thirty, Zoe Stielchek had taken over last year when my agent of nearly twenty years, Maxwell Marks, had retired suddenly due to health issues. While Maxwell had been more like a mentor to me, Zoe treated me more like a mom.

A mom whom she apparently despised. Not to mention, considered stupid and annoying and completely out of touch with the times. Never mind that in the short time she'd been my agent, my books had earned her a tidy profit without requiring much work on her part.

"She is busy at the moment," her personal assistant, Sarafena, informed me.

"Busy with a client?" I fished.

"No, she is simply eating a yogurt. Not that it is any of your business," Sarafena replied in a staccato beat, as though speaking to an errant child. "I am going to put you on hold while she finishes."

Of course, Sarafena didn't bother to ask if I *minded* being put on hold. Or if I'd prefer to call back.

As if taking second place to a yogurt cup wasn't bad enough.

I was starting to get a little steamed by the time Zoe came on the line. "Maddie, why are you calling? Didn't you get my letter? You Boomers like to get letters, right? I mean, you're not really into the electronic age yet. I thought you would be happy that I went to all the trouble to write to you."

Her words left me sputtering for a moment. "Zoe, I'm a Gen-Xer, not a Baby Boomer. And in this situation, I believe a phone call would have been appropriate." Funny, but her treating me like a Mom always led to my sounding like one.

"Oh, okay," she mumbled. "But I don't know why you're being so mean to me. I was just trying to be nice. Besides, I told you everything in the letter. What else do you need?"

I rolled my eyes. "Thank you for your letter. Now could you please tell me the details about what happened to my publisher? I thought they were in good shape financially and that my book sales were going well."

"Ummm . . . someone sued your publisher for something like a gazillion dollars. The woman claimed Paumpass House's self-help books ruined her life, and so she found a lawyer who sued for more than the company was worth. The publisher couldn't afford to settle out of court and so it went to trial. Paumpass House lost, and they couldn't afford to pay, so they went under."

"That's terrible," I gasped.

"Uh-huh. A whole bunch of my authors are out of a job. It's been really hard for me."

*Hard for her?*

I bit my lip, fighting the urge to admonish her for acting like a self-absorbed child. I could hardly believe that she'd brought out the "mad mom" in me again.

But I managed to shake it off. "I know sometimes a publisher will sell their book contracts to another publisher, like selling an asset. Did they do that in this case? Will my books be published by another company?"

"Oh, no," she informed me cheerfully. "Because I knew you'd never want that. So I fought really hard to get all the rights to your books reverted back to you. Even the electronic rights. I did a really good job."

I cringed. "I think this is something we should have talked about first."

This led to complete silence on her part for a few seconds. "I thought you'd like what I did. I don't know what you want from me."

"I want you to act like an agent," I said, choking on the words. "Do you plan to sell my books to another publisher?"

"Well, no."

"No? Isn't that what an agent is supposed to do?"

More silence. "Maddie, I'm so busy these days . . . I don't really have time to work with your books."

"My books have all been best sellers. How much time could it take to sell them to another publishing house?"

"Maddie, your books aren't cutting edge. Millennials don't like them very much."

Images of the young people I'd met at book signings flashed through my mind. "But I have a huge following among Millennials. And all generations, really."

"The problem is, your books don't have ghosts or witches or anything supernatural in them."

I dropped my head into my palm. "Because they're culinary murder mysteries."

"Yeah, but they have happy endings," she informed me as though she were educating a complete neophyte in the publishing industry. "And your main character—Blaze—is just sort of . . . well, happy. And for that matter, your books are sort of happy, too."

"What's wrong with 'happy?' My readers like that about my books. They want to escape and step into Blaze's world. They enjoy the way Blaze is sort of cavalier about everything."

"Well, *they* may like them, but *I* can't relate to all that cooking and domestic stuff. That's what restaurants are for. I want to represent more modern books. Books that are real and show the evil side of human beings. Something dark and creepy and bloody. Something dystopian. Something I can sink my teeth into."

And something I would never dream of writing. Funny, but as an author, I always thought it was my job to lift people up by the end of a book. Rather than drag them down into despair and leave them feeling depressed.

"Maddie," she went on, "Your books have run their course. You're pretty old, and it's time for you to retire. Like other old people."

"Retire?" I gasped.

"You might as well face it—nobody wants your books anymore. One day you're in and one day you're . . ." she paused and I could practically hear the gears turning in her head. "And one day you're not in."

By now I was finding it hard to breathe. "I'm way too young to retire. I'm the sole breadwinner and I've got a son about to go to college."

"Oh, well, I'm sure you could go Indie with all your old books. You might make a few dollars that way. But probably not, though, since you'll be competing with the millions of copies of your books already out there in the resale market. Whatever. I've got to think about me. And I want to have fun as an agent."

I gritted my teeth. "And nothing says 'fun' like representing dark, creepy, and bloody books . . ."

"I know, right? I'm so happy about it all," she cooed. "By the way, I didn't get the rights to all your old covers. So if you decide to sell your old books, you'll need to have new covers made."

"So let me see if I've got this straight. You're officially terminating our author/agent relationship?"

"Terminating sounds so mean. And I would never be mean. No, I'm just saying that we're not right for each other, and your books aren't right for me. Oh, and you probably won't be able to get a new agent. Not for books that have already been published anyway. Especially not at your age. But hey, I've gotta run. Stay awesome!"

With that, she ended our call.

And as near as I could tell, officially ended my career.

Now what was I going to do?

How would I support Parker and me? Because starting a whole new career at my age was going to be murder.

# Chapter Four

Once I got off the phone with my agent—or rather, the person now "formerly known as" my agent—it took me a minute or two to get my bearings. Okay, the truth was, I probably wasn't even close to getting my bearings, but at least I was able to take deep, normal breaths. Even so, that didn't change the fact that I still had to figure out a way to support my son and me. Aside from writing books, I was qualified to do absolutely nothing else. And *nothing* didn't pay the bills.

Though at least I wasn't completely destitute. Sure, we'd been living a little on the lavish side since I'd become a successful author. But I'd also been careful to tuck money away for a rainy day, and I'd gotten a nice jump on my retirement funds. Plus, my late husband, Charlie, and I had started college funds for the kids the second they were born. My spirited daughter, Lyndi, had already graduated from culinary school and was now happily cooking for huge crowds on a Navy aircraft carrier. Which also meant that her education was one less expense that I had to worry about. But despite her military service, she was a girly-girl at heart, and I fully expected to finance a huge wedding for her one day in the not-so-distant future. Then Parker was all set to start college at Texas A & M in the fall, and I was worried that I hadn't put enough away for all that. Especially if he decided to go on to graduate school.

On top of everything else, the house was going to need a new roof before long, and the water heaters were nearing their expiration date . . . and on and on and on. Just the thought of all those dollars going out the door made me dizzy.

So, yes, while I knew that Parker and I wouldn't be out on the street by morning, I was well aware that I didn't have enough money to get me through long-term. Meaning, I still needed to make a living.

And even though my finances weighed heavily on my mind, there was much, much more to losing my livelihood that made me feel like my world was coming to an end. As the saying goes, once a writer always a writer. Writing was my passion, the thing that got me up in the morning and kept me going from day-to-day. I could hardly wait to conjure up characters and scenarios with each new book, not to mention watch my main character, Blaze, hash her way through every sticky situation I tossed at her. All in all, I thoroughly enjoyed being an author. I lived for it. Early on in my career, with my husband in the military and money being so tight, it had been a real lifesaver for our family. Then later, when I lost Charlie, writing was what forced me to get out of bed in the morning and prevented me from spending my days consumed with grief.

Now I wasn't sure what I would do without it.

Much to my amazement, my thoughts suddenly turned to Blaze, and I wondered what she would do at a time like this. And since I had created her, I guess I already knew what she'd say: "When the going gets tough, the tough get cooking."

Which was exactly what I needed to do, considering Parker and I were due at the reception at the Rathburns' house.

So I raced downstairs to my oversized kitchen with its dark-granite countertops and white cabinets, décor that was repeated in my huge kitchen island. I glanced around at the seafoam-green glass tiles of the backsplash and the slightly darker hue of green echoed in the paint color on the walls. Funny, but spending time in my kitchen always made me feel grounded, no matter what was going on in my world.

I smiled and turned my oven on to broil. Seconds later, I had my bacon-wrapped shrimps sizzling on an upper rack while I reheated the honey-garlic sauce in the microwave.

With the scent of bacon filling the house, Parker instantly materialized. "Mom, that smells good. Would you mind if I have . . .?"

"Way ahead of you, son," I told him as I pulled the shrimp from the oven and put a dozen on a plate for him.

Since he'd had his last growth spurt, I'd learned it was best not to take him to a neighborhood get-together on an empty stomach. Otherwise, the child could hoover his way through an entire buffet, without leaving much for the rest of the guests.

And still be hungry.

Now he practically inhaled every morsel on his plate, though he did toss a few bites to Ellery and Agatha, who also appeared from out of nowhere, given the prospect of a between-meals snack. I was pretty sure they'd picked up on Parker's new eating habits, and they seemed to associate him with the nonstop presence of food these days. Smart kitties.

No doubt, they were going to miss him when he went off to college. And vice versa. He petted them and fussed over them while I wrapped up the rest of the food, ready to take to June's house. Then Parker carried the sauce and I took the shrimp, and together we headed for the Rathburn residence two doors down.

Along the way, I wrestled with another subject weighing heavily on my mind—when should I tell Parker that my career had gone kaput and our finances would be affected? Somehow, I didn't think today was the best day, considering a funeral and a reception for a neighbor were probably plenty for him to deal with in one twenty-four hour period.

Besides that, I needed to figure out exactly *how* to break the bad news to him. Of course, I knew it was important to be frank, but I still didn't want him to worry needlessly.

Just because I was.

We reached June's two-story, brick house and strolled up the winding walkway. Rose gardens—outlined by precisely trimmed, foot-high boxwood hedges—were in full bloom on either side of the walk. Beyond that, huge, waxy-leafed magnolia trees spread their branches toward the sky and up past the roofline.

Parker opened one of the double, front doors and held it for me as we let ourselves in to the elegant entryway. Then we followed the hallway back to the gigantic kitchen and family room, all done in varying shades of white and tan. Except for the black granite on the countertops.

That's where we found Emily Lockheed, a local real estate agent, running the show. And when I say running, I do mean running. Which was no easy feat, considering the tightness of her black pencil skirt and the height of her black stiletto heels. Emily always reminded me of the actress Morgan Fairchild in her 80s and 90s heyday.

"Oh, hi, Maddie. Hi, Parker. So nice to see you both," Emily cooed. "Is that your famous bacon-wrapped shrimp I smell? That stuff is so delicious it should be illegal. Put your platter on the end of the counter there, would you?"

"I'll do it," Parker volunteered, no doubt so he could check out all the other food.

Apparently, Emily picked up on his ulterior motives. "Don't dig in just yet, Parker. Wait until June and Tiffany get here. We shouldn't start without them."

As usual, I was amazed by how every strand of her highlighted and lowlighted blonde hair was perfectly in place. Not to mention her makeup, which always looked like it had been professionally applied by some Hollywood stylist. On top of it all, she didn't show even the slightest glow of perspiration after racing around to set up the potluck reception at the Rathburn house.

"June is a little out of it," I mentioned to Emily.

She grabbed a napkin and wiped a dab of cheese from her hand. "Believe me, it's better than having her crumbling and crying and falling apart. She really took Randall's death hard. She was practically catatonic. So I took her to my doctor, and he gave her something."

"That could explain a lot."

She nodded. "Otherwise, I'm not sure she would've made it through the funeral."

I sighed. "I've been in her shoes. I know what it's like."

Emily gave me the once over and frowned. "Are you doing okay, Maddie? You look a little . . . frazzled. Have you been working too much? When is your new book coming out?"

And that's when I choked. Both physically and mentally.

Emily gasped. "Oh, my goodness! Your new book *isn't* coming out, is it? What happened?"

I took a deep breath and tried to come up with a reasonable explanation. A public statement, if you will. But since the whole situation was still so new to me, I hadn't even had a chance to think about how I would explain things to the neighbors. Especially when I hadn't even explained it to Parker yet.

Thankfully, he was out of earshot when Emily began to dig like an investigative reporter going after the scoop of a lifetime. And because I was still in shock over losing my livelihood, I was in too much of a daze to stop her. Or change the subject when she rapid-fired questions at me until one of them hit home. Then she seemed to know exactly when she'd hit a bull's-eye. That, or she probably noticed the tears that pricked at my eyes.

"Your publisher went under," Emily now repeated, having first phrased the words in the form of a question. "But what about your agent? Will she find a new publisher for you?"

Yet before I could utter so much as a single syllable, Emily barreled on. "Your agent dumped you, too, didn't she? Oh, Maddie, I am so, so sorry. I can't begin to imagine what you're going through."

And the next thing I knew, she was hugging me. In fact, she started to rock me back and forth like a small child. That's when I spotted all the other people standing around us. Standing and listening. Judging from the look of pure shock on their faces, I could tell they'd heard every word.

I pulled back, put a cautioning finger to my lips, and glanced around the group. "Not a word to anyone. I haven't told Parker yet."

"Got it," Betty Kraukpott murmured.

"Of course," Gia Delvecchio agreed, along with several other people who nodded their consent.

Including Spencer Poe, who had joined the outer perimeter of the little cluster. *Sans* disguise.

Emily slid her arm around my waist and pulled me aside. "You know, Maddie, if you're worried about money, we could always sell your house. With just you and Parker there, downsizing is certainly an option. Especially since Parker will be leaving for college soon anyway."

"Sell my house . . . ?"

Emily smiled. "You do have the perfect house. Four bedrooms and four baths. Oversized rooms. Nice big kitchen with a U-shaped island. Huge backyard. It's exactly the kind of property that all the new execs moving to Houston are looking for."

"Sell my house . . . ?" I repeated dumbly.

"And don't forget, Abbott Cove has some of the best schools in the state. I could sell your place in a heartbeat. Our real estate market is hot right now, and sellers are getting a lot more for their homes than usual. We actually have a shortage of houses for sale, and an even bigger shortage of houses that didn't flood during Harvey. Yours happens to be one of them."

"I don't know . . ." I stuttered, wondering why I was having such a hard time forming words all of a sudden.

"These days," Emily went on, "houses are listed as either 'Never Flooded' or 'Newly Remodeled.' Since your house didn't flood, it would be considered a premier property."

"I had no idea . . ."

Sure, having lived through Hurricane Harvey, I knew firsthand how the monster storm had made mincemeat of the whole Houston area. Many of the nicer neighborhoods in Abbott Cove had also flooded during the onslaught of rain that had stalled out over the city for five horrifying days. But I didn't realize it was still having an impact on our real estate market.

"This is all so new for me . . ." I told her. "Selling my house isn't even something I've considered . . ."

"Just give it some thought. I'm here if you need me. But right now I'd better finish organizing the food in the kitchen. June and Tiffany should be here any minute."

"Thanks, Emily," I managed to mumble as I noticed Spencer Poe had moved to a back corner of the family room and was motioning to me.

I wandered over to him in a daze. Oddly enough, the mere suggestion of selling my house was enough to leave me feeling completely discombobulated. It was the first truly permanent home that Charlie and the kids and I had lived in after he left the military. And it was the first time I'd had the luxury of collecting stuff, instead of living light so we could move at a moment's notice, if necessary. Every inch of my house was absolutely loaded with memories, and I cringed at the idea of saying goodbye to all that. Selling my house felt like I'd be selling a part of my life. An important part.

I shook my head and sighed. Everything had been happening so fast since I'd gotten the letter from my agent, and I hadn't even had time to process it all. But like it or not, I was going to need to make some decisions. Big decisions. And soon.

I reached Spencer just as June, Tiffany, and Aiden entered the oversized kitchen. With the rest of the guests now fawning over them, it was the perfect time for me to talk privately with Spencer.

His eyes made a quick survey of the room before he spoke so quietly that I could barely hear him. "Well, what do you think, Mrs. Montgomery? Did you pick up on anything suspicious at the funeral?"

I nodded. "Yes, I did. I think Randall's so-called heart attack could have been an overdose of Digoxin. His last words were 'it's yellow' and 'it's snowing.' And seeing yellow or snow are both symptoms of ocular toxicity of Digoxin."

Spencer raised his eyebrows. "I am impressed, Mrs. Montgomery. Though hardly surprised by your knowledge base. Your revelation could be the ammunition I need to convince the authorities that Randall's death was no accident."

"I think it's worth looking into. And if it's true, there's still the question of how Randall ended up being overdosed. Was he on the medication, and did *he* accidentally take too much? Or did someone *give* him too much?"

Spencer's eyes darted around the room again. "Excellent observations. Either way, this information might motivate the police to perform an autopsy."

I nodded. "I think an autopsy would be a good idea."

Or at least, I *did*.

Right up until the moment when June made an announcement from the kitchen as she pointed to the digital clock on the stainless-steel oven. "Attention everyone! Randall should be completely cremated by now!" She held a glass high, as though toasting him.

Though in this case, it was probably a little more literal than most.

Confusion reigned through the crowd as eyebrows shot up and mouths dropped open en masse. A few of the people half-heartedly raised a glass while others stood frozen in place, clearly unsure how to respond.

But June seemed completely oblivious, and she giggled before going on. "His ashes will be placed in a stunning Lapis Lazuli urn that I'll be putting right over the mantel in the living room."

"She's having him cremated?" I commented to Spencer. "I don't understand. She had a 'Just (About to Be) Buried' sign on the back of the hearse. Why would she do that if she planned to have him cremated?"

"A very good question, Mrs. Montgomery. Why indeed?"

Regardless of the reason, I knew any hopes for an autopsy just went up in smoke. Again, literally. But like Blaze would have said, "There's more than one way to cook a stew."

Or solve a crime, for that matter.

Which led me right back to my original idea.

"I'm going to check the medicine cabinet in the master bathroom," I told Spencer. "To see if I can find a Digoxin prescription with Randall's name on it. Could you cover me, please?"

Spencer nodded. "Good plan, Mrs. Montgomery. I've got your back. Let me advise you to stick close to the walls. Get in and out as quickly as you can. Be prepared to hide if necessary and have an alibi ready in case you get caught."

"Got it," I told him, not bothering to ask how he knew all that.

Then without another word, I slipped down the hall and to the master bedroom, a place that I can only describe as being "extremely purple." Purple comforter, purple wallpaper, purple trim on the bedside lamps, and a purple-shag area rug over the hardwood floor. To top it off, the whole room smelled faintly of lilacs.

There was so much purple that I was pretty sure my vision would be clouded with purple afterimages for a long time to come. But I quickly became more concerned about another image that blinked across my brain—me getting caught rifling through June's medicine cabinet. And as my conscience and common sense took over, I started to question my snap decision to go off snooping or spying or investigating or whatever you might want to call it. After all, I was Maddie Montgomery, mystery writer. Not my character, Blaze McClane, amateur sleuth. My special skills included hibernating for months at a time and gluing myself to a keyboard in order to meet a deadline. My skill set did *not* include going off on some clandestine mission where I had to think on my toes and come up with an alibi.

Okay, maybe calling this a clandestine mission was a tad bit melodramatic—all right, fine, *really* melodramatic—but you get the picture. Because, truth be told, I wasn't cut out for stuff like this.

Then again, when I thought about it, I realized I'd done things in my life that other people would probably consider to be terrifying. After all, I'd gotten up on stage and addressed entire crowds at writers' conferences. And I'd been on panels for library festivals and publishing forums. Plus, I'd been interviewed on TV and radio more times than I could count.

So sure, while I did spend plenty of time alone typing away on whatever book I happened to be writing—usually in my pajamas with my hair sticking straight out—I'd still had my moments of unabashed bravery.

Which was exactly what *this* moment called for now. Especially since my hands had started to tremble ever so slightly, and my heart was pounding out a rumba beat. Loudly. But deep down, my curiosity was killing me, and I was dying to know if Digoxin had played a role in Randall's death. And if I didn't find out, I'd probably spend the rest of my life wondering.

Not to mention, if Randall really had been murdered, it was important to bring his killer to justice. Since, generally speaking, it wasn't good to have a murderer running around Abbott Cove.

So I hugged the walls like Spencer had suggested, and I quickly tiptoed through the bedroom. Then I slipped into the adjoining master bathroom where the walls were painted midnight blue. I didn't waste a single second before I raced to the white medicine cabinet that matched the rest of the cabinetry in the room. I pulled the door open and spotted several orange prescription bottles sitting on the shelves. Without hesitation, I looked them over one by one.

The first five were for June.

But the next one was for Randall. And while it only turned out to be a sleep medication, if nothing else, at least I knew I was on the right track. Especially after I pulled out bottle number seven.

Because there, in my hot, little hands, was another prescription for Randall.

A prescription for Digoxin.

# Chapter Five

I gasped and looked at the prescription bottle again, wondering if I'd read the label right. And sure enough, it was for Digoxin. The bottle was nearly empty, which meant Randall might have accidentally taken too much of the medication. But when I looked closer at the label, I realized he'd been way overdue for a refill. Meaning, he hadn't even been taking the dosage he was prescribed. Not on a regular basis anyway. While that still didn't rule out an accidental overdose, it also didn't rule out foul play.

I returned the bottle to the cabinet and closed the door, ready to make my escape back to the reception. And that's when I heard a voice.

Singing.

It was June, and she was belting out *I Will Survive*, one of the songs that had been played at the funeral.

Right away, ice-cold panic raced through my body. And I remembered Spencer Poe's advice, telling me to hide. But where? The only place I could find in a hurry was the walk-in closet, and for all I knew, that was exactly where June was headed, probably to change clothes. Worst of all, I'd seen this scene in the movies enough times—and for that matter, I'd written this scene enough times *myself*—to know that it never ended well for the person hiding in the closet.

So I focused instead on another suggestion that Spencer had given me, the idea of having an alibi ready. But what possible alibi could a person have for snooping through someone's medicine cabinet? I was just here to . . . to . . . to . . . look for an aspirin? Brush my teeth? Get a glass of water?

Of course, Blaze would have come up with an alibi in a heartbeat, in her fictitious world of culinary crime solving. Whereas I, out here in the real world, clearly had no great talent in that department. Then again, wasn't Spencer supposed to cover me? And maybe even prevent someone from coming in?

Speaking of Spencer, I suddenly heard *him* speaking in June's bedroom, and I realized he had come to my rescue after all.

"Mrs. Rathburn," he said in a voice that oozed with charm, "I was wondering . . . now that you no longer have a man around the house . . ."

"Yes?" June responded with a giggle.

"Perhaps you might like me to . . ." Spencer went on.

"Oh, Spencer," she giggled again. "I always thought there was something between us. I could feel the attraction. I could feel the heat. But of course, I was married then, so I was certainly not available. And I knew you were an honorable man and that you'd never approach a married woman. But things are different now . . ."

I tiptoed to the edge of the bedroom, just in time to see June wrap her arms around Spencer's neck and plant a big ole wet one on his lips. And judging from the way he had to practically wrestle her away, it appeared that June was a lot stronger than she looked. Spencer's usually unexpressive face registered a shock that I gauged to be about a 9.0 on the Richter scale.

And if I hadn't been in such a hurry to get out, I probably would've had a good laugh over the whole situation. But instead, I slipped past them and out of the room, all the while wondering if I should've saved Spencer from June's amorous advances somehow.

I made it into the hallway in time to hear him say, "Mrs. Rathburn, I am afraid you may have misunderstood me. I was simply wondering if you might like me to take a look at your vehicle. I thought I heard it making a rather unseemly sound this morning, and since Randall is no longer here to check it out, perhaps you might like me to . . ."

"Look under my hood?" she suggested.

And that was the last I heard as I made my way back to the kitchen. One thing was for sure, whatever Spencer's background might be—military, NSA, CIA, or who knew what exactly—it had not prepared him for the likes of June Rathburn on her new medication.

I quickly returned to the reception to find the conversation among the neighbors and other attendees in full swing, with the decibel level rising and the sound bouncing off the high ceiling. But instead of joining in right away, I grabbed a plate and helped myself to the various casseroles and finger foods that my neighbors had brought. I noticed the serving platter for my bacon-wrapped shrimp was now empty, and I made a mental note to bring extra to the next neighborhood buffet.

With Randall's Digoxin prescription still on my mind, I leaned against the island counter and ate a couple of crostini slathered with spinach-artichoke dip. It always struck me as odd how people brought their best food to a funeral. Wasn't it better to create food like this while people were still alive to enjoy it? Then again, maybe Heaven was loaded with such deliciousness . . . without the calories, of course.

I had just started in on some fried wontons when Betty Kraukpott touched my arm. "I'm not surprised to hear about your books, Maddie. Agents and publishers can be really mean. They don't appreciate talent when they see it. Maybe you should try writing blogs and self-help sites instead. Like I do."

I sighed and wiped my fingers. "It's an idea, Betty. Though to be honest, I haven't wrapped my head around everything that's happened. It's only been a few hours, after all."

Yet as I spoke the words, I wondered how Betty might know something about agents or publishers. Had she tried to get a book published herself?

I was about to ask her when she held up a plate filled with round, flat things. "The sky's the limit when it comes to blogs. I have four so far. I featured these cookies on one of my blog posts two days ago and it's already gotten 2,000 hits."

"That's a lot," Gia Delvecchio said as she joined us. "But my husband's business site gets four times that."

Emily Lockheed took a step closer and nodded to Gia. "My website gets that many hits a day, too. Even more when I have some choice properties to sell."

Right at that moment, I was pretty sure Betty bit her tongue—both literally and figuratively. Then she more or less shoved the plate of cookies in our faces.

"Here, try one," she insisted. "I invented the recipe myself. They're called Dented Two-Can Cookies."

"Toucan?" Gia repeated.

"As in the bird?" Emily crinkled her brows.

Betty snickered and began to speak to us in the same voice that she used when talking to her children. "No, *two can*. As in two cans. Dented cans. You randomly buy any two dented cans of food at the grocery store and then add them to your sugar cookie recipe. And since you'll probably end up using different cans every time you bake these cookies, no two batches will ever be alike. It's genius, actually."

Emily examined one of her many diamond bracelets. "Why would anyone buy dented cans?"

"Because it's a real money saver," Betty went on. "Grocery stores practically *give* away dented and damaged cans. For this batch of cookies I used one can of lima beans and one can of fruit cocktail."

Gia's eyes widened to saucer proportions. "Did you say Lima beans? And fruit cocktail?"

Betty nodded. "The store was about to throw them out. Can you believe it? I posted pictures of the cans and my cookies on my *Pinched and Repurposed* blog."

Gia closed her eyes for a moment. "So, you could conceivably put mushroom soup in cookies . . ."

Betty's face lit up. "Absolutely. Wow, I'll have to try that next. But here, eat one of these cookies first. Take as many as you like! As I said, no two batches will ever be the same."

While Emily stared at the cookies in horror, Gia responded by grabbing a snickerdoodle from her own plate and stuffing it into her mouth. "Sorry," she told Betty, sputtering crumbs as she spoke. "Already got a cookie."

Then Betty turned her attention to me. "From one great cook to another, Maddie, I know you'll want a whole handful of these."

I gave her the best smile I could muster and gingerly took the smallest cookie. "I'm sure your kids would be pretty sad if I ate them all." I carefully set the cookie on the side of my plate.

Betty shook her head. "Oh, no, they won't even know. I left them at home."

"With a sitter . . .?" Gia half stated and half asked.

Betty shrugged. "Well, yeah . . ." she answered, without taking her attention off me. "You know, Maddie. You and I should collaborate on a cooking blog. With my new takes on old recipes and your classic cooking skills, we could be unstoppable. We'd get even more hits and probably be number one on all the search engines."

Gia squinted at Betty. "Of course, it wouldn't hurt that Maddie is *already* a famous author."

Betty *thunked* a hand to her chest. "I don't like what you're implying. I'm only trying to help Maddie!"

Gia rolled her eyes. "Oh, *sure* you are."

To which Betty responded by stomping her foot and strutting off with her plate of cookies.

"I am so sorry to hear about your publisher, Maddie," Gia consoled me, her New Jersey accent coming through. "But at least you got to be famous for a long time. When we were looking at houses, I was super excited to find out that a big-time author lived in the neighborhood."

"That's how I convinced her to buy the house," Emily added with a laugh.

"Thanks," I sort of murmured, knowing they were just trying to make me feel better. "It's funny, but authors hardly ever experience the kind of fame and recognition that Hollywood stars or TV personalities do. Most authors can pretty much run around without getting recognized at all."

Gia's eyes went wide. "Really? I had no idea."

I nodded. "Yup, it's really nice, too, because I have a lot of freedom to come and go as I please. Without ever being hounded by the press. As long as people remember my books, that's all that matters to me."

Of course, I didn't bother to add that fame wasn't a really big motivator for me. Mostly, I just loved what I did for a living. Or rather, what I *used* to do for a living. Until the rug got pulled out from under me. And since I was still worried about Parker overhearing a conversation and learning the truth before I had a chance to tell him myself, I decided to change the subject.

"How are you adjusting to Texas?" I asked Gia. "And to Abbott Cove?"

She shrugged. "It's all right, I guess."

Emily put her arm around Gia's shoulders. "But I placed you and your husband in an absolutely stunning four-bedroom home. Complete with a game room and probably the prettiest pool in all of Abbott Cove. Not to mention, that perfect, perfect kitchen."

"Oh, yeah," Gia agreed. "The house is fantastic. But Abbott Cove doesn't feel like home to me yet."

"I'm sure it will in time," I told her. "When my husband was in the military, we were transferred all over the place. So I know what it's like to move into a new community. And I can tell you from experience that you'll get used to things here and make lots of friends before long."

Her face suddenly brightened up. "Say, Maddie, maybe we could hang out together now that you're unemployed. We could have lunch at my house. I found a great bakery that makes wonderful croissants and Italian cookies."

"Sounds nice. Let's do it. I'll bring my chicken salad with tarragon and apples."

"And I'll bring fresh guacamole and chips," Emily added.

"Oh, okay then," Gia said with a nod. "I'll give you both a call this week."

"I look forward to it," Emily replied right before she clicked away on her high heels and started straightening what was left of the food on the kitchen island.

"You know, Maddie," Gia offered, "if you seriously need a job, my husband could probably find something for you at his car lot."

I smiled at her. "That's very sweet of you. But I'm afraid I don't know much about cars."

"Vinnie specializes in selling high-end and exotic autos," she told me. "Everyone has a lot to learn when they start to work there."

"I didn't realize that was his specialty."

"Oh, yeah. Vinnie sold Randall his little MG."

For some reason, this made me choke. "You mean . . . the car Randall was driving when he crashed into that light pole?"

"Uh-huh. It was Vinnie's favorite. I was surprised he even sold it," she said just as a very jubilant June joined us.

"Randall absolutely loved that car," June pronounced with a glassy-eyed giggle. "More than he loved me. And he bought it for a song."

With June's reappearance, I guessed Spencer must have made it out of her bedroom alive. I glanced toward the family room and spotted him looking none the worse for wear. Apparently, he'd been able to fend off her advances.

Or, most of them anyway.

Though he did keep straightening his shirt and smoothing what little hair he had left on his nearly bald head. He also wore the grim expression of a man who'd just witnessed something horrific, something he was struggling to put out of his mind.

I was about to head his way when Betty Kraukpott cornered him with her plate of cookies. So I decided to catch him later and bring him up to speed on what I'd found in the Rathburns' medicine cabinet.

In the meantime, I continued to look around the room, fully expecting to see my son. "Has anyone seen Parker lately?" I asked the group of women around me.

"He's with Aiden," Tiffany seethed as she strolled up and grabbed a cupcake with pink frosting. "They're upstairs in the game room playing video games."

"I think I'll go check on him," I said, excusing myself.

I put my empty plate next to the sink, discreetly dropping Betty's cookie into the trash, before I headed to the front of the house. I was halfway up the staircase when I suddenly realized how similar the Rathburns' house was to mine. Both places had a beautifully curved staircase that served as a focal point for a dramatic, two-story entrance. Both had an office tucked away to the left on the first floor, with a formal dining room to the right. While Randall used the office area for an actual home office, I had turned that room at my house into a little library instead.

A little library that I loved dearly, with its tufted, wingback chairs and walls of shelves filled with books. Some written by my favorite author friends.

And that's when a pang of sadness practically stabbed me in the heart. I didn't just love that *library*; I loved every room and every inch of my beautiful home. I couldn't even fathom the idea of selling the place.

But if I didn't want to sell it, then I needed to find a way to make a living so I could keep on living there. Maybe working for Gia's husband at his car lot wasn't such a bad idea. While I really couldn't picture myself talking about things like power steering and paint jobs, I decided that, well, if that's what it took, then that's what I was going to have to do.

Pretty brave thoughts from someone who was a big, giant chicken when it came to making a major career change.

*But even chickens can have their day*, I told myself as I took a deep breath and climbed the rest of the stairs.

I found Parker and Aiden in another world, also known as the game room, where they were each gripping a console and blowing things up on an extremely large TV. Neither one of them seemed to notice that I'd entered the room.

"Everything okay up here?" I asked my son.

"Yeah, Mom, we're good," Parker said, without missing a beat.

"Okay, just checking," I murmured.

Normally, I might have said something about his manners and his lack of polite chitchat with the neighbors, but today was not the day. Instead, I left Parker and Aiden and headed back down the stairs. I returned to the marble-tile floor of the front entryway and walked past the office.

Randall's office.

To say I felt a stirring inside my stomach was the understatement of the century. Because there I was, just a few feet away from the home office of a man who might have been murdered. And who knew what clues a good investigator might find inside that very office? An investigator who was brave enough to sneak in and search for them, that is.

Unfortunately, I wasn't a real investigator and my bravado was certainly debatable. Though in all honesty, I had just gotten away with snooping through June and Randall's medicine cabinet. And if I hadn't taken that risk, I never would've confirmed that Randall had a prescription for Digoxin.

But maybe I'd already pushed my luck far enough for one day with my big, amateur-sleuth moment. Especially since I'd almost been caught. In fact, I probably *would* have been caught if Spencer Poe hadn't rescued me in the nick of time, as they say.

That meant the odds were probably stacked against me if I went snooping in the same house twice. In the same day. It didn't help that I'd be rummaging around in a room that was right off the hallway that led to the front door. At one point or another, everyone at the party would have to walk past that room to leave June's house. And if someone caught me searching through things, I wasn't sure I'd be able to hide or come up with an alibi. Like Spencer had suggested earlier.

Yet I knew Blaze wouldn't even bat a long eyelash at a scenario like this. She'd jump right in with both of her high-heeled feet. Especially if she was after evidence that had an expiration date.

That's when it suddenly hit me—with Randall gone, June might decide to clean out his office and get rid of some of his papers. In fact, this might be the last time when Randall's office would be intact, so to speak, probably very much like it had been on the day he died. And if anyone wanted to remove anything incriminating, they could do it at any time. Even on the way out of the reception.

So if I wanted to check out the contents of room, it was now or never. Though one thing was for sure—I didn't have time to stand around just thinking about it.

I darted a glance down the hallway to make sure the coast was clear, and then I took the plunge. Or, in my case, a quick jump into the room. I went straight for the top drawer of the filing cabinet and slid it open. Right away, I found credit card statements that showed Randall and June were not shy about spending money. They seemed to have a preference for buying tons and tons of smaller items, usually online, or so it appeared. Which could have accounted for all the boxes I saw delivered to their front porch on a daily basis.

Once I'd finished with the first drawer, I quickly went on to the next. That's where I found a file that Randall kept on the HOA—the homeowners association for our subdivision in Abbott Cove. Much to my surprise, I found violation letters inside—lots of them—for everything from a lack of edging on their lawn to his Marine Corps flag flying in their front yard. Issues that seemed overblown as near as I could tell. Because Randall and June kept their house and yard picture-perfect. The place was a virtual show home. Something you might see in a magazine.

And near the end of the file, I found letters that Randall had written back to the HOA—or more specifically, their management company—as well as what appeared to be complete documentation of all his dealings with them. It looked like battling the HOA had practically been a full-time job for him.

I returned the file to its spot, keeping an ear out for anyone who might be coming down the hall. Then I quickly slid the drawer shut and moved on to the very large and very stunning antique desk, one with a closed front panel that faced the door. I perused the contents of the side drawers of the desk in record speed, finding nothing of great interest. It wasn't until I opened the center drawer that I found something right on top that caught my attention—Randall's life insurance policy. For a million dollars. One that named June as his sole beneficiary.

But I'd barely finished looking it over when I heard footsteps headed my way. My heart began to thump against my rib cage as I slipped the policy back in place and quietly closed the drawer.

Now I had to make a quick decision—should I hide or come up with an alibi?

Though truth be told, I had absolutely no idea how to explain why I was in Randall's office behind his desk. Was I there to look at the wall color? Not likely. Or maybe check out his antique desk? Something I could do from the doorway. Or was I there to admire the ceiling height? Fat chance.

So I did the only thing I could think of to do, essentially a kneejerk reaction with no time to spare. I pushed the desk chair out of the way and ducked into the opening below the desk.

And not a moment too soon, since the footsteps kept on coming closer. From what I could tell, they were definitely heading through the entryway and probably to the front door.

Or at least, I *hoped* they were headed to the front door.

And not to Randall's office.

Otherwise, I would have to think up an alibi after all. And coming up with a logical reason for hiding under Randall's desk was going to be a lot harder than simply explaining why I was in his office in the first place.

Once again, I found myself wondering: What would Blaze do?

# Chapter Six

By now my pulse was pounding in my ears, making it hard to hear the voice that echoed down the hallway, along with the footsteps that sounded like a soldier marching to the front door. From my hiding place beneath Randall's desk, I prayed that whoever was headed in my direction would just keep on marching. And while I couldn't quite make out the words of the person speaking, one thing was clear—it was a one-sided conversation.

Not to mention, the person doing all the talking did not sound happy. Royally teed off was more like it.

Meaning, if the person coming my way should happen to spot me, it was a safe bet that they wouldn't find it delightfully amusing if I gave them some cockeyed alibi to explain my presence under the desk.

"I'm bringing them home now," said the female voice that I finally recognized as belonging to Betty Kraukpott.

And it sounded like she was talking on her cell phone. I darted a quick glance above the desk and saw her walk past the office door with her almost full plate of cookies. As near as I could guess, the "them" she was probably referring to were her baked concoctions. Or could it be something else?

"That only happened once," she curtly informed the person on the other end of the phone. "And hardly anyone went to the hospital. In fact, it was nothing but an overreaction. And I'm sure it has nothing to do with anything."

Did she say hospital? Overreaction? Now I was dying to know what had "only happened once." And who had gone to the hospital.

But mostly I was just dying to get out of Randall's office. That, and I couldn't stop thinking about the million dollars that June would be receiving, thanks to Randall's life insurance policy. It was a lot of money. Though maybe not for her, since, according to their credit card bills, June, Randall, and daughter Tiffany were no strangers to the "Buy Now" button on a variety of websites. They could probably burn through a cool million with the same speed that Parker could consume a plate of my bacon-wrapped shrimp.

If only Betty would leave the house with that same speed. Instead, it felt like an hour went by before I finally heard the front door open and shut, and Betty's voice faded away. Once she was gone, I didn't waste a single second before I jumped to my feet and raced to the door of the office. I paused for a moment and peeked out into the hallway, just to make sure no one else was coming. Then I stepped out of the room and hurried back to the kitchen.

All the while, I could hardly believe that I'd actually done two "clandestine" searches in one day. While a part of me felt sort of invigorated, another part of me was a nervous wreck. Okay, maybe not a "wreck," per se, but I was pretty sure I wasn't cut out to be an amateur sleuth. Maybe it was best if I left the investigating up to Blaze in her made-up world.

I returned to the party to see people gathering their serving dishes and containers and leaving any leftover food for June and Tiffany. And Aiden, for that matter. Though he'd yet to make an appearance at the reception. He didn't even come to the kitchen with Parker when he strolled back in, a few minutes after I'd returned.

I was proud to see that Parker showed some manners by speaking to a few of the neighbors, just like I'd taught him to do. Once he'd gotten his "token" niceties out of the way, he grabbed our platter from the island and planted himself by the entrance to the hallway. His signal that he was ready to go. Much like the others who were starting to trickle out.

I glanced out to the family room and spotted Spencer downing a drink before he got up from a leather couch. He gave me a subtle "phone me" gesture and started to head for the door himself.

That's when antennae practically popped up from June's head. "I'll walk you out," she cooed the second she spotted him leaving.

"I'm sure I can find the way," he said with a smile that was clearly forced.

"Nonsense," she insisted, taking his arm and leading him along. "After all, it's time we got to know each other better. Tell me, are you well-to-do?" She let out a very girlish giggle.

Tiffany rested her elbows on the kitchen island and dropped her head into her hands.

"Are you all right?" Gia asked, putting a hand on Tiffany's shoulder.

"I can't stand the way my mom is acting," Tiffany murmured. "I know the doctor gave her something to help her through all this, but I don't like her being all weird and drugged up. And she's acting like . . . like . . . ."

"Like she's your age?" Gia suggested.

This resulted in a great glare from Tiffany, whose head popped up with whiplash speed. Gia pulled her hand away like she'd been burned.

Then Emily stepped closer to Tiffany, taking her turn at consoling this young woman who seemed so inconsolable. "Give her some time," Emily told Tiffany. "She'll get through this. People always do."

Tiffany turned her wide, suddenly angelic, blue eyes up to Emily. "They do?"

Emily slipped an arm around Tiffany's shoulders, giving her a reassuring hug. "Yes, they do. I've seen plenty of widows and widowers, and every single one of them grieves in their own way. But yes, they always get through it. And it doesn't hurt to have a little medicinal help. For a while anyway."

Tiffany shook her head. "I can't believe Aiden and I cut our honeymoon short for this. I mean, it doesn't make any difference whether we're here or not, does it?"

For a second or two, I wasn't sure if I'd heard her correctly. But I decided to give her the benefit of the doubt, since, just as

Emily had said, everyone grieves in their own way. And I knew I probably had a few eccentricities of my own when I first lost Charlie.

"Your mom may not show it," I told Tiffany, "but I'm sure she needs you right now. And you'd probably regret it later on if you didn't give your dad a proper farewell."

To which Tiffany simply shrugged. "I guess. But now Aiden is super bored."

"He's having a good time playing video games," Parker jumped in. "He knows some really cool game sites."

Tiffany nodded. "Oh, yeah, that's how we met. Online gaming. But with all the wedding planning, I haven't had time to play much lately."

"I don't get to play much, either," Parker added. "Too much homework and stuff."

"Don't worry about Aiden," Gia said, clearly making a second attempt to comfort Tiffany. "He'll feel better when he gets back to work. Men always do. What does Aiden do for a living anyway?"

Tiffany responded with a condescending laugh. "Oh, Aiden doesn't work. He says an outdated society tries to make people into slaves by forcing them into boring, life-sucking jobs. He believes everyone is supposed to contribute to a collective that shares the wealth. Fairly."

Emily's chin nearly hit the countertop. "And how does he plan to spend his time contributing?"

"Well, he hasn't figured that out yet," Tiffany snarled just as her mother returned. "It doesn't help that he has a whole bunch of school loans. Which is so unfair."

"You'll both have to get jobs," June sang out. "And pay them off."

Tiffany shot daggers at her. "But *M-o-o-o-m!* I already have a part-time job . . ."

Something I couldn't actually say for myself at the moment. And since gainful employment was a rather sore subject for me, I decided it was a good time to duck out. Before the conversation about job hunting went any further, and Parker learned about my situation from someone else. So I said my goodbyes and walked with Parker to the front door.

June followed along behind us and gave me a goodbye hug. "Don't be a stranger, Maddie. You and I could get into some serious trouble together." Her words were followed by another bout of laughter.

"Yes, we could," I said gently, though I wasn't exactly ready to join the local chapter of the Merry Widows Club.

I let her go, and with one final wave, Parker and I took off and headed for home.

As we walked down the block, I stared at our house, trying to spot the trashcan that could supposedly be seen from the street. Or at least, according to the HOA violation letter that I'd received today. Yet no matter how hard I searched for the trashcan with my eyes, I couldn't find it. Instead, I only saw the evergreen shrub that was tall enough to carefully conceal the container. Exactly like it was supposed to do. And exactly like it had been doing since the day we moved in.

I tilted my head toward my son. "Parker, can you see our trashcan?"

He shook his head. "No. Why? Is it missing?"

"Nope. But we got a violation letter from the HOA, and they claimed our trashcan was visible from the street. Something that's against the covenants."

"Hmm . . ." was all he said as we moved closer to our two-story home.

A home that I cherished. And, as usual, I couldn't help but feel a sense of joy as I admired the pediments above the windows and the quoins on the corners. Not to mention, the Federal-style front door with its flanking sidelights and elliptical fanlight window above. They were all terms I'd learned after reading an architectural magazine. That's where I'd also learned that the style of my house was a modern version of the Colonial Revival period homes from the 1920s. And even though it was built with a rich, burgundy brick, somehow the place always made me think of the White House. Of course, it was less than a tenth of the size, and it wasn't white. Regardless, all those little details had turned the structure into a work of art.

Like Emily had said, it was the perfect house.

Parker paused for a second and quirked a dark eyebrow at our property. "I can't see the trashcan, Mom. I don't think anyone can see it from the street. Maybe the HOA got the wrong address."

"Maybe." I ducked and bobbed and moved around, trying to find an angle or position where I could see the container. But as near as I could tell, it was neatly concealed.

Just like it had been for years.

"I think I'll give them a call," I murmured as we entered the kitchen from the door on the side porch.

"Sounds good, Mom. I'd better go finish studying for my Advanced Physics test tomorrow."

"When you're done, there's something I need to talk to you about."

"Ummm . . . okay, Mom." He tossed a frown over his shoulder before he headed up the back staircase from the kitchen.

"You're not in trouble," I hollered to his retreating form.

"That's good," he hollered back.

And hopefully I wasn't, either. With our HOA, that is. I found the letter they'd sent and dialed the number at the top of the page. Then I waited while the phone rang. And rang. And rang some more.

Finally, a man's voice answered. "Haus Oversight Services. Hedley Haus speaking." His speech had the staccato beat of someone from Germany or Austria, and for a moment, I thought I had Arnold Schwarzenegger on the phone.

"This is Maddie Montgomery," I replied, fighting the sudden urge to echo his accent. "I'm calling about an HOA letter, but I'm not sure I've reached the right place."

"You have. What is your problem?" came his curt reply.

I felt an instant twinge of irritation at his attitude. "I received a violation letter today, and I believe it was sent to me in error."

"Well, I doubt that. We don't send letters in error."

His response caught me by surprise. "Never? Well, then, consider this a first."

"What is the violation?"

"The letter claims that my trashcan was visible from the street. And believe me, I've gone out to the street and looked from every angle imaginable. I assure you, that trashcan is not visible."

"Then I'm afraid you must be the one who is mistaken."

"Excuse me?" I gasped.

"Yes, I'm looking at your file now. And it says right here that your trashcan was visible."

"To whom?"

"I'm not at liberty to say."

"Why on earth not?" I practically shouted.

"We never reveal our sources, Ms. Montgomery. By direction of our attorney."

"Well, in that case, Mr. Haus, would you care to come out and take a look for yourself? And show me where you see that trashcan?"

To which he responded by letting out a loud, heaving sigh. "That won't be necessary, Ms. Montgomery. We'll let it go this time. But don't let it happen again."

"Don't let *what* happen again? I didn't do anything wrong in the *first* place."

"Well, I'm afraid we'll have to agree to disagree on that."

By now steam was practically shooting out of my ears, much like a cartoon character. "What is there to disagree about? Either the trashcan can be seen from the road or not. I'm saying there's no way anyone could see it."

"Seriously, Ms. Montgomery. What do you want from me? I've already agreed to drop the matter."

What did I *want*? Was he *kidding* me? I wanted him to quit being a jerk and admit that I hadn't broken any of the covenants. After all, I kept my yard in perfect condition. And I didn't appreciate this louse on the other end of the phone accusing me of doing otherwise.

But I also realized it would serve no purpose whatsoever to perpetuate this argument. He had agreed to drop the charge, such as it was, and that was all I really needed.

Right?

Funny, but my romance-author friends would have described a scene like this with the phrase: He was the most exasperating man she had ever met. Which was always a sign that the man in question was about to become the love interest of the story.

Thank God I wrote murder mysteries, whereby rotten people like Mr. Hedley Haus tended to get their just rewards.

"Fine," I said, chomping on the word.

Then I had to exercise about eighteen different muscle groups just to hold my tongue. Though I really wanted to let him have it. I wanted to give him a full spiel on how my HOA dues paid his salary and how he worked for the homeowners. And on and on.

But more than anything, I really longed for the good, old days when we had actual phones that could be slammed into their cradle.

Apparently, he had the same mindset, and he beat me to the punch. "Goodbye, Ms. Montgomery," he snapped before he ended the phone call.

For some reason, this made me even angrier. I put my phone on the kitchen counter and let out a loud "*Aaaagh!*"

Unfortunately, my scream came out a little louder than I'd intended. It brought Parker running from his upstairs bedroom and back down the steps to the kitchen.

"Mom, are you okay? Did you hurt yourself?"

"No, I'm not hurt . . . and yes, I am okay!" I seethed.

"Wow, you sure don't look *okay*. You look like your head is about to explode."

I had to say, my son had pegged it. Because it pretty much *felt* like my head was about to explode. I couldn't remember the last time I had been that angry. It took something pretty drastic to put me in such a state.

Yet one short phone call with the management company for our HOA had done just that. And it left me feeling mad, mad, mad.

Murderously mad.

# Chapter Seven

Since I figured it was probably better for me to calm down rather than have a stroke, I took a few deep breaths and tried to think happy thoughts. Okay, so maybe I couldn't exactly get a nice stream of happy thoughts flowing peacefully through my brain, but at least I was able to settle down a little before I addressed my son.

"Yes, Parker," I said as calmly as I could. "I got pretty irate at the HOA management company, but I will be fine. And so will they. Plus, the situation is all taken care of now."

He crinkled his eyebrows at me. "If you say so, Mom. But you sure could've fooled me."

I sighed. "Let's just say it's been a rough day, kiddo."

"Because of the funeral?"

"For starters," I told him. "Which brings me to what I need to talk to you about. Let's get something to drink and go sit in the living room and have a chat."

"Umm . . . okay, Mom."

"What would you like?"

"Whiskey!" he answered with his usual goofy grin.

"Nice try. You can have orange juice or a diet cola. Or water."

Though *I* intended to have a nice glass of wine. My favorite sauvignon blanc, to be specific.

"Cola, please," Parker conceded with an exaggerated eye roll.

Despite myself, I couldn't help but laugh. "Coming right up," I told him as I filled a glass with ice and a can of diet cola, before pouring a glass of wine for me.

Then, with our glasses in hand, we headed to the living room and sat across from each other on the oversized, gold-toned couches. A glass coffee table graced a white, shag rug that was centered between the twin sofas, while a white-mantled fireplace stood regally against the adjacent wall. Above the mantle, a Vincent Van Gogh giclée print—*Café Terrace at Night*—reigned over the elegant room.

Normally, I would've simply relaxed and enjoyed my surroundings. But this evening, "relaxation" wasn't quite the word that sprang to mind. Because the time had come for me to face the moment that I'd been dreading.

The moment when I had to fill Parker in on the situation with my books and my writing career.

Of course, the mere idea of discussing the subject with him created a whole new dilemma for me. While he was old enough to know the truth about these things and to have a clear understanding of finances, I didn't want him to be unduly anxious. Ever since his father had passed away, Parker seemed to worry about me. A lot. And sometimes I got the impression that he thought it was his job to look out for his dear old mom. Which wasn't entirely surprising, considering he had inherited his father's hero-type qualities. I was proud of Parker for having such admirable traits, but at the same time, I didn't want him to feel a sense of role reversal. Meaning, he needed to feel confident that I was still the adult in charge. And that I would take care of things.

Even though I had no idea how I was going to do just that. Not yet anyway.

Nonetheless, it was important that Parker learned the truth. And it was important that he heard it from me.

So I took a sip of wine and looked directly at my son. "Well, kiddo, I received some news in the mail today. News that was a little shocking."

His eyes went wide for a moment. "Did somebody else die?"

I shook my head. "Nope, this is about my writing career."

"Oh, okay . . ."

And then I filled him in on the details.

As near as I could tell, he took it all in stride.

"I want you to know that this will not change your college plans," I reassured him. "I want you to get your engineering degree so you can make a good living."

"But can we afford it?" he asked quietly.

"Yes. Your father and I put money away for you and your sister to go to school. And she didn't even use all that we had for her, since she went to Culinary School."

Parker grinned. "Before joining the Navy and becoming a cook on an aircraft carrier."

"Where I have no doubt they appreciate her chef's expertise."

This made him chuckle. "Since they can't exactly pull into the drive-through at Abbott's Big Burgers and grab some grub."

I smiled in return. "No, they can't."

"But what about you, Mom? Are you going to get a regular job? I'll bet there's somebody out there who still hires old people."

I rolled my eyes just as Agatha and Ellery jumped up beside me. "I'm not exactly ancient, you know. But to answer your question, I haven't figured out what I'm going to do yet. I really hate to give up writing. I've always loved my career."

He shrugged. "Then don't give it up."

I petted Ellery behind the ears while Agatha climbed onto my lap. "I don't want to, but we've been through this already. I really don't have much choice in the matter."

He shrugged. "Only when it comes to the regular kind of publishing."

"You mean, traditional publishing?"

"Yeah, that's it. It's so old school. Everyone is going Indie these days. One of my teachers is selling tons of sci-fi books as an Indie author. He's doing great."

"Funny, but you're the third person who mentioned independent publishing to me today."

He tilted his head. "Well, it only makes sense. You've already built up your brand. And you're kind of famous. You'd probably sell tons of books to the people who bought your other books. So why quit now?"

Right at that moment, I was tempted to write off Parker's opinion as the optimism of a seventeen-year-old. Someone who wasn't jaded by the ups and downs of life. But then I remembered that Parker *had* been through plenty of ups and downs already, and he was probably a little more mature than most kids his age. That, and he'd never been prone to the kind of optimism that crossed a line into being unrealistic.

Besides all that, there was something about his words and tone that sunk in. "You know . . ." I started. "Maybe I should look into this idea. I've almost got this next book finished, and I do own the rights to it. I could publish it as a trial run and see how it goes."

My son was suddenly all smiles. "I can help, Mom. I can handle all the tech stuff. Programming or formatting or whatever."

Sometimes it really paid to have a teenage son who was a tech whiz.

"Let me think about it, okay?"

He shrugged and took the last drink of his cola. "Sounds like you just did." With that, he got up from his couch and stretched.

And I knew I had just reached the limits of his attention span.

"One more thing, Parker," I said before he took off. "People will be talking about this. People in the neighborhood. So I want you to be ready."

"You know what Dad used to say, Mom. 'It's just a bump in the road.'"

I smiled and looked up at him, wondering if he'd grown another inch. "You know, Parker, I'm pretty proud of you."

He gave me a gigantic, goofy grin. "I'm pretty proud of you, too, Mom," he said in a tone that was reminiscent of someone praising a ninety-year-old in a nursing home for finishing her pudding cup.

I rolled my eyes again. "Thank you, son. Now go study for your test."

Whereby he laughed and gave me a wave before taking off.

In the meantime, I stayed on the couch with the kitties and finished my glass of wine. It was at moments like this when I missed Charlie the most. I wished he were here to see the young man our son was becoming. Plus, it would have been nice to hear any words of wisdom from him about my career crisis.

Not to mention, I simply longed to have him near me. When I was a military wife, I got used to long periods apart. Or rather, I knew how to cope with those times when he was gone. But at least I still knew he was out there. Somewhere.

Of course, it was a different story now. My missing him wasn't going to end with one of our happy reunions. Yet every now and then, I let my creative imagination rewrite the story in my mind. Because deep in my heart, I still felt like he was with me sometimes.

I glanced up at the coffered ceiling. "What should I do, Charlie? Should I look for a job? Or should I go with Parker's idea and become an Indie author?"

But the only response I got was from Agatha, who yawned and offered me her tummy to rub.

I obliged her for a few minutes, before I got up and took my wine glass to the kitchen. Then I headed to my upstairs office. If nothing else, I figured I might as well finish writing my current work in progress.

Apparently, Agatha and Ellery agreed, because they followed me upstairs, making little "*chirrup*" noises the entire way. I noticed daylight was starting to fade as I pulled up the last chapter of Blaze's newest adventure. The chapter I'd almost finished writing this morning when I was interrupted by Spencer Poe's drone. But after an hour or so of working, it wasn't a drone that broke my concentration this time. Instead it was my phone that pinged with a text, directing me to call a particular number.

Naturally, I had a pretty good idea who that number belonged to. "Good evening, Spencer," I said when he answered my return call.

"I apologize for the hour, Mrs. Montgomery. But I noticed your lights were still on and I took the risk of checking in with you tonight. Rather than waiting until morning."

"It's not a problem, Spencer. It's not so late yet, and I'm still up and working. I've decided to finish writing my latest book. I'm not sure what will happen after that, but at least I'll have this manuscript completed. And I'll be reaching my goal."

"Bully for you, Mrs. Montgomery. That's the spirit."

"Thanks, Spencer. And I appreciate the rescue this afternoon at June's house."

"Not at all. Though her behavior *was* rather surprising, was it not? Certainly, not what one might expect from a grieving widow."

I fought the urge to chuckle, remembering June's amorous advances toward Spencer. "No, it wasn't. But I wonder how much of that was really her and how much of it was a result of the medication she's been taking to help her cope with Randall's death."

"An excellent question. And speaking of medication, did you find a Digoxin prescription for Randall in the medicine cabinet? Like you were searching for?"

I felt a satisfied smile cross my face. "Yes, I did. But as near as I could tell, Randall hadn't been taking his meds on a regular basis. Because the bottle was nearly empty, and it was way overdue for a refill."

"Very interesting, Mrs. Montgomery."

"And," I went on, "I also found Randall's million-dollar life insurance policy. Naming June as the sole beneficiary."

"So the plot thickens. Where, if I may ask, did you find this item?"

"In Randall's office. I jumped in there and did a quick run-through of all the files and drawers."

"Quite outstanding! You have truly taken to this spy . . . or rather, I mean . . . this investigative work. I am thoroughly impressed."

"Well, you probably wouldn't be if you knew how close I came to getting caught. And I have to admit, I'm not exactly comfortable when it comes to nosing around in our neighbors' private affairs . . . Let alone their drawers and cabinets."

"Not an easy thing for you to do, I am sure. But you must agree when I say that something is rotten in the state of Denmark. And the circumstances surrounding Randall's death are undoubtedly suspicious."

I sighed and hesitated. "Yes, there are definitely some red flags there. But you have to understand that I am not a detective. Amateur or otherwise. And I'm just not cut out for sneaking around like this."

"But if not you, Mrs. Montgomery, then who? Particularly with your knowledge of investigative procedures when it comes to murder."

"Yes, but . . ."

"If this were one of your novels, would your lead character not proceed to look into the case? And considering the police refuse to take any action, would she not see it as her civic duty?"

"Sure. But remember . . . I'm not my character."

"But what about Randall? Does he not deserve the same justice that any of us deserve?"

"Well, sure he does . . ."

"One might even say that it is un-American not to delve further into this situation."

And that's when I started to falter. Because I knew I was a goner the second he tossed the "un-American" card into the conversation. After all, I was the widow of a man who'd volunteered to serve Uncle Sam, and in a sense, that meant our whole family had served as well. So just like that, I knew I'd officially been talked into investigating Randall's death. As an amateur sleuth.

"All right, Spencer," I conceded. "I'll look into it."

"You have my utmost gratitude, Mrs. Montgomery. Now, let me ask, what do you perceive as our next step?"

I drew a blank for a moment. "Well . . . it might help if I could see an accident report."

"Consider it done. I shall deliver it to you by tomorrow evening."

Of course, I didn't even ask him how he planned to get this. Mostly because I didn't want to know, for fear it might involve some means other than the usual . . . legal . . . methods.

"One last thing," he told me. "Please watch your back. Both you and young Parker. It is a distinct possibility that we have a murderer running loose in the neighborhood."

And with those words, he signed off, leaving me holding my phone while his final sentiments echoed through my brain.

Without a doubt, I knew he was right. If Randall had, in fact, been murdered, there was a hard and fast truth when it came to an amateur investigating the crime. It was a truth that I knew all too well, having spent years writing murder mystery novels. While most people barely noticed when some regular Joe or Josephine looked into a suspicious death, there was always one person who *would* notice. Someone who wouldn't appreciate it one bit. Namely, the murderer. And if that person had already crossed a line and killed once, a second murder was hardly out of the question. Especially if it prevented them from going to jail.

That meant an amateur sleuth was always in the crosshairs and in more danger than anyone else.

And this time, that amateur sleuth happened to be me.

Chills raced up and down my spine as I ran down the stairs to make sure all the doors and windows were locked. Then, for the first time in a long time, I set the alarm on the high-tech security system that Charlie had installed years ago.

# Chapter Eight

Needless to say, I slept fitfully that night. When I did finally fall asleep, I was tormented by nightmare after nightmare. Most of them featured people wearing disco clothes and sitting upright in coffins as they were being rolled down church aisles—and all coming after me. Somewhere off to the side, my former agent appeared too, eating stacks of yogurt cups and laughing uproariously. She kept pointing at me with a plastic spork and hollering that I was old and next in line for a coffin.

I woke with a start to find Agatha and Ellery smooshed tightly against my legs, one on either side of me. A position they did not relinquish easily when I tried to move my legs and get up. But with a little chin scratching and prodding, I finally managed to maneuver my way out of bed.

Then I threw on my bathrobe, tied my hair up in a messy bun and brushed my teeth. My feet felt like they weighed about a thousand pounds each as I dragged my body to the kitchen to fix breakfast. Operating on autopilot, I soon had hash browns seasoned with fresh thyme sizzling in a skillet, while I whisked eggs and prepped broccoli and grape-tomato halves for omelets.

Okay, I know what you're probably thinking, that I was spoiling my son by cooking for him like he was a pampered passenger on a cruise ship. And yes, I know Parker was old enough to grab some cereal or something on his own. But after his father died, I'd made it a point to cook meals for Parker most days. All with the idea of giving him some extra stability while he was learning to live without his number one hero and role model. Plus, I didn't want Parker to be starving all morning long, given his propensity to consume about 80,000 calories a day. Even so, I tried my best not to overdo it, and I didn't give my inner helicopter mom clearance for takeoff. Mostly because I didn't want to raise a helpless kid who wouldn't know how to navigate the real world one day.

Parker tossed his backpack on the counter while I put steaming plates of food on the table. "Mom, you're not looking so hot this morning. You gonna be okay today? You want me to stay home?"

I smiled. "Nice try, kiddo. But you were out of school for the funeral yesterday, and I do believe you've got an Advanced Physics test today."

He *thunked* a hand to his chest and turned his eyes up to the heavens, or in this case, the ten-foot ceiling. "For you, Mom, I'd do anything. I'd make the sacrifice and skip the test."

I fought hard not to laugh. "Sorry, but I spotted that ploy from a mile away. There'll be no skipping. And you know you'll ace that test just like you always do."

"*Geesh*, Mom. Sounds like a lot of pressure to me," he slid onto his chair, grabbed his fork and managed to down his first bite—all in one motion. "You're lucky I'm not really insecure like a lot of kids. Or you could be doing some serious damage to my self-esteem." A grin spread across his face before he dug into his food again.

I raised an eyebrow. "You may not be secure about some things, but your science and math ability have never been in question. You can practically do that stuff in your sleep. So when it comes to taking your test, it's just a matter of stepping up to the plate . . ."

". . . and getting the job done," he finished with a groan. "Yeah, yeah, yeah. Just like Dad used to say, 'No guts no air medals.' You know, Mom, maybe *you* should take that advice and step up to the plate."

"Me? How that's?"

"You know . . . you should be an Indie author. And publish your own books."

I blinked a couple of times, wondering when my son had become old enough to turn the tables on my advice giving. To make matters worse, with my added grogginess this morning, I couldn't seem to come up with a good comeback. Of course, it didn't help that he had a good point.

But at least he had the *good* manners not to belabor that point. Instead, he finished his breakfast, wiped his mouth, and dropped his napkin onto his plate.

"Done!" he hollered as he raised his arms above his head like he'd just won a professional eating competition.

Something that might not be a bad idea, considering the volume and speed with which he ate. In fact, entering him into regular eating competitions might save me a whole lot of money in groceries.

He took his plate to the sink, washed his hands, and grinned again. "Gotta run, Mom!"

"Have a good day!" I hollered as he zoomed out the door.

But he had barely shut the door behind him when I jumped up from my chair and raced over to lock it.

"Oh, great," I said to the kitties who'd been sitting on their perch and watching Parker leave the house. "I'm becoming as paranoid as Spencer Poe."

To which they responded with swishing tails and disapproving glares. A rare reaction for the pair.

I returned to the table to finish my own breakfast, and more importantly, to down every drop of coffee in my cup. Then I made a beeline to my coffee maker to start brewing cup number two. I was just adding cream to the steaming concoction when my phone rang. It was a number I didn't recognize.

Hopefully it wasn't Spencer calling me already. Because frankly, I didn't need to add any talk of murder to my morning.

"Hello," I managed to mumble.

"Maddie, it's Gia," came her jubilant voice through the phone. "Would you like to come over for lunch today? Around twelve o'clock? Emily said she can make it. And I've picked out a nice Italian wine."

Well, *that* was fast. I really hadn't expected to hear from Gia for a day or two. Though I had to say, maybe lunch with the girls was exactly what I needed. Something to take my mind off everything else.

So I gave her a cheerful, "I'd love to. I'll bring my chicken salad with tarragon and apples."

"Sounds absolutely delicious. See you then."

I got off the phone, downed some more coffee, and decided there was no time like the present to make my salad. Soon I had chicken breasts browning in a skillet while I cored and chopped Honeycrisp apples. Between working in the kitchen and the coffee finally kicking in, I felt much better by the time I covered the completed salad with cellophane and headed for the shower.

Once I was properly groomed, painted, adorned, and attired, I climbed my curved staircase and went straight to my office. I booted up my computer and called up the final chapter in Blaze's newest adventure. Of course, I set the alarm clock on my phone so I wouldn't lose track of time. Like I tended to do when I was writing.

Then I sat back and relaxed. I put my fingers to the keyboard and went off into the world of Blaze McClane as I wrote:

*"Square-jawed and golden-haired Detective Angus Steele flashed his high-beam smile at Blaze. 'You've done it again, darling. You've caught the bad guy, and you even got it on film.'*

*'And best of all,' Blaze added, 'my soufflé is still standing.'*

*'It smells scrumptious. I wonder if I should take it in for evidence,' he teased.*

*Blaze put her hands on her hips. 'Ha! That marvel of chocolate and beaten egg whites is going nowhere. Everyone knows that a soufflé must be served immediately. Otherwise it could dissolve into a puddle of goo.'*

*Much like her heart did, whenever Angus was near.*

*She gave him an appreciative glance before she spooned out portions of the soufflé for him and for her, as well as the other police officers who were busy working the scene.*

'Do I not even get one single bite?' Count McMatton whined with all the indignation of his upper-crust upbringing.

Sparks flared in Blaze's green eyes. 'Certainly not! Not after you tried to kill me! And my soufflé. And believe me, you won't be eating anything nearly so delicious in the prison cafeteria, either.'

To which the group around her erupted with laughter.

Minutes later, Count McMatton was led away in cuffs while the officers went back to work. All except for Angus, of course.

He slid his arm around Blaze's tiny waist and brought his lips next to her ear. 'You know, my love, maybe we should make this relationship official.'

She wriggled out of his grasp. 'I've told you many times, Angus, that I'm not a fan of living together.'

'I don't want us to merely live together. When I say official, I mean "official." I want us to tie the knot.'

'You mean . . .'

'That's right, darling,' he said in his sultriest voice. 'I want us to get married.'

'Married?' Blaze repeated."

"Married?" I echoed.

And that's when I sat back and stared at my computer. Strangely enough, I was probably just as shocked as my character had been at the sudden appearance of the *M*-word. It certainly wasn't anything I'd intended to write. But apparently, I'd been caught up in the moment and my fingertips had done the talking. Not an unusual experience for any writer.

Still, it put both Blaze and me at a crossroads. Did I really want her to get married? It was an important question for any author regarding a lead character in a book series. Particularly if that character happened to be a female amateur sleuth. After all, a husband might frown on his wife running out in the middle of the night to investigate a clue. Or he might make a fuss if she tailed another man, even if it was in the interest of solving a crime.

On the other hand, Blaze and Angus had probably reached the stage where their relationship needed to move on. One way or another. Yet the very thought of sending Blaze down the aisle made my stomach turn somersaults. Why?

Probably because I knew that marrying off a lead character often signaled the end of a series. Which led me to do some serious soul-searching, whereby I had to ask myself—did I want to continue writing my Blaze McClane series? Or had I come to the end of her story? And hence, most likely the end of my career as a mystery author?

It was the moment of truth, as they say. Yet if I wanted to keep Blaze's adventures going, I would have to publish the series independently. Just like Parker was pushing me to do. And like Spencer Poe had suggested.

But was I up to the challenge and all that went with it?

Thankfully, I was saved by the bell. Or rather, by my phone that went *ping*!

It was a text from Parker. "Can I bring a friend for dinner tonight?"

His request made me smile, since I truly enjoyed having Parker's friends over to our house. Most of them were intelligent and upbeat, and usually quite respectful of me. Besides that, when Parker and his friends were at my house, I had the added benefit of knowing my teen wasn't out there driving around and up to some kind of mischief.

"Sounds dandy," I texted back. "We'll order pizza."

"Can't you make something fancy?" came his electronic reply.

*Fancy*? I crinkled my brows and tried to wrap my head around the fact that my son wanted something "fancy" to feed his friend.

In my state of shock, I responded with, "Would Boeuf Bourguignon and garlic mashed potatoes be okay?"

"Cool. Make extra, please," came his reply. "I'm hungry."

Hadn't I just fed that kid a few hours ago?

"No problem," I messaged back. "Do I know this friend?"

"Maybe. Think so. Gotta run."

Maybe? What kind of a response was *maybe*? I thought I knew most of Parker's friends. So why hadn't he given me a name?

That's when it dawned on me—maybe Parker was bringing a girl home to dinner. It could account for his wanting me to cook something "fancy." Something that might impress someone special to him.

My heart skipped a beat at the thought. The idea of Parker bringing a girl home both delighted and worried me at the same time. Sure, it would be nice for him to have a girlfriend. A first love. Being in the military, I'd known plenty of couples who had started out as high school sweethearts and watched their romances evolve into wonderful, lasting marriages.

On the other hand, the prospect of some girl breaking Parker's heart got my dander up. He'd already dealt with plenty of grief after losing his father. Heartbreak from a breakup could hit him harder than most kids his age.

Then again, it might be a good idea for me to *actually* meet the girl before I jumped on the fast train to Crazyville.

I sighed, just as the timer went off on my phone. Here I was, getting all worked up over two romances—Blaze's and Parker's—one that was fictitious and one that was only suspected. Truth be told, I probably had enough real-life drama to deal with, and I certainly didn't need to go around "inventing" more. So I turned off the timer, slipped my phone into the pocket of my capris, and headed for the kitchen. Then I grabbed my chicken salad and, after being careful to lock the door and set the alarm, I walked down the block to Gia's house.

Which was right next door to Spencer's two-story home.

I glanced up at his place as I walked past, to see if I could spot any signs of life, but there was no visible movement whatsoever. Even Evinrude wasn't out buzzing around today. Though I did spot a few vertical wires that were barely hidden against some tall trees in his yard. Wires that I could only guess were some kind of antennae. I also wondered if I was being fully monitored and videoed as I moseyed past and headed up Gia's flower-lined walkway.

Much to my surprise, Emily answered the door when I rang the bell at the sprawling, single-story home that wrapped around a huge corner lot. It had so many arches and columns that it made me think of a Roman villa rather than a suburban, Texas dwelling.

Emily led me back to the kitchen, which had white marble countertops over the main cabinets and a contrasting black marble countertop on the island. The cabinets were antiqued to look old, in huge contrast to the appliances that were state-of-the-art. Gia had put her own touch on things by adding a red stand mixer, red hand towels, and red canisters. Not to mention, lots of red dishes and vases.

She greeted me with a hug. "I'm so happy you could come today, Maddie."

"Thanks for inviting me," I told her. "Your house looks gorgeous."

"It does, doesn't it?" Emily agreed with an exaggerated nod.

"Thank you," Gia gushed. "We were so lucky it came on the market when we were house hunting."

"It just *barely* came on the market," Emily corrected her. "It was one of my listings, of course. Good thing you snapped it up before anyone else even knew it was available."

Gia smiled. "I'm glad Emily was on top of things."

"A good realtor has to be. You snooze you lose," Emily added as she helped herself to an olive.

"Well, I'm happy it worked out, because it's nice to have you in the neighborhood," I said to Gia. "Now, where would you like my salad?"

"Right there," Emily pointed to a spot on the island next to a platter piled with fresh croissants. "Gia has been giving me a lesson on Italian wine." She lifted a glass of red.

Gia grabbed a large-bowled wineglass and filled it halfway for me. "I grew up around wine, so naturally I picked up on a thing or two."

I took a sip after she handed me the glass. "Mmm . . . this is excellent."

"Nothing but the best," Gia said with a laugh. "Let's take this food to the dining room and dig in."

So we did just that. We moved it all to the ornate room that featured an accent wall embellished with gold leaf. It was opposite a wall of nearly floor-to-ceiling windows, with a perfect view of the pool and lush backyard.

After we took our seats, we each took a sliced croissant and began filling it with my chicken salad. Plus we added olives and Emily's guacamole and chips to our plates. Certainly a lunch feast fit for civilized neighbors.

"I've got a question for you two," I said after I'd savored my first bite. "Have you ever noticed my trashcan from the street?"

Gia crinkled her brow. "Your trashcan? Nope. I can't say that I have."

Emily responded with a shrug, her mouth full of food.

I took a sip of my wine. "Well, I got a letter from the HOA that said the container was visible. I called the phone number on the letter and the guy I spoke with was obnoxious."

Emily nodded. "Hedley?"

"That's him," I told her.

"He's not actually part of the HOA," Emily told me. "He just runs the management company that was hired by the HOA. To police the neighborhoods and make sure the covenants are enforced."

Gia wiped her mouth with a napkin. "Either way, he had no business being nasty to you, Maddie. I'm sure our HOA dues pay his salary."

"They do," Emily said before she took another bite of her lunch and downed it with a big gulp of wine. "But there's not much you can do about an HOA. They have way more power than most people realize. They can fine you tons of money for not complying with the covenants. And if things get ugly enough, they can even take your house. Was your letter certified? Or was it just by regular mail?"

"Regular mail," I told her.

She nodded. "Well, that's a good thing. If they start sending certified mail, then you *should* be worried. Because that's when things get serious and the lawyers get involved. And that's also why lots of people move out of HOA-controlled neighborhoods. Believe me, I've helped plenty of people sell their houses for just that reason, and then I've helped them find homes in neighborhoods that aren't regulated by HOAs. There are several of those communities right here in Abbott Cove."

"I can see why someone would consider it," Gia added. "If they got harassed enough."

I sat up straight and took another sip of my wine. "Well, I personally have no plans to move any time soon."

Emily dabbed at her mouth with her napkin. "Even with your current career and . . . financial . . . situation?"

I swallowed another bite of my sandwich. "Even with that. I love my house, and I feel so at home there."

"Like I said before, you have the *perfect* house," Emily said with a nod. "It takes a lot of guts to hang on to it like you are."

Gia touched my arm. "By the way, I talked to Vinnie last night, and he said they could definitely use you down at the car lot."

"That's very thoughtful," I told her. "But I'm considering the idea of . . ."

But before I could finish my sentence, we heard a door open from what I could only guess was the vicinity of the garage. The door must have been flung pretty hard against a wall, because it made a loud "*thwack!*" sound, and the house even shook.

This was followed by a man's baritone voice, yelling, "Babycakes! I'm home! I snuck away for lunch. Come show me what you got! I didn't pay for all that plastic surgery for nothing!"

With that, Gia's eyes went wide, and she jumped up from her chair. She did her best to call out, but her mouth was full of food and she only ended up sputtering. She waved her hands wildly, just as a man with thick black hair and even thicker black eyebrows came around the corner.

He grinned from ear to ear. "There you are, Dollface! Daddy's got a present for you. Look what fell off the truck today. Now take everything off and try this on!"

With that, he tossed her something that sparkled and twinkled as it flew through the air, across the room and into her open hand. Whereby she quickly wrapped her fingers around it and dropped it into her cleavage.

But there was no use trying to hide it. Because I'd already seen what it was, and I was pretty sure Emily had, too.

The man who had entered the house had just tossed Gia a diamond tennis bracelet. And from what I'd seen, those diamonds were all pretty good-sized.

# Chapter Nine

With the appearance of this dark-haired, diamond-tossing man, my chin nearly dropped to the top of Gia's carved and inlaid table. To make matters worse, the man still hadn't noticed Emily and me sitting there. No, he was much too busy staring at the precise spot where Gia had dropped her new bracelet. He didn't even seem fazed by the way she was frantically waving her arms. Clearly, he was focused on one part of her anatomy, and one part only.

I guessed the man must be Vinnie. Or at least, I *hoped* the man was Vinnie. To tell you the truth, I wasn't sure. I'd never actually met him before, and since they'd moved in, I'd only ever seen him from a distance.

Thankfully, Gia finally managed to swallow her food. "Vinnie, honey, we have guests!"

"We do?" he gasped and looked around.

That's when he finally spotted Emily and me. Then his eyeballs practically popped out of his head and his face turned so red I was afraid he might have a heart attack.

Emily gave him a little wave. "Hello, Vinnie. So nice to see you again. Wow, I sure wish I had a husband who came home and surprised me at lunch like that. None of my exes ever did anything so romantic."

"Well . . . uh . . ." Vinnie sort of stammered, before he sighed and threw his hands up in the air. "Ladies, what can I say? I'm a lucky guy to be married to a gal like Gia. How can I resist running home to see her for lunch?"

"That's very sweet," I said, hoping to ease his embarrassment.

After all, I always appreciated a man who openly showed love and adoration for his wife. And keeping the spark alive in a marriage was truly important. Charlie had surprised me plenty of times by showing up unexpectedly at lunch for a romantic rendezvous, though he'd never, ever tossed jewelry at me like someone flinging a tennis ball to a golden retriever. In fact, that little gesture would not have gone over well in our household. Instead, whenever he gave me jewelry, it always came in a box or a case. And there was usually gift wrapping involved.

But to each their own.

I stood up and held out my hand. "So you're Gia's husband. I'm Maddie Montgomery from down the street a few houses. It's nice to meet you."

His face perked up. "Oh, yeah. The famous author. Gia's read your books. I'm sorry to hear about your publisher."

"Me, too," I said with the best smile I could muster.

Funny how one embarrassing moment could so quickly lead to another. Now I wondered, was there anyone in Abbott Cove who hadn't heard about my situation already?

Yet oddly enough, the one person who wasn't embarrassed in the least was Gia. From what I could tell, she appeared to be downright proud of her husband and his unexpected arrival. Though I had to wonder why she hadn't retrieved her bracelet and put it on. It was quickly becoming the elephant in the room.

Gia gave her husband a glowing smile. "Honey, would you like to join us? Maddie brought some chicken salad and Emily brought chips and guacamole."

But he just waved her off. "Naw, that's okay. I'll grab something at work. I should probably get back there anyway."

I raised an eyebrow to Emily and angled my head toward the door, trying to get her take on whether we should vamoose and give Gia and Vinnie their privacy.

But Emily just scrunched up her face and shook her head. "So, Vinnie . . . How's business? I saw a car on your lot that knocked my socks off. I think I'm going to need it. It's a Bentley."

Antennae practically popped out of Vinnie's head as he turned his attention to Emily and tuned into her words. "Oh, a lady with very discriminating taste! We have a couple of pre-owned Bentleys on the lot. They're one of the best car brands you could ever buy. And I'll make you a good deal, since you found this house for us, and it's made my Gia so happy."

Then the next thing I knew, Vinnie had planted himself on a chair while Gia filled a plate full of food and plopped it down on the table in front of him. Using his large, hairy hands, Vinnie dug into his meal in much the same fashion that Parker might attack a plateful of food. And, just like that, the whole conversation suddenly became all about cars. Of course, Gia knew most of the vehicles on her husband's lot, and I quickly learned that Emily could identify nearly every brand of car on the road. It seemed like I was the odd one out, since I honestly didn't have that much to contribute to the discussion.

Finally, I added the only interesting tidbit that I could come up with. "My late husband left me his favorite car. But I haven't taken it out of storage."

"What kind is it?" Emily asked half-heartedly.

I wiped my mouth with my napkin. "It's a Continental Mark II. Black."

Vinnie's mouth dropped open, and I was sure he started to drool. "A '56?"

I took a sip of my wine. "Yes, he inherited it from his father."

Vinnie let out a low whistle. "That was a very classy car in its day. Do you wanna sell it? I don't sell vintage cars on my lot, but I trade with other dealers. I'm sure one of 'em could find you a buyer. It's a rare car."

Emily's eyes went wide and she turned to me. "I'm *sure* Maddie would never dream of selling her late husband's car. That would be like selling off his memory. He probably planned to pass it on to Parker one day. Can you imagine how upset Parker would be if Maddie sold it?"

"Why is it still in storage?" Gia asked. "Shouldn't you be driving it?"

I shrugged. "Well, I guess I don't have a good answer for that. I just never got it out of storage after Charlie passed away."

"You shouldn't leave an old car like that sitting and rotting in a storage unit," Vinnie insisted. "Why don't you get it out and bring it by the shop. I'll have my mechanics check it over and make sure everything's working okay."

"Well . . . all right," I said with a slight smile. "I guess I will."

Funny, but I hadn't seriously thought about Charlie's vintage car in a long time. And maybe it *was* time that I retrieved it. After all, I had room to park it in my garage now, and given my current financial status, it would be nice to eliminate the monthly storage fee.

"And while you're at the lot," Vinnie went on, "I've got some other cars you might wanna look at. In case you'd like to make a trade-in."

I had to say, I was pretty amazed at how quickly Vinnie could work a room. In a matter of minutes, he had Emily on the hook for a high-dollar Bentley, and he had me bringing Charlie's car in for servicing—which would leave me with nothing else to do but peruse the other cars on his lot while I waited. Plus, I couldn't forget that Vinnie had sold a car to Randall, too.

The very car that Randall died in.

Though I remembered June telling me that it was a vintage car. A fact that seemed odd, considering Vinnie just told me he didn't sell such vehicles.

I smiled at him. "Randall bought a car from you, didn't he? An old MG?"

Much to my surprise, Vinnie responded to my question with complete and utter silence. As well as a clamped jaw and hostility that practically steamed from his ears.

Apparently, I'd hit on a sore subject. A *very* sore subject.

"Yes," he finally said with a forced smile, one that didn't even come close to reaching his eyes. "Randall wrecked that car. And it was a beauty. It was my uncle's car."

Gia touched her husband's arm. "I'm still surprised you sold it to him. I didn't think you'd ever added it to your inventory. I know it was your favorite."

"Oh well, easy come, easy go," Vinnie replied with a hollow laugh as he sprung up from the table. "Hey, will you look at the time? I'd better get back to work."

Putting his hands on Gia's shoulders, he smiled at Emily. "I'll see you soon, Emily. And you, too, Maddie. Nice to meet you."

"Nice to meet you, too . . ." I barely managed to say before Vinnie reached down and gave Gia a kiss on the lips.

A very long, sloppy kiss.

When he came up for air, he waved goodbye to us all and raced from the room.

Emily grinned. "Boy, oh boy, Gia, you are one lucky girl. None of my ex-husbands ever showed that kind of passion. Not for me, or for anything, really."

Gia glowed with pride. "Vinnie's a one in a million, that's for sure." She smoothed her hair and looked directly at me. "You know, Maddie, maybe *you* should think about finding a man for yourself. Maybe you should start dating."

I choked on my wine. "Me?"

"How many years has it been since Charlie died?" Emily asked.

I gulped. "A couple . . ."

Emily dipped a chip into what was left of the guacamole. "You've gotta get back in the saddle, Maddie. I know this great online dating site . . ."

I held up my hands. "Whoa . . . hang on a minute. I'm not sure if I'm ready for this. And I'm not sure how Parker would handle it. Plus, I need to figure out what I'm going to do about my career."

Gia winked at Emily. "Not if you marry a rich man. Then you won't need to worry about a career."

I laughed. "Ladies, I'm afraid this is a conversation for another time. Because I've got to run. Parker is bringing a friend home for dinner, and he wanted me to make something 'fancy.' So I need to get cooking. Literally."

"*Ooooh*, fancy!" Gia said in a singsong voice. "He's really growing up."

"He is," Emily chimed in. "He'll be out of the house and on his own before long."

"Don't I know it," I added.

And with that, I got up from the table, and Emily and Gia followed suit. After a few minutes of farewells, I wrapped up the rest of my chicken salad and headed for home.

Yet as I walked out to the street, I couldn't help but feel oddly discombobulated. Somehow, I expected to feel lighter and happier after a little "girl talk." And while I was sure Gia and Emily had meant well when they encouraged me to get Charlie's car out of storage and to start dating, the truth was, it had thrown me a smidge.

Okay, it had actually thrown me a *lot*.

Probably because a very big part of me wondered if they'd been right. Maybe I wasn't getting on with my life.

Then again, maybe I didn't really want to.

Besides, I had bigger fish to fry at the moment. And my frying pan was getting a little crowded, considering I had to figure out how to make a living in my late forties. Not to mention, delve in to the suspicious circumstances surrounding a neighbor's death. A death that might have been a murder.

I glanced up at Spencer Poe's house as I walked past, and I thought about ringing the bell. But I decided to hold off since I didn't have any big news for him just yet.

None that I could put my finger on anyway.

Even so, there *was* something sticking in my craw, as they say. I couldn't help but wonder why Vinnie reacted the way he did when I brought up the MG that Randall had bought from him. To be honest, I thought Vinnie seemed more upset about the loss of the car than the death of Randall. If Vinnie hadn't wanted to sell his family heirloom, then why did he?

Somehow, I got the feeling there was more to the story.

And I knew there was one person who might shed some light on the situation—Randall's widow. So instead of going straight home, I made a beeline for June's house, using my chicken salad as an excuse.

She answered the door, and I was instantly stunned when I saw the color of her hair—a radiant red. Probably the same color as her daughter's. And much as it was a shock, I had to admit, it made June look about ten years younger.

"Maddie, darlin'!" she practically hollered. "It's wonderful to see you again! What do you think of my new hair?"

"June . . . it's . . ." I sort of faltered. "It's gorgeous. You look like you were practically born to be a redhead."

She nodded and let me in. "That's what everyone says."

I smiled at her. "I had some extra chicken salad, and I thought you might like it."

"How nice!" she cooed as I handed her the bowl. "You are such a great cook, Maddie."

"Thanks, June. And . . ." I started to say before I hesitated, trying to think on my feet. "Since Randall's car was totaled, I wasn't sure if you had a working vehicle. So I wanted to let you know that I'd be happy to give you a ride somewhere if you ever need one."

She giggled. "That's so sweet, darlin', but I've still got *my* car. And Tiffany has hers."

"Oh, good," I said in my most casual, chatty tone. "By the way, I never understood how Randall managed to buy that car. It sounded like Vinnie didn't want to sell it."

"That's what I heard, too. But Randall could be very, very persuasive. And he never, ever gave up. He was like a dog with a bone. You probably didn't know it, Maddie, but he could be a real fighter if he thought something was wrong. Or unfair. You should have seen the way he went after the HOA."

"So you think he was fighting with Vinnie, too?"

She shrugged. "I don't know *what* was going on. But I know there was some bad blood between them. Randall was fighting mad about something, and it involved Vinnie. And the next thing I knew, he owned Vinnie's favorite car."

"Wow, I had no idea. Randall was always so nice to us."

"That's the way he was, Maddie. He was really nice to most people. He only went after the ones he called 'the bad guys.' That sounds so funny, doesn't it? The bad guys?" She let out another giggle.

"I guess it does," I told her, though I really found it more surprising than funny. "Anyway, I hope you enjoy your chicken salad. I've gotta run!"

"Okay, thanks. See you later."

With those words, I left, only to find Emily coming up the front walk just as I was walking down to the street.

"Visiting our new widow?" Emily asked.

"I was," I told her. "Just checking on her. And I thought she might like the rest of my chicken salad."

Emily nodded. "Good idea. I decided to check on her, too. She really fell apart when Randall died."

"It's hard to lose someone you love," I agreed.

"You would know," Emily said and gave me a quick hug.

Then she knocked on June's door while I headed for home. As I went, June's words played over and over inside my head. Especially the part about there being bad blood between Randall and Vinnie. Yet despite all that, Vinnie had sold his favorite car to Randall. So what *exactly* had gone on between the two of them?

I was still wondering about it when I made a quick detour to our community mailboxes at the end of the cul-de-sac. I stuck my key in my box, opened the little, metal door, and removed the various envelopes and flyers. There were ads from several of my favorite stores. And there was the usual political party flyer folded neatly inside an envelope. Last, but not least, there was a letter from our HOA.

"This must be an apology letter," I muttered as I traipsed over to my driveway.

That's when it dawned on me—maybe I had overreacted just a smidge the day before. Maybe I was a little too hard on Mr. Hedley Haus. It was entirely possible that I had judged him all wrong. And if he was big enough to apologize, then maybe I should do the same, so we could put the past behind us and move on to a much more civil relationship.

With a little chuckle, I tore the envelope open and pulled out the letter. As I unfolded it, I fully expected to see the words "apology" somewhere in the first sentence.

But instead, I saw words that sent my pulse pounding.

Notice of Violation.

# Chapter Ten

To say I was steaming mad right at that moment was like saying the Hope Diamond was a big gem. Meaning, it was a massive understatement. Especially after I read a little farther down on the letter and saw the words: "Front door not painted an approved color."

"What?" I practically shouted as I walked into my house.

First of all, the door was stained, not painted. And second, I'd had it restained every few years using the exact same color. A color the HOA must have approved in the first place. Plus, the color still looked deep and rich, since it had been restained barely six months ago. So, why, oh why, did the HOA suddenly decide that it was the wrong color, after it'd been like that since the mid-'90s, when the house was built?

It made no sense. And to top it off, the management company for the HOA had upped the ante this time—they were giving me ten days to comply or they intended to start fining me $200 a day.

Well, one thing was for sure, Hedley Haus knew how to get my dander up. I'd only heard from his company twice, and both times I was ready to flip my lid. I couldn't help but wonder if Randall had felt the same way, given the file he'd kept on the HOA.

I also wondered if Randall had done exactly what I did—namely, stomp into the kitchen and call Hedley.

This time, it was a woman who answered the phone. "Haus Oversight Services. Carla speaking." Her voice was surprisingly sweet and upbeat.

"Hello, this is Maddie Montgomery, and I'd like to speak with Hedley Haus."

"I'm sorry, but Mr. Haus is out at the moment. He's running his rounds."

"You mean, he's checking out the neighborhoods?" I clarified.

"Yes, that is correct, ma'am."

"Well, could *you* possibly help me?" I suggested in a rather brusque tone.

"I'll do my best. I'm his personal assistant. What seems to be the problem?"

I rolled my eyes and explained the situation to her, doing my level best to keep my temper in check.

"My goodness, that's odd," she said with what sounded like genuine surprise. "You're sure you haven't painted your door recently?"

"Yes, Carla, I am quite sure." For good measure, I trotted out to my front entryway and pulled the door open. "I'm looking at it right now. And I assure you, it is stained and not painted, and it's the same color that it was the day we bought the place."

She went silent for a moment or two. "Ms. Montgomery, could I please put you on hold while I get to the bottom of this?"

"Sure," I conceded, though I really didn't want to waste my time sitting on the phone when I had better things to do.

So I returned to my kitchen, with the kitties following and hovering around my feet. I switched to speakerphone and set my phone on the counter while I started to collect the ingredients I needed to cook dinner. If nothing else, at least I smiled when I thought about Parker's request for something "fancy" to feed his friend. A friend whom I guessed was actually a young woman.

That immediately made me think of my daughter, Lyndi, and what she'd been like at that age. She had a pretty sophisticated palate by then, mostly because she'd spent her childhood taste testing the various recipes that I'd created. She started cooking the minute I thought she was old enough to operate kitchen appliances, and eventually she loved to cook even more than I did. Then *she* invented her own recipes, and I became *her* taste tester. And when I thought about it, I realized Parker must have been in on a few of those sessions, too. Because frankly, how many teenage boys even knew what Boeuf Bourguignon was? Apparently, the beef stew seasoned with bacon and cooked in red wine had been a big hit with him. Then again, who could resist that dish with a side of garlic mashed potatoes?

After what felt like an hour, Carla finally returned to the phone. "I'm so sorry, Ms. Montgomery, but I'm afraid there's been a mix-up. It appears the letter you received should have gone to another address. Evidently, a letter for a different violation was mailed to your residence a few days ago, and for some reason, the computer program used your address for this letter, too. There must be a bug in the program somewhere. In any case, no, you're not in violation. So please disregard that letter."

"Thank you. I will," I told her, trying my best to show an ounce of good manners, when I really just wanted to scream.

But all's well that end's well, right?

Minutes later, I took my frustrations out on a big, white onion, chopping with such speed and ferocity that it was probably illegal in some states. Then I repeated the process on some bacon strips that I sliced into lardoons. By the time I moved on to chopping, flour coating, and searing some cubes of chuck roast, I was starting to feel like my old self again.

It wasn't long before I had the whole concoction loaded into my cast-iron casserole pan. I put the matching red-enameled lid on top, always amazed at how much the dang thing weighed, considering it was almost as heavy as the pan itself. In fact, I wondered if I'd have to start lifting weights to stay strong enough to keep using my casserole pan—one of my favorite pieces of cookware.

In any case, I left the stew simmering in the oven while I ran upstairs to work on my manuscript. And the very second I scooted my chair under my desk, the words flowed right out of me:

*"Blaze sighed as Angus enveloped her in his arms and pulled her tightly to him. He put his lips firmly onto hers, and she let herself fall into his kiss, just long enough to buy some time and come up with an answer to his question. His proposal of marriage.*

*Finally, she pulled back and looked him squarely in the eyes. 'Angus, darling, I'm not sure it would work. Do you remember how you reacted when I traveled to Tokyo and took on a roving band of diamond thieves?'*

*He raised one of his perfectly symmetrical eyebrows. 'Well, okay, maybe I got a little upset. But who can blame me? That group was dangerous. Deadly dangerous. And I was afraid you were in way over your head.'*

*That's when she shook the very head he was referring to. 'But I wasn't, was I? I solved that murder mystery just like I solve every murder mystery. I helped the Tokyo police catch the crooks, and those crooks went to prison for a long, long time.'*

*Angus crossed his arms. 'What's your point?'*

*'My point is, my dear, that even though I love you with all my heart, I'm afraid you would be a terribly overprotective husband. And I don't want anything to hold me back, not when I have so many more adventures ahead of me . . .'"*

I had barely finished typing the words when I felt a huge, involuntary intake of air, like I'd been swimming underwater and suddenly surfaced in my swimming pool. Probably because I'd basically answered a very big question for myself, one that had been weighing me down—but yes, I really *did* want Blaze to continue on and get some more escapades under her belt. And I really *did* want to continue writing her books. That much I was sure of.

As for converting those books to ink on paper, well, that part I *wasn't* so sure about. It would only happen if I took the plunge and published them on my own. Something that made my heart start to race. Not only did I know next to nothing about the Indie publishing world, but the lack of guaranteed income terrified me.

Whereas gainful employment elsewhere could provide me with a steady paycheck. Gia had mentioned that her husband might hire me to work at his car lot, but oddly enough, he hadn't said a word about it at lunch. And there was still the possibility that I could find a job at some other business. Though neither of those options really appealed to me.

Meaning, there could be a huge disconnect between what I *wanted* to do and what I *had* to do. But any way I looked at it, I needed to figure out which path to take at this fork in the road.

Thankfully, I was saved from having to face the music when I heard Parker's car come up the driveway. Seconds later, his footsteps sounded in the kitchen, followed by his shouting, "Mom, I'm home! I didn't get arrested or anything!"

I rolled my eyes and went downstairs to greet my son. "That's good. Because I'm fresh out of bail money."

This brought forth his usual goofy grin, and I knew he was pleased with himself for getting the elicited response. I also thought he seemed pretty self-assured for a young man who had invited a girl to dinner. *If* it was a girl he'd invited.

"Wow, that beef stew smells good, Mom. Can I have some now?" He picked up Agatha and cradled her in his arms.

I shook my head and laughed. "No, I haven't made the mashed potatoes yet. Besides, we've got to save this for dinner. You know where your after-school snack stuff is."

"Yeah, yeah, yeah. Apples and carrots and yogurt. *Geesh*, it would be nice to get a cookie every now and then." He sighed as Agatha gave him a sympathetic purr. "What time is dinner anyway?"

"Six o'clock. Just like always."

"Good," he said with a smug smile.

"Is that what time you told your friend to come over?"

"Five-thirty."

"Does this friend have a name?"

"Uh-huh. Sure does. By the way, that's not what you're wearing, is it?"

I gaped at my son and then looked down at my white capris. "Since when do you care about what I'm wearing? Are we going to start dressing for dinner now?"

"No, but you could put on something . . . you know . . ."

I raised an eyebrow. "No . . . I *don't* know . . ."

"Well . . . maybe something prettier."

While a part of me wanted to ream my son, another part of me realized that maybe he wanted to make a good impression. And that's when it hit me—if he was bringing a girl home, maybe she was more important to him that I'd suspected.

So I put a smile on my face. "I'll dress up if you'll dress up."

He set Agatha down and saluted me. "Consider it done, oh, mom of mine." And with that, he raced up the back stairs to his room.

Leaving me standing there baffled. "What gives?" I asked the kitties.

Their only response was to stare after Parker. Until they finally decided to run up the stairs in full pursuit.

Now I was absolutely dying to meet Parker's "friend." For all I knew, one day she might even be . . . "My daughter-in-law," I said aloud.

I couldn't help but smile. Though I knew Parker was still so young, I also knew that a high school romance could turn into a lifelong love.

I kept on smiling as I peeled potatoes and set them on the stove to boil. I minced a few cloves of garlic, ready to add to the potatoes.

Then I made a beeline to my closet and put on a navy blue knit dress. I worked a little magic with a curling iron and dabbed on some pink lipstick. Then I added a strand of pearls.

*Not too bad*, I decided, as I inspected myself in the mirror. Right before I returned to the kitchen, checked the potatoes, and then drained them. I had barely added the milk, sour cream, and garlic when the doorbell rang.

"Parker," I yelled to the top of the stairs. "Your friend's here!"

When I heard no response from him, I headed to the front door myself. I put on my sweetest, most welcoming smile, all ready to meet Parker's special friend. I wondered what she might look like, and, don't ask me why, but I somehow envisioned her as being petite. So I instantly dropped my eyes downward and turned the knob.

Imagine my surprise when I opened the door and was forced to move my gaze upward, until my eyes met the vivid blue eyes of the very tall Mr. Yarborough, Parker's forty-something-ish Physics teacher.

He held his hand out to shake mine. "Hello, Mrs. Montgomery. So nice to see you again. And thank you for inviting me to dinner. It was very kind of you."

*Wasn't it, though?* I fought the urge to roll my eyes. No wonder Parker had been keeping mum about the name of his "friend" who was coming over. Especially when he had done such a great job of railroading me into this meeting—or whatever it was meant to be—with his teacher.

"Please come in, Mr. Yarborough." I smiled with all the graciousness of a good hostess and held the door open wide for him. "And please call me, Maddie."

"And I'm Nick. I normally would've brought a bottle of wine, but I don't like to encourage my students. If you know what I mean."

"I do."

"So I ran by the bakery and got these instead," he said as he produced a box full of sugar cookies that were decorated like spring flowers.

I laughed. "Parker will be so happy. He doesn't get to eat many cookies at home."

Nick rubbed his neatly trimmed dark beard, one that matched his neatly trimmed dark hair. "Oh? He always brags about what a good cook you are. I just pictured you whipping up cookies right and left."

"I'm afraid not," I told him. "Because Parker can down a dozen in one setting."

And speaking of Parker, he came racing down the front staircase, wearing navy dress pants, a white shirt and one of his father's old ties.

"Oh, forgive me," Nick said, glancing at his own sports coat over a button-down shirt, along with a pair of jeans. "I should've dressed up a little more."

I shook my head. "Not to worry. We don't normally dress like this for dinner. Parker, would you like to get your teacher some sweet tea? While I finish cooking dinner?"

Parker grinned. "Sure, thing. Come on in, Mr. Yarborough."

And with that, we all headed into the kitchen. Parker poured tea for us, and I mashed the potatoes. Then I pulled my ridiculously heavy casserole dish from the oven. Using both hands, I removed the cast-iron lid, and the smell of Boeuf Bourguignon filled the kitchen.

For a moment or two, I thought Nick was going to faint from the delicious scent. But much to his credit, he managed to recover and hold it together.

"I've read lots of your books, Maddie," he told me. "You're a fantastic author. But I understand you're thinking of switching to Indie publishing. That's how I've been publishing my sci-fi books for a while now, and Parker wanted me to talk to you about it."

I slid my eyes in the direction of my son, whereupon my gaze was met with an enormous grin.

"Dandy," I said to him.

Now I finally understood the real reason for this dinner.

# Chapter Eleven

Much to my amazement, Parker's teacher ate almost as much as my son did, though thankfully, not at quite the same speed. For the first serving anyway. But once Parker had practically licked his plate clean—figuratively, of course, since I would never let him do that in real life, (especially not when we had company)—he raced off to the kitchen for seconds. Though he did have the good manners to take Nick's plate to the kitchen for a refill, too.

"I just want you to know," Nick said to me, "I'm not in the habit of downing so much food in one setting. But this dinner is so delicious I can't help it."

I smiled and took a sip of my tea. "Very sweet of you to say. Parker, on the other hand, eats like this three or four times a day. Sometimes I can't believe how much food that kid can put away, without putting on an ounce. I'm starting to wonder if I should take him to the doctor."

Nick gave me a knowing smile. "Most of the boys in my class are like that. I even allow them a quick break for a snack, because I know they can't concentrate when their stomachs are growling."

"I'll bet they appreciate it."

He laughed. "You figure these things out when you work mostly with adolescent boys."

"I can imagine," I added just as Parker zoomed back into the room with Nick's plate.

He set the food in front of his teacher before putting his own plate—piled high with my "fancy" beef stew and garlic mashed potatoes, of course—at his spot at the table. Then he plopped down in his chair, inhaled a few bites, and proceeded to change the subject. Specifically, he asked his teacher to tell me about Indie publishing, and Nick seemed more than happy to oblige.

It wasn't long before I began to understand why Parker liked his teacher so much. Nick seemed to have found his calling, both as an educator and an Indie, sci-fi author, and I honestly envied him for that. Only a week ago, my life had also been headed on a trajectory that was unquestionable in my mind. Now I longed for that sensation of being so sure about my career path again.

Though Parker seemed to think he had it all figured out for me. Because he was practically on a mission to point, or rather, *push* me in the direction of independent publishing. In fact, he even brought his laptop down to the dining room table after we'd finished eating. And while we all ate sugar cookies and drank decaf coffee with plenty of cream, Nick showed Parker the various sites and publishing services that I would need to get started.

"Formatting a book doesn't look too hard," Parker said, right after taking a nice, big gulp of his coffee and downing it like he'd been drinking it every single day of his life.

Even though I didn't let him drink the caffeinated kind just yet. But what he did when he went away to college was his business.

"Yes, formatting is the easy part," Nick assured him. "But you've also got to consider all the marketing and advertising. A book won't survive unless you advertise."

And so it went. The two kept on talking while I cleared the table.

I returned just in time to hear Parker say, "My mom's got a new book almost ready to go. And she's already built her brand, so that'll help a bunch."

Nick smiled at him and then turned his eyes up to meet mine. "That's right, Maddie. You're starting out in such a fantastic position. Authors like you are actually poised to make more money as Indies."

"I like the sound of that, but I have to admit, it's a whole new world for me. And . . . it's a lot to take in," I said with a sigh. "I'll have to give this some more thought."

Nick tilted his head toward Parker. "It might seem a little overwhelming at first, but you've got some great help here."

"That I do," I agreed and smiled at my son.

Nick glanced at his watch. "I guess I'd better get going. It's a school night and I've still got homework to grade."

"I'll be getting all A's, right, Mr. Yarborough?" Parker half asked and half stated. "Since I brought you home to dinner?"

This made Nick laugh. "You get all A's anyway, Parker."

"That's the game plan," he said with a huge grin. "See you at school, Mr. Yarborough. I'm gonna go do the dishes now."

And that's when my chin practically hit the table. In fact, I was speechless for a moment as I watched my tie-wearing son head into the kitchen. Presumably to wash the dishes. Voluntarily. Something he'd never done in his entire life. Now I really did wonder if I should take him to the doctor.

"You've raised a great kid there, Maddie," Nick said softly. "I don't know of many kids who go off to do the dishes without complaining."

I crinkled my brow and stared in the direction of the kitchen. "Neither do I. And I'm not sure I know who *that* kid is, either."

Nick chuckled and took his time heading to the front door. "I really do hope you'll consider publishing your own books. You'll love having the creative control."

"I suppose that would be a nice bonus."

He put his hand on the doorknob and paused. "You know, we could talk about this some more over dinner sometime. I don't cook like you do, but I do make great reservations."

"Sure," I said, without really thinking.

Then I looked into his blue eyes that practically bore into mine. Wait a minute, had he just asked me out on a date? And had I just agreed to it?

Before I could say another word, he leaned over and gave me a kiss on the cheek. The motion was so swift and so casual that I almost didn't realize it had happened, though I was well aware of the slight tickle of his beard. Much to my surprise, I felt a warmth in the pit of my stomach, and I remembered the sensation of kissing Charlie.

And how much I missed that.

"Thank you for dinner," Nick said smoothly before he opened the front door. "It was really delicious. Parker was right about you being a sensational cook."

"Thank you . . ." I managed to murmur.

"I'll call you," were his final words, and then he was out the door.

Leaving me standing there. My hand immediately went to my cheek, to the exact spot where he had kissed it. And not surprisingly, my brain insisted on going into "instant replay" mode as I shut the door and took my time about finding Parker in the kitchen.

When I got there, I pulled up a stool at the island and watched my son put a soap pod into the dishwasher dispenser. "*Soooo* . . . you didn't mention that you were bringing Mr. Yarborough over for dinner."

"I didn't want you to get all weird about it. And say no."

"Excuse me?" I laughed.

"Well, I wasn't sure you'd listen to what he had to say about publishing your books and everything."

"It sounds like you really want me to go the Indie route. You seem pretty determined to talk me into it."

He turned and leaned against the counter, folding his arms in front of him. "Yeah, Mom, I know how much you want to keep writing books, so I think you should do it."

"Is there any more to it?"

He shrugged. "I dunno. Maybe."

"Care to elaborate?"

"Well . . . it's like this. I'm going to college in the fall. And sure, Texas A & M isn't very far away, but you'll be here all by yourself. Alone. Dad's gone. Lyndi's at sea, and I'll be gone, too. And if you quit writing, you won't even have that to keep you busy anymore. You've always gone to a bunch of conferences and book signings and all kinds of things since you started writing books. Plus, you've got author friends all over the place. So if you don't even have all that, then you'll be here all lonely and sad with no one to take care of you."

"So you feel like you need to take care of me?"

He examined his tie. "Well, yeah. Dad would want me to."

I couldn't help but smile. "That's very sweet of you, Parker. Your dad would be proud of you for that. And while I truly appreciate the concern, you don't need to worry about me. I'm not quite as decrepit as you think."

"I dunno, Mom. You're pretty old."

I rolled my eyes. "Exactly how old do you think I am?"

"*Really* old," he assured me with his usual goofy grin.

Once again, his words made me laugh. "Parker, I'm not ninety, you know. And just out of curiosity, were you also trying to line me up with your teacher? So I wouldn't be 'all lonely,' as you put it?"

"Maybe. Sort of. He's a nice guy, Mom. I really like him."

"I can see that. But Parker, I want you to be thinking about college, and then someday, your career. So I don't have to worry about *you* for the rest of my life, okay?"

"Okay, Mom, but only if you'll do one thing."

I raised an eyebrow. "And what's that?"

"Let me use the programs and sites Mr. Yarborough showed me for this Indie thing. And publish that book you've almost got finished."

I laughed. "All right, Parker. It's a deal. I will."

"Awesome, Mom. Now I've got to go finish my homework."

"Sounds good, kiddo. Thanks for doing the dishes."

He grinned and raced up the back stairs to his room. With both cats following him.

Just as Nick had said, Parker was a great kid. Or rather, a great young man. Soon to be a grown-up. And yes, the thought of him being a full-fledged adult tugged at this mom's heart. Because I was really going to miss the person he was right now.

But I didn't have long to think about it before my phone started to play the theme song from Peter Gunn. I immediately wondered if it was Nick calling already. Though I truly hoped it wasn't, since he'd just left my house and, honestly, that would have been a little quick for me.

Okay, make that *really* quick.

But when I saw the words "Unknown Caller" on my phone's readout, I knew exactly who would be on the other end of the line when I answered.

"You've had a busy day, Mrs. Montgomery," came the gravelly voice of Spencer Poe. "I saw you come and go from the Delvecchios' house. I was going to phone earlier, but I noticed you had company this evening."

For a moment or two, I felt a twinge of annoyance. While I knew full well that Spencer followed the goings-on in our neighborhood, I wasn't sure how comfortable I felt being the subject of so much surveillance.

"Yes, I haven't had a free moment all day," I told him.

"Please forgive me if it appears that I have been spying on you, Mrs. Montgomery. But I am more convinced than ever that Randall was murdered, which means we likely have a dangerous person lurking about. And because I have requested that you look into the matter, I do feel an obligation to watch over you, as it were. Out of respect for the Colonel."

Apparently, Parker wasn't the only one who felt I needed to be taken care of. And to think, I wasn't even fifty yet.

"Of course," I said with a smile. "And I do have some information for you. After having lunch with Gia—whereby her husband showed up—I learned there'd been some bad blood between Randall and Vinnie Delvecchio. Somehow or another, Randall got Vinnie to sell him a car that he didn't want to sell. A car that had been in his family."

"That does sound rather suspicious," Spencer replied. "Randall must have had some kind of leverage over Mr. Delvecchio. Though I am surprised that Randall never mentioned it to me, since we were certainly friends."

I poured the remains of the decaf coffee into a mug. "That *is* odd. I wonder why he kept hush-hush about it."

"There is only one reason that I can think of, Mrs. Montgomery. Perhaps he was blackmailing Mr. Delvecchio. Otherwise, I cannot imagine why Randall would not have said something to me."

"Blackmail?" The word made me gasp.

Which was sort of strange, considering I must have written about blackmail a zillion times over the years in my books. Yet here I was, in a real-life situation, and the mere concept of it shocked me.

"You must understand," Spencer went on. "Randall had a definite moral compass and he abhorred injustice. So if he had committed blackmail, it would have been to teach someone a lesson. And to make them think twice about repeating some behavior. But it would not have been something Randall embarked upon lightly."

"I wonder if his actions got him murdered," I said quietly.

"Possibly. Perhaps we might consider pursuing that angle."

I added cream to my coffee. "And I know the perfect way to do that. Or rather, the perfect way in, you might say. I've decided to get Charlie's car out of storage."

"The Continental Mark II? Why, I was not even aware the vehicle was in storage. Though I think it is an excellent idea, Mrs. Montgomery. No doubt the Colonel would want you to enjoy his cherished automobile."

I smiled at the thought. "And Vinnie invited me down to his lot to have the car checked over."

"Excellent. It will be the perfect opportunity to learn more about Mr. Delvecchio, and to make sure your vehicle is in tip-top condition. I would be happy to accompany you if you wish. For your safety, of course."

I stirred a nice helping of sweetener into my coffee and put the spoon in the sink. "Thank you, Spencer. That's very thoughtful. And speaking of learning more, I'll bet you got a copy of the accident report."

His voice was oddly hesitant as he answered me. "Yes, I did obtain a copy of the report."

"Did you learn anything significant?" I asked carefully.

"The crash was consistent with someone having a heart attack and losing control of a vehicle. The car was smashed beyond repair, which was not surprising, considering the make and type. It was not a vehicle that would have survived much of a wreck."

I took a sip of my coffee. "Hmmm . . . so there's really not much to go on there."

"No, except for one detail that did stand out to me," he replied, suddenly lowering his voice to a stage whisper.

And for the life of me, I couldn't imagine why. My first inclination was that he thought his phone was bugged. Though if it had been, simply talking more quietly wouldn't have made any difference. But I also wondered if Spencer had stepped into another room in his house, maybe one that he hadn't "swept" lately, like I'm sure he did the rest of his house on a regular basis.

Then again, maybe he just dropped his voice out of some kind of habit.

"Well, you've got my curiosity up," I told him. "This detail must be a real humdinger."

"I would say so. It has to do with a witness to the accident."

"Anyone we know?"

"Yes, Mrs. Montgomery. Someone we do know. A neighbor."

I set my coffee mug on the counter. "I had no idea one of our neighbors was there at the time of the wreck."

"This was the first I became aware of it myself. According to the report, Mrs. Betty Kraukpott witnessed the entire event. She was the first person on the scene of the accident."

That's when I nearly dropped my phone. Betty was there when Randall died? If Betty had seen the accident, then why didn't she say anything to anyone?

# Chapter Twelve

I was still wondering about Betty long after I got off the phone with Spencer Poe. In part, because I promised him I would pay her a visit in the morning and see what she had to say about witnessing Randall's accident. But on top of that, I was more than a little shocked that she hadn't said a word about being at the scene when he died. She was one of those people who told everybody *everything*, and keeping mum about something so significant was truly out of character for her. Especially when I factored in her snide remark at Randall's funeral, when she said something about his having had a heart attack thanks to the cost of Tiffany's wedding. It seemed like a pretty calloused comment for someone who'd just watched a man die.

Which also led me to wonder if she'd taken any steps to try to save him, since he'd obviously been alive to utter his final words. So had she administered first aid, or tried to revive him when he was gone?

Or, on the flip side, had she taken actions to *ensure* that he went on to meet his maker?

That's when a cold chill raced up and down my spine.

Maybe Betty had been keeping mum because she had something to hide. Meaning, she could have given Randall an injection or slipped him a dose of Digoxin right there at the scene of the accident.

But if that were true, what motive could she have possibly had for wanting to finish the man off? And in essence, commit an act of murder?

Whatever the case, there was obviously much more to the story than Betty was letting on.

I shuddered, thinking of Spencer's words about a killer being loose in the neighborhood. As a knee-jerk reaction, I closed all the blinds on the first floor and armed my home security system. Then I poured myself a glass of wine and took it upstairs to my office.

A minute later, I parked myself in front of my computer. Even though it had been a long day, and I was ready to put my feet up, I had something I needed to take care of first. Something important.

So I called up the last chapter of Blaze's new book, and without any hesitation at all, I added the final paragraphs:

*"Angus frowned. 'Blaze, my love, are you saying what I think you're saying?'*

*Blaze stared up at Angus with adoration in her eyes. 'I'm afraid so. My answer to your proposal of marriage is no. For now anyway.'*

*He responded by taking her hands in his. 'Deep down, I suppose I already knew the answer. But that won't stop me from asking you again from time to time.'*

*She nodded and smiled. 'I wouldn't have it any other way.'*

*Then he put his arms around her, and together they turned to admire the forensic team who was busy at work in her home. It wasn't the first time she'd had a forensic team working there. And for that matter, it wasn't the first time a murderer had broken in and tried to silence her once and for all.*

*And, she thought, I have a feeling it won't be the last."*

"Neither do I," I said aloud as I typed in my favorite words of all—"The End."

Then I sat back and sighed, right before I smiled from ear to ear, as they say. It was the same, involuntary smile that I always got whenever I finished writing a novel. Funny, but I've often heard people describe the joy of reading a good book. I've experienced it myself plenty of times.

But it doesn't begin to compare to the joy of writing one.

I took a sip of my wine and made sure I had everything saved properly. I would start on the rewrites in the morning and get the manuscript ready to send to my editor.

And that's when I stopped cold. Because it suddenly hit me that I didn't *have* an editor anymore.

"Well, I'll simply have to hire one," I said to Ellery and Agatha who had slipped in while I was working and now sat vigilant in the window seat, staring outside. Possibly watching for the return of Evinrude.

Or, watching someone lurking on the street below.

And much as I was inclined to give in to my budding paranoia, I fought the urge to get up and look out the window. Instead, I started an online search for freelance editors.

Seconds later, Parker knocked on the door and poked his head in my office. "Working on your book?"

My smile returned. "Just finished the first draft."

He grinned. "Good job, Mom. I'll start working on the other stuff tomorrow. The stuff Mr. Yarborough showed us."

"Thanks, Parker, but no rush. There's plenty of time before this manuscript will be ready. And school work comes first."

"Okay, Mom. I'm going to bed now."

"Sleep tight," I said as he waved and took off. "See you in the morning."

Yet little did I know, it was a morning that came a whole lot sooner than I'd expected. Especially after I stayed up much too late searching the Internet for editors and cover designers. And when I finally did get to bed, I jumped at the sound of every creak and crack outside my bedroom window. I barely managed to crawl out from under the covers after only a few hours of shut-eye, whereby I dragged myself to the kitchen and practically started an IV infusion of caffeine. I was on my second cup of coffee by the time Parker downed his last bite of breakfast and took off for school. Thankfully, the caffeine started to kick in just shortly before I wobbled to the shower and got ready for the day. And once I was reasonably presentable, I started to feel halfway human again.

In fact, I was even feeling a little full of myself, amateur sleuth that I'd suddenly become, when I headed out the door and made a beeline for Betty's house. I congratulated myself on being well armed with questions and strategies, and completely ready to get to the bottom of things.

But all that came to a screeching halt when I reached the outer edge of Betty's front walkway. Sure, I had a good view of her property from my side of the street, but it had been ages since I'd *actually* approached her front door. And from the vantage point of my house—a view that was impeded by plenty of trees in the center island of our cul-de-sac—I hadn't been fully aware of just how "overgrown" her front yard actually was. So now, as I started moving forward again, slowly stepping past the virtual Amazonian forest of gigantic shrubs and huge lily-like plants that appeared to have reproduced at an alarming rate on her property, I sort of felt a little, well . . . creeped out. It was almost like I expected some woman-eating beast to burst forth from all that foliage and gobble me up like Parker eating a hamburger.

Of course, the rational side of me said I needn't worry about anything quite so large bounding out to get me. No, instead I should have been more concerned about all the wriggling-and-crawling-type creatures that probably called Betty's personal jungle their home. It didn't help that I could barely tell where her garden ended and where her walkway began. That's because the normally light-colored cement sported a layer of dark mold—not entirely unusual for the Houston area—though most of us had it removed through that modern miracle known as power washing.

And as I inched ever closer to her house, I truly wished I hadn't just slipped on a pair of flip-flops before embarking on this big adventure. I became acutely aware of my bare toes by the time I finally stepped up to the brick façade of her front entryway and spotted a vivid green mold that had sprouted at ground level and spread upward about a foot. Something even the spiders in their webs dangling from above wouldn't touch.

Okay, I have to admit, I don't consider myself to be a complete neat freak, but the entire area was bringing out my inner Mr. Clean. It took every ounce of willpower I had to resist the urge to cut back that overgrown garden and hire someone to power wash the whole shebang.

Which made it that much more difficult to ring her bell. Because all that mold and grime and overgrowth seemed to impair my ability to think, and for the life of me, I couldn't remember the specific questions I had wanted to ask Betty.

Which left me no choice but to wing it.

Unfortunately, "winging it" wasn't exactly my forte. Though Blaze wouldn't have had a problem when it came to coming up with questions on the fly. In fact, if this had been one of her scenes, she probably would've had the foresight to bring along some diluted bleach in a spray bottle to kill any mold and insects along the way.

If only I had done the same.

Nonetheless, I managed to take a deep breath (but not too deep for fear of inhaling any mold spores) and hit the doorbell. Much to my surprise, June's daughter, Tiffany, swung the door wide open.

"Yes?" she murmured in a tone that ranged somewhere between bored and annoyed.

I stopped gaping and plastered a smile on my face. "Good morning, Tiffany. I didn't expect to see you here. Is Betty home?"

She sighed and looked down at her skinny jeans. "I'm babysitting. Betty is out somewhere."

"I didn't realize you were a babysitter."

"I *told* everyone I had a part-time job. And this is it."

"Oh . . . how nice," I murmured, only seconds before the crash of breaking glass came from somewhere inside the house, followed by gales of laughter.

Tiffany jerked her head up. "I don't believe this. Why me?"

"Maybe you'd better go see what happened."

"I can't take these little brats anymore. I just can't do this."

Which meant what? That she planned to abandon them?

"Maybe you should call Betty," I suggested.

Tiffany shook her head. "She's out taking pictures or something. She told me not to bug her."

"Would you like me to go in and take a look?"

"So I'll lose out on my babysitting money? No way," Tiffany snarled.

Then before I could say another word, she stepped back into the house and shrieked, "Beauregard, Bianca, and Bristol! Come here right this minute!"

Thankfully, there was something in her tone that made the three little terrors come running to the front door. They all had some kind of dark goo in their hair and on their faces, and judging from the smell, I could only guess it was chocolate pudding. Or some reasonable facsimile of, given Betty's "unique" cooking concoctions. The trio then stood there barefoot, wearing grimy, mismatched clothing, as they all stared up at Tiffany.

I regarded them much like I would have my own children when they were that age. "We heard a loud crash inside the house and it sounded like something broke. Would you like to tell us what happened?"

Whereby one child looked at the other and so on.

The little girl, Bianca, finally spoke up. "It was something Mommy was working on. For her blog. She said it was going to make us rich."

"Yeah," the oldest child added, the boy named Beauregard. "That's right. And everyone who has been mean to Mommy is going to be really sorry."

Though probably not as sorry as these kids were going to be when their Mom got home and saw what they had broken.

"Do we need to clean it up?" I looked at their dirty faces and resisted the urge to march them inside and clean *them* up.

But Tiffany shook her head and started moving down the front walk. "No, I'll just take them to my house."

And without a word, the children simply shrugged and followed along. Bianca grabbed the hand of the youngest boy, Bristol.

I pulled the front door shut and took up the rear of the little procession. "Tiffany, do you think this is a good idea? They're not wearing shoes."

"They're fine," she informed me. "I go barefoot around here all the time. So does Betty."

An image of Betty blogging about some homemade, antifungal cream suddenly flashed through my mind. And despite the warmth of the day already, I couldn't help but shudder.

Even so, I kept my eyes on Betty's young ones to make sure they tagged along like they were supposed to. Thankfully, they had decided to behave and followed Tiffany without deviating from the course.

We were all smack dab in the middle of the street when Tiffany suddenly stopped and turned to me with tears in her eyes. "Maddie, can I ask you a question?"

"Sure," I told her, reminding myself not to be too judgmental, since, after all, Tiffany had just lost her father.

"Do men sometimes ignore their wives? I mean, my dad never ignored my mom. She always complained that he spent too much time with her. Did your husband ever ignore you?"

"Well, that's a hard one to answer," I told her as I made sure the children continued to cross the street. "My situation with my husband was different. He was in the military, and we always knew that he might have to leave at a moment's notice. Plus he was deployed several times. So we didn't always have the luxury of being together when we wanted to be."

"Well, Aiden and I are together, but we're not really together."

To be honest, I wasn't exactly surprised by this news. After all, I'd seen Aiden in action, so to speak. Though "inaction" was probably the better word.

"What's going on?" I asked her gently as we all reached the curb on the other side of the street.

Tiffany pulled out a wad of tissues from her jeans pocket, accidentally dislodging another piece of paper along with it. She let the paper fall to the street, without giving it a second glance, and used the tissues to dab at the huge tears that now rolled down her cheeks.

I immediately picked up the paper and shoved it into the pocket of my own capris, something I realized was becoming a uniform of sorts for me. Maybe I needed to start switching up my dress code a little.

Tiffany sniffled some more and then blew her nose. "All Aiden ever wants to do is play his stupid video games. He doesn't even stop and talk to me when I go into the room. And he wouldn't come to bed last night after I yelled at him a couple of times. I don't know what to do."

"Well . . ." I started to say. "Have you thought about going to a marriage counselor?"

"A marriage counselor?" Tiffany scoffed. "Are you kidding? We just got married. We're newlyweds. Newlyweds don't need marriage counselors."

"Are you sure? Marriage can be a huge adjustment for people. And sometimes young couples can use a little help," I added just as we reached June's front door.

But Tiffany didn't respond as she opened the door wide to let everyone in. June appeared almost immediately and shot her daughter a questioning look.

Tiffany's tears increased tenfold. "I can't handle these little brats today. You take care of them."

June giggled and shook her head. "Nope, this is your job. You're getting paid for it. Not me."

That's when Tiffany started to yell at her mother. "Why should I have to work anyway? I'm going to inherit all that money from daddy."

Now June tilted her head back and roared with laughter. "*You* didn't inherit a thing, darlin'! *I'm* the one who gets everything."

"But that's my money, too!" Tiffany shot back.

"Oh, no it's not," her mother replied with more giggles.

In the meantime, Betty's three darlings decided that *now* would be a really good time to run up the elegant, curved staircase. So they went racing up just as fast as their little legs would take them, shouting and laughing all the way.

While I stood there, wondering if June really wanted those kids up there. I felt like I should say something, but I didn't want to butt in while Tiffany and June's odd argument escalated even more. Though to be honest, it was a little hard to tell if they were really arguing or not, with Tiffany yelling and June laughing as though her daughter were telling her the funniest jokes on the planet. But the pair finally went silent when, about a minute later, the most high-pitched, bloodcurdling scream I've ever heard in my entire life came from somewhere on the second floor.

The shrieking continued as three terrified young children raced back down the stairs, crying, and apparently running for their lives. Yet the screaming upstairs didn't let up, and, as near as I could tell, it was coming from the vicinity of the game room.

What in the world had happened?

Once again, the words that Spencer Poe had said a few nights ago echoed through my brain: "It is a distinct possibility that we have a murderer running loose in the neighborhood."

So had there been another murder, right here in Abbott Cove? In our very own neighborhood?

# Chapter Thirteen

With fear etched across their little faces, the children flew down the steps to the first floor and ran right past us, making a beeline for the family room. And that's when I took off running *up* those very stairs. Had someone else been the victim of foul play? Was someone injured or dying upstairs?

And for that matter, could I even get there in time to save them?

I had almost reached the second floor when I heard a voice hollering, "I'll kill you, you little monsters! I'll kill you! You will die for this!"

The voice belonged to a man.

A young man.

One who suddenly appeared at the railing of the second-story landing.

I stopped dead in my tracks and glanced back at June and Tiffany. Much to my amazement, they didn't seem the least bit fazed by the whole situation.

"Is that . . . Aiden?" I managed to ask.

It was a valid question, considering the guy looking down on us was a far cry from the young man I'd seen at his wedding. Or at his father-in-law's funeral. *This* Aiden was wearing stained sweat pants and a stained and ripped t-shirt. His silky hair was in tangles, and half a tortilla chip was plastered to his cheek. And after I got a good whiff of his distinct "lack of hygiene"—something that was very noticeable even from where I stood—I guessed he probably hadn't showered in a while.

In any case, as near as I could tell, he wasn't bleeding or injured or even remotely close to dying.

At least not from some accident or attack.

Yet judging from the veins popping out on his forehead and the way his normally pale skin had turned a dangerous shade of red, I wondered if death from natural causes might still be a possibility. Though his lungs certainly seemed to be healthy enough, given the volume with which he continued to shriek. Honestly, I don't think I've ever seen a grown man so angry or upset before, and well, it sort of reminded me of Parker when he was two and having a major temper tantrum. A behavior I nipped in the bud long, long ago, thank God! And now I wondered if someone had skipped that phase of child-rearing where Aiden was concerned, and maybe this was his normal behavior, since, when I thought about it, other than seeing Aiden up at the altar on his wedding day where he simply participated in the "repeat after me" section of the ceremony, I really hadn't heard many words out of the young man. Ever.

But he didn't seem to be at a loss for words now.

"I'll kill them!" he hollered again. "Do you know what those little animals did? They poured my entire cola into my modem! And the whole thing just shorted out. It's dead. Completely dead. Those little jerks were only in the room for five seconds and they ruined everything! Now what am I going to do? We don't have Internet!"

Tiffany shrugged. "Oh well."

Then, like a charging bull, Aiden ran down the stairs, pushed past me, and headed straight for his wife. "It's bad enough that I have to live in this house. And now *this* happened!"

For some reason, June found her son-in-law's meltdown to be rather hilarious, and she started to giggle without showing any signs of stopping. "If you don't like it here, go find your own place," she finally managed to spit out between guffaws. "You're married now, and you two shouldn't be living here anyway."

Aiden immediately turned his nastiness toward his mother-in-law. "We'll move out just as soon as we get the money that the old guy left us."

"Old guy?" I repeated as I stepped down to the main floor and joined them.

Whereby he directed his gaze at me, his eyes wild and blazing. "Yeah . . . you know . . . the old guy. Old what's-his-name."

I couldn't help but choke. "You mean . . . your father-in-law? Randall?"

"Yeah, him!" Aiden shouted, just inches from my face, demonstrating that he was an equal opportunity bully. "We're supposed to inherit half his money."

Tiffany nodded in agreement with her husband, but kept her eyes on June. "See, Mom? That's what I was telling you! As soon as we get our share, then Aiden and I can get a place of our own."

June giggled. "What do you mean, 'your share'?"

"You know, my half of the money that daddy had in the bank," Tiffany went on. "And his investments and things like that. And this house."

Again June laughed uproariously. "Where did you ever get an idea like that? You don't get half of anything, little girl."

"What Tiff said is right," Aiden added. "We're supposed to get half. I learned about it in school."

June grabbed the staircase banister for support as she bent over laughing. "Well, maybe you should've paid more attention in class. Because you've got it all wrong. You don't get a dime."

And that's when a tearful Tiffany practically started to hyperventilate. "But it's not fair. That's supposed to be my money, too! Aiden said so. And I know Daddy wanted me to have it. You'll see when we have that reading of the will thing. When is that, anyway?"

"There won't be any reading of the will," June went on, practically hiccupping by now. "They only do that in the movies, darlin'. Your daddy and I had joint ownership of everything, so everything is in my name, too. The house, the car, the bank accounts, and all our investments. I own it all. Plus I'm the sole beneficiary of your daddy's life insurance policy."

For a second or two, I thought Tiffany might faint.

Aiden threw his hands up in the air. "Well, if I'm stuck here, I'm gonna need Internet!" He pushed past me a second time and headed into Randall's office. "Where is the account information for your Internet provider? They better send out a new modem today!" Then without waiting for an answer, he began to dig through files and drawers with such speed that I feared he might spontaneously combust.

That, or I wondered if I might blow a fuse myself, considering the way he was treating both June and me. But at least I had the option of leaving. June, on the other hand, lived here. And for a minute or two, I wondered if she was safe in her own home with this out of control young man.

I stepped into the office with him. "Maybe you'd better take a minute to calm down, Aiden."

But he didn't bother to respond with so much as a monosyllabic grunt. In fact, he acted like I was completely invisible. And he continued to act that way even as June and Tiffany joined us in the office. Tiffany remained silent, too, while she dug around and found the Internet account information. Then she handed her cell phone to her new husband, and he dialed what I assumed was the number for customer service. I could hear ringing through the phone and, right after he punched in a few numbers, I was pretty sure he was put on hold.

Standing there, I spotted Randall's file on the HOA, the very one I'd seen the day I'd been snooping around his office. Something I wasn't exactly proud of. But the file was now sitting on top of the desk.

"June, I know Randall had quite a battle going with the HOA. Is this a file he kept on it?" I asked ever so innocently.

"Yes! He was always fighting with them." She batted her lashes and let out a girlish giggle. "And I like a big, strong man who stands up and won't back down from a fight. One who defends his fair maiden. Don't you?"

I crinkled my brow. "Well, yes, I suppose I do. As long as those big, strong men don't go around *starting* fights. Would you mind if I borrowed Randall's file? I've been having a little HOA trouble myself lately, and I would appreciate any pointers I might pick up."

"Oh sure, Maddie, help yourself," she said with a smile.

"Thanks," I told her. "I'll bring it back when I'm done."

I grabbed the file and stepped into the hallway, ready to leave. June came with me, and together we walked to the front entry.

I was just about to open the door when she gave her wrist a good sniff and then put it in front of my nose. "What do you think, Maddie? I've always wanted to buy this perfume. So I just decided to do it. I had it overnighted. It was super expensive. But it's so nice, don't you think?"

I took a little sniff. "It's a very pretty scent, June."

And certainly, a welcome change from Aiden's Eau de Body Odor. In the background, I could hear him angrily explaining his Internet situation to the poor customer service person who had been unlucky enough to answer his call.

"June . . ." I started to say before I hesitated, trying to find words that struck a balance between watching out for her well-being and minding my own business. In the end, I simply went with, "Are you okay?"

"Okay? Darlin', I've never felt so good," she replied with more giggles.

I had to say, from what I could tell, she was definitely feeling "good," all right. But she wasn't herself, considering all the things she'd been saying and doing lately. And when I thought about it, I realized that what I'd seen was probably just the tip of the iceberg when it came to her new antics. Sure, I was happy her medication was helping her through the difficult stages of grieving, but I also hoped she didn't plan to stay on it for very long. Not only was I concerned that she might blow all the money from the life insurance policy, but I was also afraid she might do something she couldn't "undo" later. Things that could come back to haunt her.

In the meantime, I wanted to make sure she was safe from her son-in-law.

"I'm a little concerned about the way Aiden is treating you," I said gently.

"Oh, him," she laughed again. "He won't be a problem."

"Well, if he ever is, you know I only live a couple of doors down. You're always welcome to come over if things get ugly."

She scrunched up her forehead and looked at me as though I'd just told her I'd flown in from another solar system.

So I didn't pursue it any farther. Instead, I gave her a quick hug and opened the door.

Betty walked in just as I was walking out.

Without so much as a "hello," she glanced up at the staircase. "Does anyone know where my kids are? I got home and found the front door unlocked and Tiffany and my kids were gone."

I nodded to her. "I think you'll find them in the family room."

June chuckled and spun on her heel. "I'll go make them some lunch."

"Awesome!" Betty said with a huge grin.

And much as I wanted to ask her about witnessing Randall's car wreck, I didn't want to question her in front of June. So I decided to wait until I could catch Betty alone, and I headed back to my house with Randall's file in hand.

But I had barely stepped to the curb when Evinrude came buzzing in my direction. He landed on the street, winked his little lights at me a couple of times, and dropped a few envelopes and flyers onto the cement.

I smiled at his bug-like face. "Hello, little drone."

As always, his appearance was followed by my Peter Gunn ringtone. I pulled my phone from my back pocket, knowing full well who was calling.

"Hello, Spencer," I said. "Thanks for dropping off my mail."

"You're welcome, Mrs. Montgomery. Thankfully, I'm not the bearer of bad news this time."

"That's good to hear. Hopefully the HOA will leave me alone after my last two phone calls with them. Though I can't shake the feeling that I haven't heard the last of them."

"I can't say that I blame you, Mrs. Montgomery. HOAs are a far more powerful form of government than many people realize."

"Including me," I told Spencer. "Now it seems like I'm "realizing" it more every day. In any case, I'm afraid I don't have any news for you about Betty. She was out all morning and I haven't been able to catch her alone yet."

"I appreciate that you have tried, Mrs. Montgomery. But I had another reason for calling. I wondered if you would like me to go with you to retrieve the Colonel's car. Not to sound condescending, of course, but since the car has not been started in a few years, I would be happy to give it a quick going over. To make sure everything is running well enough for you to get home safely."

"That's very thoughtful of you, Spencer."

"If you would like, I am available to go right after lunch," he said as Evinrude gained altitude and headed for home base.

"Well, umm . . . yes, that sounds great. I'll grab a quick bite to eat and be ready to go."

"Don't forget a key to the storage unit and to the vehicle itself."

"Oh, right . . ." I murmured, remembering that I'd put them in the safe in my master bedroom closet.

"I will pull up in front of your house at thirteen-hundred hours and wait for you there, Mrs. Montgomery."

"Well, thank you. I'll see you then."

And sure enough, just minutes after one o'clock, I was sitting in the passenger seat of Spencer's huge, black SUV. One that was strangely nondescript on the outside, thanks in part to the darkened windows that prevented anyone from seeing all the electronic gadgetry on the dashboard. There were so many buttons and switches and dials that I even wondered if the vehicle had ever been used for presidential motorcades. For a moment, I toyed with the idea of tapping on the windows to see if they were made of bulletproof acrylic. But I held back and minded my manners.

Instead, I opened the folder that I'd brought along, the one labeled "Charlie's Car." I found the address of the storage complex, and Spencer plugged it into his navigation system on steroids. Right away, a voice gave us directions and we were off.

Trepidation rose in my throat at the very thought of seeing my late husband's car again. Mostly because I'd skillfully managed to avoid this day for a long, long time. In my mind, that car was so completely linked to Charlie that it was hard for me to picture it without him. He had loved that vintage automobile; he enjoyed tinkering with it, and whenever he had time, he brought it home and we all went for a ride. Charlie nearly always drove it when we went out to dinner, or to the symphony or to the theatre downtown. Sometimes he even donned a stingy-brimmed fedora, along with a dark suit and thin tie, giving him a real "Rat Pack" look.

Truth be told, there were just so many memories attached to that car . . . and so many emotions attached to those memories. Amazingly enough, the idea of revisiting those days gone by terrified me. Or rather, I was afraid of the way I would react when those memories came to the surface again. Would I fall apart, and go right back to the paralyzing grief that I'd felt shortly after he died? I'd been through that agonizing pain once already, and I hardly wanted a repeat performance.

It had been so much easier just to leave the car in the climate-controlled unit and keep it out of sight and out of mind.

But despite my fine-tuned sense of denial, the time had come for me to face the past and the pain. To rip off the band-aid, so to speak. And I was as ready as I was ever going to be. In fact, a very big part of me actually wanted to see the Continental again.

Spencer turned into the drive of the storage complex, and I gave him the code to punch into the keypad that opened the electronic gate. Seconds later, we parked in front of the huge unit. I stepped out with my key in hand and unlocked the padlock holding the door in place.

Then I lifted the garage door. Sunlight and dust immediately filtered into the sparse room. And that's when I saw it. Charlie's car. Protected by a fleece-lined car cover.

Yet oddly enough, what stood out to me the most was the silence of the moment. I don't think I'd ever been inside that unit without the presence of laughter or conversation or some kind of joyful noise. Now there was none. Only the eerie silence that comes with the loss of someone who had once been so full of life.

Someone who had once made *my* life so full.

Still, much to my surprise, no tears welled up in my eyes. I didn't fall apart like I feared I would as I moved toward the car and carefully slid the cover off. The shine of the black paint reflected even the minimal light in the room. Oddly enough, I smiled and almost laughed at the sight of Charlie's car. If it had been a living being, it would have had the same cavalier grin and swagger that my husband had been known for. On top of it all, I'd forgotten just how beautiful the Continental was.

Nearby, Spencer let out a low whistle. "The Colonel most definitely knew his cars. Let me confirm that everything is in good working order before you start it up."

And the next thing I knew, Spencer popped the hood and started to examine the engine with a flashlight. I opened the driver's side door, slid onto the front seat, and ran my fingers over the dashboard.

Then just like I had feared, the familiar smell inside the car brought memories flooding back to me. I thought of all the times when Charlie had taken us to Abbott's Big Burgers for our favorite fast food. And I thought of all the drives to the beach on Galveston Island and back. Of course, everywhere we went, everyone always commented on Charlie's car, and they always wanted to know "what" it was, too.

My reminiscing quickly took me away from the here and now, and carried me back in time, and brought a smile to my face. I was barely aware of Spencer's flashlight beam shining against the metal walls of the room. Though for a second or two, it did register that this behavior might be unusual. Even for him.

But I didn't budge from my reverie until Spencer called out with, "Mrs. Montgomery, did you know there was a lockbox in here?"

A lockbox?

I answered him with, "No, I didn't know."

I got out of the car and joined Spencer in the back corner of the unit. And sure enough, I saw the dull metal box that he pointed to. One that I knew nothing about. It was sitting right next to a couple of file storage boxes that I also knew nothing about.

Which left me to wonder—why did Charlie leave a lockbox in this storage unit?

And more importantly, what was inside?

# Chapter Fourteen

I could practically hear time ticking by as I just stood there, dumbfounded, staring at that lockbox. It was about twelve inches by eight inches and butted up next to one of the two cardboard file boxes. All things I knew absolutely nothing about. Things I would've learned about years ago if I'd taken the plunge and emptied out this storage unit. But that's what a girl gets when she goes around avoiding something for years.

I reached down and, just for the heck of it, tried to pull the top up on the metal lockbox. On the off, off chance that it might be unlocked. But no such luck. The lid held tight.

So I turned to the file boxes, and I was just about to remove the lids when Spencer put a protective arm out in front of me. "Allow me, Mrs. Montgomery. These boxes have cutouts that work as handles, and you never know what might have slithered into a container that has been sitting undisturbed for quite some time. Snakes and spiders and mice have been known to make themselves at home in such environs."

Before I could respond, he nudged the lids off with the toe of his shoe and shined his flashlight into each box. Then he carefully reached inside and pushed the files and other items from side to side and then front to back, making a very thorough inspection. When nothing creepy or crawly made a snarling or biting appearance, he stood back while I glanced at the contents of the boxes. I saw mostly file folders that were filled with papers and a few photos, but nothing that stood out to me as being terribly noteworthy. Charlie had been involved in a private security company after he retired from the Air Force, and I guessed the things in the boxes probably pertained to his work. Whatever the case, I knew I'd have to go through them later when I had more time.

And light.

"Would you like me to load these in my vehicle and transport them home for you, Mrs. Montgomery?" Spencer asked quietly while his eyes scanned the room.

I shook my head. "Thanks, but I'll just put them in the trunk of the Continental. It's almost bigger than the first home that Charlie and I rented."

This brought forth a chuckle from Spencer. "I'm sure it is roomy, all right. That fine automobile was in a class of its own, back in the day. They don't make them like that anymore."

"No, they don't," I agreed as I walked to the rear of the car and popped the trunk open.

Then we loaded up the boxes, and Spencer went back to inspecting the car. And while he put some air in the tires, I walked around Charlie's treasured Continental, staring at it, and giving it a loving caress or two.

"Go ahead and start it up," Spencer said at last.

So I slid back into the driver's seat and did just that. The car purred to life, and for some reason, I felt like purring myself. My reaction to the sound was instantaneous, and in a flash, I was back in time and enjoying life with my husband again. A whole parade of happy memories streamed through my mind, making my heart pound with joy. Funny how I had feared those memories before we arrived, and now here I was, loving every second of them.

And much as I longed to stay lost in my reverie, reliving days gone by, I didn't want to take advantage of Spencer's kindness in bringing me over to the storage unit. So I got out of the car, and I found him walking along one of the corrugated steel walls. He was shining his flashlight from top to bottom as he went, just like he'd done before.

Was he checking for bugs, possibly? Not the kind that crawl or fly, but the kind that spy?

"Is anything the matter?" I asked him.

He crinkled his forehead. "I could have sworn I heard something . . ."

Which made me wonder if it was time to get him back home. While I didn't know exactly how old Spencer was, I had a sneaking suspicion he was at the age where an afternoon nap might be a good idea.

"It's probably just a mouse or something," I said gently.

He switched off the flashlight. "Perhaps, Mrs. Montgomery."

I gave him a smile. "I'm ready to go now. Would you mind showing me how to lower the hood?"

He took another glance around. "Most certainly. Let's get the Colonel's prized automobile where it belongs. I will follow you home to make sure you do not have any problems."

"Thank you so much. I really appreciate your help."

Minutes later, I backed the car out of the storage unit, and Spencer closed the huge garage door. Then I fastened the old-fashioned seatbelt—without a shoulder harness, of course—and put the car in gear. Thankfully, it had automatic transmission, though I knew many automobiles of that era did not. While I'd learned how to drive a manual transmission when I was a teen, these days I was probably more than a little rusty when it came to such skills.

Fortunately, I got a feel for driving the Continental right away. The steering was a little stiffer than my SUV, and the pedals weren't quite as responsive as what I was used to, but all in all, it drove like a dream as we headed toward the office of the storage unit complex. After a quick stop inside—where I closed out my account—I was off to the streets of Abbott Cove with Spencer Poe driving behind me in his amped-up SUV.

I pushed the lever for the electric window and let in some fresh air, completely ignoring the dusting of pollen on the sidewalks and trees. With the sun shining in through the curved windshield, the wind in my hair was just too exquisite to pass up.

Naturally, I got plenty of stares along the way home. Some appreciative and some, well . . . quizzical. A couple of kids from Parker's class even pulled up beside me at a red light.

"Wow, Mrs. Montgomery, your car's really tricked out," one boy hollered. "Can Parker bring it to school? So we can take it out riding around?"

I laughed and shook my head. "Sorry, guys, not *gonna* happen. This car won't be spending the day in the high school parking lot. But you kids are welcome to come over and look at it."

"Nice!" the boy hollered back before the light changed.

Moments later, I arrived at my house and eased the Continental into the third stall of the garage. Very, very carefully.

In the meantime, Spencer Poe parked in front of my house and walked up the driveway to join me. "Would you like me to carry your boxes inside for you, Mrs. Montgomery?"

I popped the trunk, just as my son turned his car into the driveway and pulled up about ten feet from us. "Thanks, Spencer, but Parker's home from school. He can do it."

Not that any of the boxes were too heavy for me to carry.

Parker shut off his engine and bounded out to join us. "Dad's car is here!" He grinned from ear to ear while his eyes took in every inch of Charlie's car.

"Excuse me, young man," I said. "But where are your manners?"

"Oh, right," he murmured. "Hi, Mr. Poe, how are you?"

Spencer smiled, like a grandfather to a grandchild. "I'm fine, son. Did you have a good day at school?"

"Oh, yeah," Parker answered. "I aced my test."

Spencer's gray eyes beamed. "Your father would have been very proud of you, no doubt."

I raised an eyebrow to Parker. "And he would've been even more proud to know that you carried these boxes in for me."

"All right, all right," Parker moaned. "Hey, can I take Dad's car to prom?"

"Prom? We'll see," I told him as I handed him the lockbox.

He almost dropped it. "Wow, what's in the mini-safe? Gold bars? This thing's heavy."

Without saying a word, I just laughed. Though it probably came out sounding a little forced. Mostly because, for all I knew, there *actually* was a small gold bar or two inside that box. Or gold coins. Or silver. I really wished Charlie had mentioned the box to me, including where he kept the key. Then again, maybe he *had* planned to tell me about it, but never got the chance.

Parker took the lockbox inside and came back for one of the file boxes.

I grabbed the other box and shut the trunk. "Would you like to come in for a glass of sweet tea, Spencer? Parker always has an after-school snack. You're welcome to join us."

Parker let out an exaggerated sigh. "Yeah, but just so you know, I don't get any of the good stuff. Just healthy junk. Like apples and carrots and things. As much as my mom cooks, you'd think she'd bake me some cookies once in a while."

I could tell Spencer was fighting hard not to laugh. "Thank you for the offer," he said. "Perhaps another time. But right now I am afraid I must be getting home."

I smiled at him. "I appreciate your help this afternoon."

Especially since I knew how much Spencer hated to leave his house.

"Anytime, Mrs. Montgomery. And I appreciate all that you are doing with . . . looking into Randall's . . ." He hesitated and darted a glance in Parker's direction.

I nodded my understanding so he didn't have to say the words. "I'll try to catch Betty tomorrow."

"I shall be anxious to hear what you find out." He touched his forehead like he was tipping a hat and then headed for his SUV.

Parker and I took the boxes into the house, hitting the garage door button along the way.

"Where do you want this stuff?" my son asked.

"Good question. Let's take it up to my office," I told him.

He gave me his usual goofy grin. "Your wish is my command, oh, mom of mine."

I laughed. "Very nice. Though I suspect you're just angling to take the Continental to prom."

He grinned even more. "It would be a great way to impress a girl."

Well, he had me there.

"Dad told me that's how he got *your* attention. He took you out for a date in that car."

"Yes, he did. I didn't realize your dad told you about that."

We reached my office and dropped the boxes in the corner.

"Dad told me lots of stuff. I still miss him, you know."

"Me, too," I agreed softly.

"Gotta go do homework, Mom."

"Sounds good. Dinner at six," I said to his retreating back.

Just as my phone rang.

"Hello, Maddie?" came a husky voice on the other end of the line. "This is Nick Yarborough."

A tingling sensation raced along the backs of my arms, a sensation that had been dormant for so long that I barely even recognized it. "Oh hey, Nick. How are you?"

"Great! I was wondering if you'd like to go out to dinner tomorrow night."

So much for flirtation and small talk.

Something I probably could've handled much better than such a straightforward, direct request. A request which, for some reason, made my mouth freeze up. Sure, it was flattering to have an attractive man like Nick ask me out. And he was nice enough, and we probably had a lot in common.

*But he's no Charlie Montgomery*, a voice in the back of my mind sang out loud and clear.

Yet I was also well aware that there would never be another Charlie Montgomery. So maybe it was time I took the plunge and went out on a date.

But was I really ready for this?

Nick must have picked up on my hesitation, because he quickly added, "You know, so we can talk about books and things. It's always great to get together with a fellow author."

"Sounds good," I said, forcing a smile into my voice.

"I'll pick you up at six-thirty. I'm guessing you like Italian food since you served that upscale beef stew last night, cooked in red gravy."

Of course, I saw no need to correct him and tell him the recipe was actually French, so I simply responded with, "Italian would be wonderful."

"Great, I'll see you then!"

We said perfunctory goodbyes and, just like that, I had a dinner date for tomorrow night.

Yet much to my surprise, a twinge of annoyance tugged at my temples. The whole phone call had felt oddly reminiscent of making a doctor's appointment, or calling to get my oil changed. It was a far cry from anything that I might consider to be, well . . . romantic.

Then again, since I hadn't gone out on a date in decades, maybe I didn't understand how things were done these days. And considering I hadn't even gone out on *this* date yet, maybe I needed to hold my judgment until the night was over.

Still, as Parker had just reminded me, Charlie had completely swept me off my feet when he took me out to dinner in the Continental. Meaning, *that* first date was going to be hard to beat.

But Charlie had always been full of surprises. In fact, he was still surprising me now, two years after his death. This time with a lockbox and two file storage boxes that I knew nothing about.

I sighed and stared at those boxes. And because I didn't have a key to open the lockbox, I decided to check out the file boxes first. I lifted one lid and noticed the dust on top too late. While outdoor pollen rarely bothered me, this dust sent me into a convulsive sneeze. And then another one.

I instantly reached into my pocket for some tissues. As I pulled them out, the piece of paper that I'd picked up in the street this morning came with them. The very piece of paper that Tiffany had accidentally dislodged herself when *she'd* been reaching for a tissue.

Naturally, I grabbed the folded paper to throw it in the trash, but I stopped when an airplane logo caught my eye.

"This looks like . . ." I murmured as I unfolded the paper.

And just like I'd thought, it turned out to be a boarding pass for a flight from Aruba to Houston. At first it didn't seem out of the ordinary to me, since Tiffany had told me that she and Aiden were forced to cut their honeymoon short.

But then I looked at the date on the boarding pass.

That's when my chin nearly hit the floor. Because the boarding pass was dated two days before Randall's accident. That meant Tiffany and Aiden had been back in Houston on the day that Randall died.

Secretly.

And as far as I knew, neither one of them had an alibi for Randall's murder.

# Chapter Fifteen

Funny, but as I gaped at that boarding pass, I wondered when I'd fully graduated to the belief that Randall had been murdered. For the life of me, I couldn't pinpoint the precise moment. But regardless of when the conversion had taken place, one thing was clear—I now believed exactly what Spencer Poe had believed in the first place. That, in and of itself, was more than a little disconcerting. Much as I thought Spencer was terribly sweet to watch over Parker and me, I truly hoped I wouldn't find myself shining a flashlight along a corrugated steel wall one day. And I prayed I would never be afraid to leave my house for fear some government agent might sneak in and plant a listening device in my credenza.

Though at the moment, I had much bigger things to think about than wondering if I was on my way to becoming the next Spencer Poe. Especially now that I held a boarding pass in my hand, proving that two of the key players—whom I should probably start calling "suspects"—were actually in town on the day that Randall died.

So why did Tiffany and Aiden pretend like they'd flown home just in time for Randall's funeral? And complained about having to cut their honeymoon short? Generally speaking, innocent people didn't bother with so much deception.

Was it possible they'd come home early to kill Randall? Somehow I found it hard to believe that Tiffany could murder her own father. The man who gave her everything. Sure, she was a surly, spoiled, and selfish young woman, but that didn't make her a murderer.

Though Aiden clearly had no attachment to his father-in-law. In fact, he didn't really seem to have an attachment to much of anything, except for the video games that he was absolutely addicted to. It truly made me wonder how he and Tiffany had even managed to date, let alone tie the knot.

Plus, I couldn't forget that Tiffany and her new husband would've had access to Randall's medication. If they'd been in town, they could have easily sneaked back to the house and dumped a few extra pills into Randall's morning coffee.

I shuddered at the thought of his daughter doing him in. I only hoped I was way, *way* off base in even wondering if she or Aiden could have committed such an unspeakable act. But there was only one way to find out—I'd simply have to question the pair tomorrow. Carefully. They'd be next on my list of suspects to talk to, right after Betty.

Until then, I turned my attention back to the file storage boxes and the lockbox before me. I glanced through the folders inside the first box, and from what I could tell, they mostly contained records of Charlie's work expenses. As well as paperwork on various installations that he'd done around the state. To be honest, none of it really meant much to me at all. And nothing stood out as being unusual.

The same went for the second box. The files inside looked like they held nothing but business papers. And sure, while I wondered why Charlie kept them in his storage unit, I really didn't see anything too nefarious about the whole situation. He'd probably just emptied everything out of his SUV one day, maybe because he needed the room inside his vehicle for equipment. Just thinking about it sent a stabbing pain through my stomach, considering he died in a fiery crash in that very car.

I took a few deep breaths and tried to force the image from my mind, turning my attention to the lockbox instead. Again, I wondered what was inside. As a general rule, people only put valuables inside "mini-safes," as Parker had called it. So what had Charlie put in there? And more importantly, where had he put the key?

I knew he'd kept duplicates of virtually every key he owned in our safe in the master bedroom closet. And there was quite a collection of those duplicate keys. A few months after he died, and I started the process of sorting through his things, I found several of those keys that didn't seem to go to anything. One of them was probably the key to this lockbox.

Without waiting another minute, I raced downstairs to the safe to retrieve all those extra keys. Then I returned to my office and tried each of them twice. Yet none of them opened the lockbox.

So where was the key?

I sighed. Surely there must be a way to open a lockbox without one. Unfortunately, any truly viable options—other than methods used in old cartoons—escaped me at the moment. Though I kept wondering about it as I headed for the kitchen to cook dinner. Parker, who was normally a quiet guy, had plenty to talk about when we sat at the table to eat.

After touching on everything from his test score to an upcoming science project, he finally flashed me one of his goofy grins. "So, Mom . . . did you get any phone calls today? Maybe from someone asking you out to dinner?"

I raised an eyebrow. "How do you know about that?"

"Mr. Yarborough pulled me aside, and he wanted to know how I'd feel if he took you out. Sort of like he was asking me if it was okay or not."

Score points for Mr. Yarborough.

"Well, that was thoughtful. So how *do* you feel about me going out to dinner with him?"

"He's a good guy. I like him. And if you start dating him, you won't be all lonely when I leave for college."

So we were back to that again. Parker worrying about what would happen to me when he left home. His concern probably wasn't all that abnormal, considering he'd already lost one parent, and now he likely felt protective toward the one he had left.

Namely me.

I smiled at my well-meaning son. "Yes, I'll be sad when you leave, kiddo, and I'm really going to miss you. But I'm also very proud and happy to see you going to college. Plus, you won't be that far away. You'll be home for Thanksgiving and Christmas. And summers."

"Uh-huh. I know. Promise me you'll give the guy a chance."

"Okay, Parker, I will. But keep in mind, your father was the love of my life. There is nobody who could ever take his place."

"I know, Mom. I know. Dad is a tough act to follow."

"He is. And again, I don't want you to worry about me when you go to school."

"Umm . . . well . . . in that case, can I show you something on my computer? I want you to see what I did today."

"Of course."

Then he took off with the two cats running behind him, and like a whirlwind, he was back in his chair with his laptop before I even had a chance to finish clearing the table. "See, Mom," he said after he called up a screen. "I've got this all set up so you can publish your new book. When it's ready to go, I'll get it formatted and uploaded."

I took a closer look as he scrolled and clicked, showing me that he'd set up an account, along with pre-ordering, advertising, and all kinds of things I knew next to nothing about. But after we went through it, step-by-step, I was much the wiser. Not to mention, on my way to starting a career as an independently published author.

"Parker, this is fantastic," I told him. "When did you have time to do all this?"

He yawned. "Between classes. And at lunch."

"Well, that's awfully sweet of you to do this for me. I feel much better about the whole situation. Now we'll see if I can actually sell some books."

He got up and stretched. "You will, Mom, you will."

Like I've said before, sometimes it truly pays to have a tech-savvy teenage son. And as he ran off to his room to head for bed, I had to admit to myself—I *was* going to miss that kid. Terribly.

And the truth was, yes, I probably would be a little lonely without him.

Which was a very good reason for me to up the ante on my social life, by giving his teacher a chance, as Parker had put it. Yet the very thought of getting involved with a new man kept me awake for hours that night. If nothing else, I was happy to see that my angst didn't affect Ellery and Agatha's ability to sleep as they cuddled in next to my legs.

Okay, maybe I wasn't *that* happy about it. It might have been nice if they'd stayed awake with me as I fussed and fretted. Because I couldn't ignore the fact that I hadn't been on a date in a long, long time. I wasn't even sure how I was supposed to act on a date. Charlie and I had been so comfortable together that I rarely even gave our relationship a second thought. But tomorrow night, I would be going out with a man who wasn't my husband. It felt too weird for words.

I woke up the next morning to the sound of birds singing. And as I plodded out to the living room, I noticed an awful lot of nest building going on outside the big picture windows. Bird couples were clearly vying for materials and prime locations. It wasn't exactly the kind of scene I needed at the moment, not when I was already worked up about just going out for a simple dinner.

Apparently, the kitties didn't think much of it, either, as they swished their tails and glared at those birds. I left my two felines standing guard in a windowsill, and I trudged onward to the kitchen.

At least now, in the light of day, I was able to focus on Randall's murder, instead of thinking about tonight's date. So as soon as Parker headed for school, I showered and made a beeline to Betty's house. This time I caught her at home, right after her husband, William, left for work. And this time, I also had the forethought to wear closed toe shoes.

Betty answered the door in an outfit that appeared to be made from repurposed plaid pajamas. She'd added a wide denim waistband and some buttons to the pajama pants, and black chiffon sleeves to the button-down top. Then she'd tied a matching plaid strip around her head and through her updo, finishing it off with a huge bow.

Her eyes went wide when she saw me on her stoop. "Maddie, I'm so glad you came over!" she gushed. "I just pulled a fresh pan of eggplant carob-chip muffins from the oven, and I was about to start my photo session. I hope you're here to talk about collaborating on a blog."

"Well . . ." I started to say, and then hesitated.

I knew I needed to pick my words carefully. Because I suddenly became very conscious of a major drawback to being an amateur sleuth—I had no legal authority whatsoever to interrogate a suspect. Which meant that Betty had no obligation to open up to me at all. In fact, she could tell me to take a hike if she wanted to. And then she could slam the door in my face, and I'd never, ever find out what I wanted to know.

So the whole situation had to be handled with some serious finesse.

I instantly thought of Blaze and how she might maneuver her way through a scenario like this. Of course, she'd ease into her questions in a roundabout fashion. And she'd be so charming that her suspect would never even realize they'd been interrogated.

Naturally, I decided to do the same. I mean, if the technique worked for a fictitious character, then hey, what could possibly go wrong?

*Only a hundred and one things*, I told myself.

Even so, while Betty led me into her dining room that had been converted into a photo studio, I *ooohed* and *aaahed* over her house. And I admired the wide range of cameras and lenses that she had set up and ready for action. Upstairs I heard her kids jumping and hollering.

Funny, but I couldn't remember the last time I'd been inside Betty's home. Sure, I saw her and her husband at plenty of neighborhood potlucks and gatherings, but she didn't return the favor by hosting anything herself.

"Would you like some coffee?" Betty asked me. "I've started adding eggshells to it."

I nodded. "Oh, I've done that myself. If you add eggshells to the grounds before you brew the coffee, it can take some of the acidity out of it."

She smirked. "Well, *everybody* does that. People with no imagination. But being a highly creative person like I am, I've found that if you lightly mash the eggshells and then add them directly to the coffee itself, it makes for a very interesting surprise with each cup."

No doubt, *surprise* was the word.

I tried not to choke and forced a smile onto my face. "I can imagine. But I'll pass on the coffee. I just had breakfast and probably way too much coffee today already. Thanks anyway."

"Oh, okay. Then let me show you some of the backgrounds I use for my photo shoots." Without hesitation, she began to unroll a wide assortment of screens that could be fastened to a large board that was sitting on a long table.

"These are nice," I commented as I perused everything from bubble backdrops to sparkly, flashy screens in all colors. "Very pretty."

"It makes such a difference with my pictures. I especially like to use background colors that clash with whatever I'm shooting. It kind of gives the brain a jolt, so people really wake up and take notice of whatever I'm photographing. It's much more eye-catching."

"Umm . . . interesting," was the best I could murmur. "Sounds like you really enjoy taking pictures."

She gave me an enthusiastic nod. "Like you can't believe! I can spend hours just to get one perfect photo."

"How wonderful. I'm so happy to see you in such high spirits. I was afraid you might be . . . umm, you know . . . upset. So I came over to check on you."

She crinkled her forehead. "Upset? Why on earth would you think I'd be upset?"

"Well . . ." I said carefully, letting my words dangle and hoping she'd take the bait.

Thankfully, she did just that. "Well . . . what? What are you getting at, Maddie?"

I leaned back. "Well . . . I heard that . . ."

She leaned forward. "Yes, what did you hear?"

"That you were *there*," I finished with a sigh.

"There? There *where*?"

"You know . . ." I went on. "Randall's car wreck. I heard you were there when it happened. Is it true, Betty? Did you see the whole thing? That must have been awful."

She stared at me with a blank expression. "Who told you that?"

I shook my head. "I can't remember for sure. It was in a crowd of people somewhere," I lied. "But somebody had read a copy of the accident report, and all I could think of was, 'Poor Betty.'"

"Oh, I'm fine," she told me.

"So you were there? And you saw it?"

"Yeah, I saw it."

I *thunked* a hand to my chest. "Betty, I'm so sorry . . . Are you okay? Is it giving you nightmares?"

She waved me off. "No, I'm fine. No nightmares. I'm far too busy for stuff like that. Besides, I gave birth to all three of my children at home. So a little blood and guts doesn't faze me one bit."

"Oh, I'm glad to hear you're all right. I'm not so sure I'd be as strong as you are. What happened exactly?"

"Nothing much. He was driving up to the intersection and the light was green. He saw me, and he pointed at me, like he was mad. Then he hit the gas and went through the intersection, and the light turned yellow just as he went through. He put his hand to his chest, and the next thing I knew, he went careening off the street and smacked right into a light pole."

My chin practically dropped to the floor. "That must have been horrible! Was he still alive when you reached him?"

"Kind of. He looked at me and said, 'It's yellow.' And I said, 'Well, duh, of course it was yellow.' Then he said, 'It's snowing,' right before he slumped over and died."

I shook my head. "My goodness. I'm guessing you tried to resuscitate him."

"Naw, I knew he was gone. It was too late. I just called nine-one-one."

"Well, if nothing else, I'm sure Randall appreciated having a friend there during his final moments. It probably gave him great comfort."

To which she responded with a huge, heaving sigh. And pure silence.

An odd response for Betty.

"You and Randall got along okay, right?"

She shrugged. "I wouldn't say we were exactly . . . pals."

"Oh, I didn't realize. So there was trouble between the two of you?"

She furrowed her brows. "We had our clashes. Just like most people. It's not always easy getting along in a neighborhood, you know. And Randall wasn't exactly what you'd call 'understanding.' He could get upset. Over little things."

"Really? Like what?"

"Oh, I don't know," she said with barely concealed annoyance. "It's not important now."

"Well, I'm glad the car didn't hit you," I added, pouring a little sugar on my words. "It sounds like it came pretty close."

She glanced around the room. "I did have to jump out of the way. And I dropped my camera on the sidewalk and it broke. That was a big loss."

"Were your kids with you?" I went on. "That couldn't have been easy for them to see."

"Oh, no. I left them with a babysitter."

I crinkled my brows. "Isn't Tiffany your regular sitter?"

"Yeah, but she was still on her honeymoon. So I got someone else."

"It must have been pretty important for you to go wherever you were going. I guess you had an appointment somewhere," I supplied.

"No, I was just out walking."

"Walking?"

"Around the neighborhoods. I like to take pictures. Which is what I should be doing right now. I have a blog post to get up by this afternoon."

And just like that, I knew she'd given me the brush-off.

I nodded. "Then I'd better not keep you from your work."

I gave her a smile, and when she didn't return it, I was pretty sure I'd pushed her to tell me much more than she wanted to. And I was also pretty sure she wasn't happy about it.

But I kept my own smile plastered to my face as I thanked her for showing me her home studio. Then I let myself out, mostly because she didn't bother to see me to the door.

Though frankly, I was oddly relieved to get out of there. Especially since the conversation left my head spinning as I toddled down her front walk. It wasn't *what* Betty said; it was more what she didn't say. Or *wouldn't* say. From what I could glean, she and Randall hadn't seen eye to eye about something. In fact, I got the impression that she'd done something to really set him off. Yet from her stance, she didn't seem to think he should have been so upset. So what had happened?

Stranger still, she didn't seem the least bit upset over witnessing his accident. If anything, she came across as being completely detached about it all. Like she saw car accidents every day of her life. In fact, she was obviously more upset about her camera than the death of Randall Rathburn.

It was enough to make my skin crawl as I reached the edge of her mold-lined front walkway. I stepped into the street and glanced back at her house, only to see her standing at the window, watching me. Then she dipped out of sight.

Despite myself, I shivered and kept on walking. Suddenly my own house didn't seem far enough away from Betty's.

Once I reached the middle of the cul-de-sac, I paused, taking in the neighborhood and trying to warm up in the bright sun. That's when I noticed a new metal sign in front of June's house.

The shock of it nearly bowled me over. I shook my head and blinked a couple of times, to make sure I wasn't imagining things.

But sure enough, what I saw was real.

For there, staked into the grass, close to the street, was a bright red and white sign. And it proclaimed, loud and clear, for all to read: "For Sale."

So when had June decided to sell her house? And for that matter, when had she decided to move?

# Chapter Sixteen

For a minute or two, I stood frozen in the middle of the street, absolutely stunned. June was selling her house? Funny, but she hadn't said a word about it the last few times I'd seen her. The whole thing seemed a little sudden. Okay, *incredibly* sudden. And now I couldn't help but wonder if this was something June really wanted to do, or if she was just making a rash decision while under the influence of her medication. I also couldn't help but wonder if she might wake up, so to speak, once she was off the drug, and completely regret her decision.

Naturally, my immediate reaction was to run right over and have a nice, neighborly chat. But June had been so out of it lately that I wasn't sure I could get through to her. Not only that, but I didn't want to get in the way of the photographer who was standing in front of her house taking pictures. Though it didn't seem to stop the pack of people who piled out of the *Stella's Home Staging* van and started hoofing it in the direction of June's house, having parked in front of the house next door.

All in all, it meant June would be pretty busy at the moment, making it an especially bad time for a visit. Besides that, it was really none of my business if June wanted to sell her property. She was a grown-up. And she was free to move as far away as Timbuktu if she wanted to.

But that didn't mean I wasn't concerned about her.

I finished crossing the street to my own yard when I realized I'd have to scrap any plans to question Tiffany and Aiden. Temporarily, anyway. Though the idea of waiting made me uneasy, since I had a sneaking suspicion they hadn't been in on the decision to sell June's house. And I wondered how they would take the news.

I strolled up my front walkway and stepped into my house just as my phone rang.

It was Gia. "Maddie, did you hear the news? Or rather, see the news? About June moving?"

I plopped down on the second step of my staircase. "I just saw the sign. I had no idea she was planning to move."

"I heard she wants to go to one of those fifty-five-plus communities. I guess there's one here in Abbott Cove."

Ellery and Agatha joined me on the stairs. "Well . . . she might be very happy in a place like that. She'll have lots of people her own age to run around with. Plus, I've heard they have tons of activities."

"And, she could even meet her next husband," Gia gushed. "Those places are supposed to be full of widows and widowers."

"In that case, it might be right for her. Except I've heard the HOAs in those communities are extra strict, and young people are only allowed to visit. Meaning, Tiffany and Aiden won't be able to go with her."

"*Thaaaat's rrrright,*" Gia said in a singsong voice. "Which is just another reason for her to move. To get rid of those freeloading kids."

"I guess it's one way to push your kids out of the nest—sell the house out from under them. Then move to a community where they're not allowed. I wonder where Tiffany and Aiden will go."

"I don't know," Gia said. "But you can bet there will be some serious drama going on over there! Grab a bowl of popcorn, and sit back and watch the show."

I sighed. "To tell you the truth, I really hate to see it. They've been through so much already with Randall's death."

Gia responded with a few moments of silence, followed by a not-so-smooth change of subject. "Maddie, did you get your vintage car out of storage? Because Vinnie says his mechanic can take a look at it this afternoon."

"Wow, that would be terrific. And, yes, I did bring Charlie's car home yesterday."

"Perfect. I'll tell Vinnie you'll be down. He says he's got a job for you. I guess one of his people is quitting and going back to school."

"Thank you, Gia, that's very thoughtful of you and your husband. But I've decided to take a leap of faith and publish my books independently. So I'm going to keep on writing for a living."

"Oh, pishposh," came her surprising reply. "The job he has in mind won't take you away from your writing. He'll give you the details when you go down there. I'll tell him to expect you right after lunch."

And with that, she ended our conversation. I didn't even have a chance to make it clear that I wasn't interested in outside employment. Then again, maybe she didn't want to give me that chance. Maybe Vinnie needed someone to fill a slot and it would save him a lot of time and trouble if I simply took the job.

*Whatever* that job might be.

No matter. When I ran into Vinnie at the car lot, I'd just be firm and let him know that I wasn't interested in working for him. Case closed.

That left me with the next item of the day to deal with—figuring out what I was going to wear for my date with Nick. So I went straight to my closet, with the kitties at my heels, and began to peruse my dresses. I pulled out a red dress, held it up to my body, and looked it over in the mirror. *Too flashy*, I decided. Next I pulled out a black dress and repeated the process. *Too elegant*, I told myself. I finally settled on a soft blue number with a drop waist, something that was a scale above a day dress and yet still nice enough to wear for a casual dinner. Then I grabbed a pair of two-tone pumps to go with it.

Task completed. In a matter of five minutes.

Which struck me as being incredibly strange. I thought back to my younger years when I was figuring out what to wear for a date with Charlie. It took me hours and maybe even a full-blown shopping trip to come up with the right outfit. In some ways, that was part of the fun of dating. So shouldn't I be having some of that excitement now, maybe even feeling a little giddy, about my first date with Nick?

Then again, maybe agreeing to this whole dinner date had been a bad idea. Maybe I wasn't really ready to take this step.

But it was too late now. It would be horribly rude to back out at this hour. Besides, it was just dinner. Dinner wasn't a big deal. I'd gone to dinner with plenty of people over the years, and it was usually nothing but good food and—hopefully—good conversation.

Or so I told myself.

I was about to head up the stairs to my office when my phone rang again. I immediately wondered if it was Nick calling to cancel our date. In a way, I sort of hoped it was.

But it was Spencer Poe instead. "Hello, Mrs. Montgomery. I am checking to see if you might like to take the Colonel's car in to Mr. Delvecchio's garage sometime soon. As I said before, I would be more than happy to accompany you. And I would be happy to watch over his mechanic to make sure he does not pull a fast one. And to free you up to investigate, of course."

"Thanks, Spencer. Gia just called and set up an appointment for this afternoon. And yes, I'd appreciate it if you came with me. That sounds like a great plan—if you'll keep an eye on the mechanic and the Continental, I'll go question Vinnie. And see if I can find out if Randall had something over him."

"Excellent. Shall I come by your house at thirteen hundred hours again?"

"No need, Spencer. This time I'll pick you up."

"Then I will watch for the Colonel's car, Mrs. Montgomery."

We ended the call, and since I still had plenty of time before lunch, I decided to take another stab at finding the key to Charlie's lockbox. So I climbed the stairs to the attic and located some of the boxes where I'd stored his old things. Though I figured the odds of my finding a key up there were slim to none, I really didn't know where else to look.

But the instant I opened the first box, I knew I was in trouble. Because I couldn't help but notice how everything smelled so much like . . . well . . . like Charlie. Amazing how things that were boxed up could retain that scent. His scent. Yet here it was, two years after I'd lost him, and his memory was so real to me that sometimes I still had a hard time believing he was gone. In a weird way, his absence just felt like another deployment, from our younger years when he was in the military. Or maybe a business trip, like he'd taken plenty of times after he'd retired. A part of me still felt like he'd be coming home again any day now.

And another part of me knew this was just a game I played with myself, one that probably wasn't doing me any good. Talk about being the Queen of Denial. Cleopatra had nothing on me.

Regardless, one thing was painfully apparent—I hadn't gotten over Charlie. I definitely hadn't moved on, like everyone seemed to think I was supposed to do. To make matters worse, tonight I was going out on my first date since I'd become a widow. Even though Nick was attractive and intelligent and thoughtful, my heart just wasn't in it. Instead, my heart was right here in this dusty attic, with all these boxes and all my memories of Charlie.

Would that ever change?

And for that matter, did I really want it to?

I sighed and rummaged around through his things a little bit more. But just like I'd expected, there was no key to be found.

So I repacked it all and closed the boxes again. Then I headed back down the attic stairs, feeling shaky and close to tears. Thankfully, Agatha and Ellery were there waiting for me as I sank down to the floor. I cuddled them both for a few minutes, until I felt a little more calm, and the waves of grief washed on by.

Funny, but in this neighborhood, you might say there was a tale of two widows. One who couldn't move on, and another who was ready to move out before the body was even cold, so to speak.

The thought of it made the little hairs on the back of my neck stand on end. Sure, I knew we all dealt with grief in our own way, but even the toughest person would have a hard time packing up and selling off the memories they'd made, before starting over like nothing had ever happened. In less than two weeks.

And that's when I suddenly wondered about my neighbor and her moving plans. Did she really have a fifty-five-plus community all picked out? Or was she actually planning to hightail it out of the country? Perhaps to some place with no extradition treaty?

Oddly enough, but until that moment, I hadn't seriously considered June to be a suspect in her husband's murder. I had known her for years. She'd been a kind, reliable neighbor and a friend. Plus, she didn't seem like the type who could kill her own husband, a man who had treated her like a queen. Then again, maybe I'd been letting my feelings cloud my judgment.

With so many questions still rattling around inside my head, I downed a quick lunch. Then I jumped into the Continental and backed out of the garage.

Spencer Poe had a big smile on his face when I picked him up at his house. "It always brings me such joy to see the Colonel's car, Mrs. Montgomery."

I smiled and nodded in return. "It seems like he should be opening the door and jumping in any second now, doesn't it?"

"It truly does," he said quietly and gave me a sympathetic, fatherly glance. "Did you get a chance to talk to Mrs. Kraukpott this morning?"

I put the car in gear and told him about my visit.

By the time we were on Abbott Cove Boulevard—the main road in, out, and through Abbott Cove—Spencer was shaking his head. "There certainly are a number of red flags with that situation, would you not agree, Mrs. Montgomery?"

"Yes, I think so, too," I said as I spotted Vinnie's car lot up ahead, just outside the Abbott Cove city limits. "I wish I could've learned more about the conflict between Randall and Betty. But I sensed she was getting suspicious and starting to clam up. So I didn't push. I figured it wouldn't do any good if I completely alienated her."

Funny, but as I listened to myself, I couldn't help but notice how much I sounded like Blaze. Had I officially taken on my character's characteristics? Or had I simply given her mine?

"A sound decision," Spencer encouraged me. "Since you are not operating in any official capacity, you do not have the authority to compel a suspect to open up. You have to rely solely upon your wit and their willingness to cooperate."

I tilted my chin as I listened to him speak. If I thought I sounded like Blaze, then who did Spencer sound like? Because, right then and there, I thought he sounded a lot like a . . . cop.

"Spencer," I said carefully, "when you were in the military, were you ever an MP? Or a JAG?"

"Oh, Mrs. Montgomery, I was many things, and it was a long, long time ago."

With those words, I knew the subject was officially off limits. For now, anyway. And it was the last we spoke of it as I drove into the lot and carefully wove the Continental through rows of cars, and then to the garage on the left of the big, metal building.

A dark-haired man wearing a navy polo shirt and jeans waved me into a bay. As near as I could guess, he was probably the mechanic that Vinnie had mentioned, though there were a few other men in the garage as well.

And every single one of those men stopped what they were doing and stared the second I rolled on in. I stepped out of the car to a major wolf whistle. Okay, I have to admit, once in a while it's nice to know that I can still inspire that kind of a reaction, just to let me know that I've still "got it." And I couldn't help but smile and blush a little.

That is, until I realized the whistle wasn't for me.

No, the only thing these men were gaping at was the Continental.

And to be honest, I wasn't quite sure how to take this revelation. While I generally—on principle, of course—didn't appreciate being ogled, it was somewhat disconcerting to be outdone by a car. Though considering the classic beauty of the Continental, I decided not to take it personally.

The mechanic, who wore a name badge that read "Joey," waltzed right over. "Glory Hallelujah!" he exclaimed as he came to stand beside me. "That's the most beautiful thing I've seen all day."

"It's pretty stunning," I agreed, feeling like a proud parent.

Spencer got out and joined us, extending his hand to shake with Joey's. "I am Mr. Poe and this is Mrs. Montgomery. I will be staying out here while she goes inside to chat with your boss."

Joey laughed and tilted his head toward me. "So you're leaving someone here to guard this baby. Scared I'll take her for a joy ride, ma'am?"

"Yes, I am," I laughed in return. "I know my son is itching to drive it, and apparently, so are a lot of other people."

"I'll just have to settle for being a not-so-secret admirer," he said with a grin, though he didn't take his eyes off the Continental. "And don't you worry, ma'am, I'll take good care of her."

"Thank you, Joey," I murmured as Spencer raised an eyebrow and gave me a barely perceptible nod, which I knew was my cue to head into Vinnie's office.

So I did just that.

I went in the side door from the garage and down a hall. The entire place reeked of motor oil and was just barely clean enough to pass inspection. Provided, of course, that anyone ever inspected the place. Off to the right was Vinnie's expansive office that looked out onto the car lot. And to the left was an even more expansive lobby with a couch and chairs, and a counter toward the rear.

I knocked on the open door to Vinnie's office while I mentally conjured up the questions I wanted to ask him.

"Hello, Vinnie," I said in my sunniest voice.

He looked up from his computer and motioned me toward a turquoise chair in front of his desk. "Come in, Maddie! Come in! I'm glad you're here."

I stepped into his office, which was clearly a whole lot nicer than the rest of the building. Somehow I imagined Gia must have put her decorating touch on this room.

I took the chair that he'd indicated. "I just wanted to let you know that I brought the Continental in. I really appreciate your mechanic looking it over. And as near as I can tell, so does he."

"Very likely," Vinnie said with a gigantic smile. "I'll bet he's never seen one before."

"My husband always told me it was a pretty rare car."

He nodded, still flashing his high-beam smile. "These days, it's even more rare."

"In any case," I went on, "I want you to know, I insist on paying for the inspection."

Vinnie stiffened and frowned like I'd just insulted him. "Nothing doing. What are neighbors for? Besides, Gia told me you've fallen on some hard times. I heard you might even have to sell your house."

"Well, things aren't quite *that* bad," I clarified, wondering where he'd gotten the idea that I was nearly destitute. "And I definitely won't be selling my house. Parker and I will be fine because . . ."

But he didn't give me a chance to finish. "There's nothing to be ashamed of, Maddie. Everyone goes through a rough patch now and then. I'm here to help out by giving you a job. One that pays well and won't take up too much of your time."

"Vinnie, that's very thoughtful, but . . ."

"No worries, Maddie. It'll be easy, and a big help to me. But let me explain. If a car isn't selling here, I like to send it over to my lot in New Orleans, and then bring a car from that lot back over here. Hoping it'll sell locally. I trade cars back and forth a couple of times a week. So that's all I need you to do—drive a car over there and then drive one back. Always at night, of course, when there's not much traffic. And so I don't miss out on a sale by not having either car on a lot during the day."

I crinkled my brow. "So the job entails my transporting cars back and forth between car lots? From here to New Orleans? That's it?"

He held his hands out and the big smile returned. "That's it. Easy-peasy, right?"

"I'll say. I didn't realize car dealers moved their cars that way. I thought everyone used auto transporters."

He leaned back in his chair and frowned again. "Are you kidding? Those guys are piranhas! They'll charge you an arm and a leg just to move a car a couple of miles. The big dealerships probably use them. But I don't."

"Well, either way, I really appreciate your offer, but I'm afraid it's just not for me."

He sat up straight and put his hands firmly on the armrests of his huge, leather chair. "Whoa, maybe you should stop and think about it for a minute. I could really use your help. One neighbor to another. The kid who used to drive for me is going to start night school, so he's quitting. That means I'm in a bind here."

"I'm sorry, Vinnie, but I'm afraid I can't help you. I've got a teenage son, and I can't leave him alone at night."

Not to mention, I had more books to write now that I was going to be an independent author.

Vinnie gave me a knowing wink. "Oh, I get it. If you're gone your son would invite all his buddies over and they'd tear the place apart."

"Something like that," I lied, though the truth was, Parker was *nothing* like that.

"No worries. I'll just keep an eye out from down the street, and make sure he's not throwing a major rager of a party." The big smile was back, though it didn't quite reach his eyes this time.

I laughed. "No thanks, Vinnie. You'll just have to find someone else for the job. Surely there are lots of people out there who would really like this kind of work."

And then, right on cue, the frown reappeared, along with plenty of anger in his dark eyes. "You can't seriously be saying no to this offer. With your financial situation? I'm handing you some big-time cash on a silver platter. How can you turn this down?"

"Maybe June's son-in-law might like this job. I've heard he owes a lot of money in student loans."

"Who?"

"You know, Aiden. Married to Tiffany. June and Randall's son-in-law," I said sweetly, doing my best to work Randall's name into the conversation, in hopes of steering it in another direction. "Say, did Randall ever transport cars for you?"

And that's when I felt his dark eyes practically bore right through mine. Or more specifically, right through my skull. If I had steered the conversation anywhere, it had been straight into a very dead end.

"Thanks for nothing," he said with a scowl.

His heavy, black eyebrows came down in a *V* across his forehead as he waved me off. Like swatting at a fly. And essentially waving me out of his office. He folded his arms and turned to stare out the window, making it clear that he was *extremely* upset with me.

Needless to say, I was more than a little surprised at his reaction. Or *overreaction*, in this case. Was it my question about Randall that had triggered this response? Or was he just upset because I'd said no to his offer? For that matter, what did he expect? That I would instantly take some job driving cars back and forth to New Orleans? A ten or eleven hour trip in the middle of the night? Maybe he thought I should've gushed over his "generosity." Sure, on the one hand, it had been nice of him to offer, but on the other hand, it wasn't the kind of job that would work for everyone.

Unfortunately, it was also clear that I'd hit a big, giant wall when it came to my real reason for coming down to his car lot in the first place. Obviously, Vinnie wasn't going to spill his guts about his relationship with Randall, and I wasn't going to find out what Randall had over Vinnie.

Not today, anyway.

So I got up from the chair and said a quick goodbye, one that was met with stone-cold silence on Vinnie's part. Then I headed back down the hallway to the garage. I tried not to sigh, coming to the full realization that being a *real* amateur sleuth was a whole lot more difficult than what I wrote about in Blaze's books.

Along the way, I spotted a ladies room and decided to duck inside, since I'd downed way more coffee today than I should have. And by the time I walked out, I heard Vinnie talking to someone else in his office. Amazingly, it sounded like he'd made a remarkable recovery from whatever I'd said or done to offend him so terribly. And though I realized I was taking a risk by eavesdropping, I also knew that spying on other people's conversations was practically job skill number one for any amateur sleuth. So I leaned against the wall, scooted closer to his office, and listened.

"I'm sorry to see you go, Dillon," a very jovial Vinnie said. "You sure you don't want to stay on?"

"Thanks, Mr. Delvecchio," a young man's voice answered. "It's been real fun working for you. But I want to finish up my degree, so I'm taking night classes. That means I can't drive for you at night anymore. Tonight will be my last run."

"Fine. Then here's a picture of the car you're going to pick up in New Orleans."

"It looks just like the car I dropped off there last week," said the young man whom I guessed must be Dillon.

Vinnie cleared his throat. "Yeah, well, sometimes a car doesn't work out at one place. So we bring it back."

"Oh, okay, whatever you say, Mr. Delvecchio. Thanks for letting me drive early today, instead of at ten, like usual. Do I take the car to the car lot or to the pawnshop?"

"The pawnshop this time. I'll have Louie there waiting for you. He'll have the other car ready for you to drive home."

I peeked out from my hiding place just enough to get a side view of Dillon. He appeared to be in his early twenties with shoulder-length brown hair.

He nodded at Vinnie. "Okay. Then should I bring the other car back here? Or to your pawnshop?"

"Bring it back here. The place will be locked up, so just lock up the car and leave it on the side street. In fact, you can park your own car there before you go."

Dillon pointed in the direction of the street that was adjacent to the lot. "Already got it there, Mr. Delvecchio."

"Good boy, Dillon. I'll pay you tomorrow when you drop off the keys. I've got an extra set so no big rush to get here in the morning."

"Cash?" Dillon asked hopefully.

"Like always," came Vinnie's cheerful reply.

Dillon chuckled. "Good. Because I don't want to pay taxes."

This time Vinnie was the one who laughed. "I won't tell if you won't tell. You remember the rules, right?"

"Yup. I remember. Go straight to the pawnshop in New Orleans. No eating in the car. And no pictures or selfies, and no talking or texting on my cell phone. I can drink a cola if I use a cup holder, and I can stop for a bathroom break if I need to. If the car breaks down or if I have a flat, don't call a car service or a tow truck. Call you instead. Don't drive over or under the speed limit. And don't open the trunk."

"Good job, Dillon. That should cover it. Here's the keys."

I saw both men stand as Vinnie passed a set of car keys to Dillon, and I figured now was a good time for me to amscray. So I tiptoed down the hall and out the side door and into the garage. Because I had a pretty good idea that I wasn't supposed to be privy to the conversation that had just taken place between Vinnie and Dillon.

And I also had a pretty good idea that the cheerful, happy-go-lucky exchange that I'd just overheard was far more nefarious than what it appeared to be on the surface. The odds that Vinnie was simply hiring drivers to move cars from one lot to another were pretty slim, from what I could deduce. Especially since he was making his drivers go at night, and he was paying them in cash.

No, I think it was safe to say that Vinnie was moving a whole lot more than just cars. No doubt there was something illegal stashed inside the trunk that Dillon wasn't supposed to open.

And I intended to find out *what* exactly it was that Vinnie was transporting across state lines.

Tonight.

# Chapter Seventeen

Naturally, I filled Spencer in on everything I'd heard—or and for that matter, *overheard*—at Vinnie's office while I drove us home in the Continental. As a mystery writer, I learned long ago to pay close attention to conversations, and I even became adept at practically memorizing what people had said to each other. I listened intently for things like speech patterns, cadence, and use of slang, noticing how each person had their own particular way of talking. And frankly, it taught me some very valuable lessons when it came to writing realistic dialogue. Now, much to my surprise, that listening skill had come in handy this afternoon, making it easy for me to repeat both *my* conversation with Vinnie and then *Dillon's* conversation with Vinnie. Word-for-word. No doubt, another important ability for any amateur sleuth to have in her skill set.

When I'd finished giving Spencer the "lowdown," which included my plans for later tonight, he nodded gravely. "I never would have suspected Mr. Delvecchio of carrying on such an operation. And I would say it is quite possible that his activities are somehow linked to Randall's murder."

"That's what I think, too," I told him. "But there's only one way to find out. I need to see what's in the trunk of one of those cars that Vinnie's been transporting across state lines.

And if I'm successful tonight, then maybe we'll have a better idea of what he's been up to."

I gave the Continental a little gas, feeling more comfortable by the minute when it came to driving the vintage car. Thankfully, it had checked out just fine at the shop, and the mechanic gave me the okay to drive it all over Abbott Cove. In fact, he suggested that I take the car out on a regular basis to keep it running properly.

So I intended to do just that.

Provided I survived the night, of course. And I wasn't just talking about my date. No, I was thinking about what I had in mind for *after* my date. Namely, a stakeout near the car lot while I waited for Dillon to get back into town.

"I would be much more comfortable if you would allow me to accompany you tonight, Mrs. Montgomery," Spencer said. "This mission could become dangerous."

*Mission?* Somehow that struck me as an odd choice of words.

"It is quite possible that Vinnie and his cohorts are part of a narcotics smuggling pipeline," he went on. "And those are not people to mess with. If the Colonel were still with us, he would not be pleased to know that I let you step unaccompanied into a dodgy situation."

"I appreciate your concern, Spencer, but I'll be fine. I'm just going to look inside the trunk of that car and see what's in there. Then I'll take a couple of quick photos and vamoose. Besides, it'll probably be a pretty late night."

"At the very least, please take my vehicle," Spencer insisted. "It is completely nondescript, and it will blend right in."

"Well . . . all right. I guess I could do that."

"Excellent," he said, nodding. "Be sure to park a decent distance away and avoid streetlights. You will find a pair of night-vision binoculars in the glove compartment, should you need them. And I can monitor the vehicle's movements from my computer system at home to make sure you are all right."

"Umm . . . okay. That sounds good."

"And one other thing, Mrs. Montgomery. Since Mr. Delvecchio instructed that young man to leave the vehicle locked, that means the trunk will be locked, too."

"Oh . . . right . . ."

"Have you ever broken into the trunk of a vehicle before? Or picked a lock?"

I was all set to say no when an old memory popped into my brain. Because, the truth was, I *had* picked a lock before—very early in my writing career. When Blaze needed the ability for a certain scene, I found someone to teach me the technique, so I could make it sound realistic for my readers.

"It's been a long time since I've done anything like that," I admitted to Spencer. "But yes, I think I could manage. I had to research lock picking for one of my novels, and I tried it out a couple of times. Though not on the trunk of a car."

"It will be like riding a bicycle, Mrs. Montgomery. And while you're working on the lock, just remember to stay low and out of sight. Keep your senses on full alert. It should be quiet that time of night, so you will be able to hear if anyone approaches. And like I said before, have an alibi ready in case someone comes along and inquires as to what you're doing."

"Got it," I told him as I turned the Continental onto our street, wondering once again how he knew all this stuff.

And, as before, I decided not to ask him about it. I pulled into his driveway and dropped him off, right after we made arrangements for him to deliver his car to my house later on. Then I headed home.

But as I drove past June's house, I spotted Emily standing next to the "For Sale" sign in the yard. She flagged me down, and I stopped and rolled down the passenger side window.

Her diamond jewelry sparkled in the bright afternoon sun as she leaned over and poked her head in. "Wow, Maddie, this is such a pretty car. Did you take it down to Vinnie's like he suggested?"

"Yes, I did. Everything checked out just fine and dandy."

"Glad to hear it," she said with a smile. "I'm absolutely dying to buy that Bentley on Vinnie's lot. Maybe I'll be able to afford it after I sell June's house."

"I still can't believe she's moving," I said, shaking my head.

"Oh, I can. She wants to downsize and move into a fifty-five-plus community. She'll be surrounded with people her own age, so she'll have a built-in social life. It's really the best thing for her, now that Randall's gone."

"I hope she's really happy there. It just seems sudden, that's all. What will happen to Tiffany and Aiden?"

Emily laughed. "That's for them to worry about. They're grown-ups. Though June will probably have to pry Aiden from his gaming chair and kick him to the curb. He and Tiffany have been giving June a pretty bad time about her decision."

"I'm sorry to hear that."

"I just hope they won't cause any problems tomorrow."

"Tomorrow?"

She pointed toward the yard sign. "We're having an open house in the afternoon. You should stop by. And you should think about selling your house, too."

I laughed. "I've already told you, Emily, that I'm staying put. Though I will come to the open house."

"Okay, but you know I'm here for you if you change your mind and decide to sell after all. If money gets tight, I can have your house sold in a heartbeat."

"Thanks, Emily. Nice to know. Now if you'll excuse me, I've got to go and get ready for a date tonight."

Emily gasped. "Maddie, I'm so proud of you. It's wonderful that you're getting on with your life! Who's the lucky guy? Anyone I know? You're not going out with that old guy . . . Spencer . . . are you? I've seen you hanging out with him a bunch lately."

I rolled my eyes. "No, Emily. I am not going out with Spencer. If you must know, I'm going out with Parker's teacher. Nick Yarborough."

Her well-defined eyebrows perked right up. "Nick? You're going out with Nick?"

For some reason, not only did her reaction surprise me, but it bothered me a little, too. "Yes, I am. So how do you know Nick?"

"He's been doing a lot of house hunting lately. Ever since his divorce, he's been stuck in a horrible, undecorated apartment."

Funny, but I hadn't realized that Nick was divorced. Though I wasn't sure why it surprised me so much. Lots of people were divorced. Did I really think that an attractive, intelligent man like Nick, a man in his mid-forties, had never had a serious, long-term relationship?

Just another reminder that I had been out of the dating scene for a long time.

I took a deep breath and glanced at the mailbox cluster at the end of the cul-de-sac. "Well, I hope he finds something he likes."

"I'm sure he already has," she said slyly.

Which was my cue to go. So I said a quick goodbye to Emily and headed for home, feeling strangely unsettled. I parked the Continental in the garage before I headed to the mailbox. For once, all the mail in the box was for me.

Including a letter from the HOA.

I ripped it open as I returned to my yard. Hopefully, Hedley and company were simply sending me a letter to apologize for the two violation letters they had already sent by mistake. After all, most people were decent and just trying to do a good job, right? And everyone makes mistakes, of course. Including yours truly.

So imagine my complete and utter shock when I unfolded the letter to see the words at the top that read "Notice of Violation."

I nearly fell over in the middle of my driveway. *Now* what was the problem? I quickly skimmed the letter to read "trashcan visible from the street." And this time, not only were they charging me with the violation, but they were *literally* charging me. If I didn't "correct" this heinous desecration against the perfect aesthetics of our neighborhood in ten days, they were going to start fining me $200 a day.

Just like I had before, I glanced at the place where I always kept my trashcan, to the very spot where it had been kept since the day we moved in. And *also* like before, I couldn't so much as see the outline of the trash container.

But I did see Betty coming out her front door and heading to the mailbox.

I waved her down like a woman on a mission and walked over to join her. "Betty? Say, have you been getting letters from the HOA? Like I have?"

She inserted her mailbox key and opened the little, metal door. "Letters from the HOA? What kind of letters?"

"You know, violation letters."

She crinkled her eyebrows. "Huh? What do you mean?"

"The homeowners association sends out letters if you've violated the covenants. I'm guessing from your reaction that you've never gotten one."

Her eyes went wide and she took a step back from me like I'd just told her I had the plague. "Maddie . . . you *violated* the covenants? What did you do?"

I shook my head. "I didn't do anything. It's all a complete fabrication."

"Oh . . . okay . . ." she said, taking another step back. "What are these covenants?"

"They're simply rules established by the HOA, supposedly to keep the neighborhood looking nice. And to keep property values up."

She stepped back yet again. "Maddie, what you do is your own business. If you've broken the law or something, I really don't need to know . . . You live your life and I'll live mine." Terror filled her wide eyes.

And with that, she turned and ran back to her side of the street, like she was fleeing from a serial killer. She trotted straight up her moldy walkway to her cobweb-filled front entryway, bounded inside her house, and slammed the door behind her.

Leaving me to wonder—given the state of Betty's property, how was it possible that she'd never, ever received a single HOA violation letter? And how was it possible that she didn't even seem to know what a violation letter was?

It was a question I hoped Mr. Hedley Haus could clear up. Because I marched right into my kitchen and immediately called the HOA management company.

After about ten rings, the phone was finally answered with, "Haus Oversight Services. Carla speaking."

"Hello, Carla, it's Maddie Montgomery calling. I've gotten another HOA letter, and I'd like to know why."

To which she responded with a heavy sigh. "I'm afraid I can't help you, Ms. Montgomery. You'll have to talk to Hedley."

"All right," I said, chomping on the words. "Please let me speak to him."

"He's not in. You'll have to call back later," she intoned, mere moments before she hung up on me.

Apparently, such rude behavior was standard operating procedure for Haus Oversight Services. Worst of all, I reminded myself that my HOA dues were essentially paying for her to treat me so badly. Though my phone encounter had been brief, it was enough to make me hopping mad.

And I do mean mad.

But since I couldn't do much about it at the moment, I decided a little commiseration might be in order. So I grabbed Randall's HOA file that I'd brought home from June's house and went through the contents with a fine-tooth comb, as they say. One page at a time. And little by little, I managed to piece together the ongoing battle between Randall and Hedley's management company. The violation letters ran the gamut—from complaining about a visible trashcan to saying the front-yard shrubs were six inches too tall. Then there was the complaint about Randall and June not power washing their walkway and driveway. Something that couldn't have been farther from the truth, considering Randall owned a power washer and had annoyed me with the noise more than once while I was trying to write. In any case, with each letter, there was also the threat of a fine attached. Yet I couldn't tell if a fine had ever been collected.

Somehow I doubted it.

But whether it had or not, it was apparent the situation had been nasty from the get-go and just kept on getting nastier. There were certified letters back and forth, and Randall had even consulted an attorney, though I couldn't tell if he ever mentioned that little tidbit to Hedley. Eventually, Randall requested photographic proof of the violations, and from what I could find, the only photograph provided was grainy and looked like it had been taken from quite a distance. Oddly enough, the photo was at an odd angle and height, like someone must have climbed atop a large ladder to get the shot. And frankly, it proved absolutely nothing.

The battle seemed to come to a head when Randall attended an HOA meeting. According to Randall's typed-up transcript, the HOA board members had been completely in the dark about the whole tug-of-war, and the news that Randall relayed was, in fact, news to them. To top it off, Hedley remained quiet throughout the meeting, and simply denied any wrongdoing at the end. The meeting closed with a promise by the HOA board to thoroughly investigate the entire situation.

Just as soon as everyone had the time.

And that was as far as it went. There was nothing more in Randall's file. Probably because he had passed away. Or more accurately, been murdered.

Yet as near as I could tell, those so-called violations had never been resolved. Meaning, they were still pending. Or were they? June didn't mention them when she let me borrow Randall's HOA file. And honestly, she seemed sort of oblivious about any open violations. Was it her medication that made her so unaware? Or had the violations simply been rescinded since Randall's death?

None of it made any sense.

Though the words that Randall had scrawled in angry, red letters at the top of one of the notifications did make sense: "Move to a community with no HOA!"

To tell you the truth, I had no idea that he and June had ever thought about moving. So maybe it wasn't such a snap decision for June to put her house on the market after all. Maybe she was only following through with something that she and Randall had already considered.

Yet that didn't exactly add up, either. Not if June intended to move to a community for people aged fifty-five and older. Those places were notorious for having some of the strictest HOA rules around. And if June and Randall hadn't been happy with our HOA overreach, she definitely wasn't going to be happy in an age-restricted community.

I shook my head and sighed. Because reading Randall's well-documented file only brought up more questions than it answered. Even so, it did give me an idea for my next step when it came to dealing with my own HOA nightmare. I needed to demand "photographic proof" of my supposed violation. And I planned to do just that.

In person.

After all, if Hedley and his management company wouldn't talk to me over the phone, then I intended to pay them a visit. First thing in the morning.

Yet the mere thought of meeting Hedley face-to-face sent chills running a road race up and down my spine. Because, according to the file that I held in my hot, little hands, Randall had also confronted Hedley in person. And, for all I knew, that very action just might have gotten him killed.

# Chapter Eighteen

I slammed Randall's HOA file shut with a loud *thwack!* The sound echoed across the kitchen only seconds before Parker walked in. Or maybe I should say "bounced in," with his usual Friday happy dance.

But he froze the minute he spotted me. "Aren't you supposed to be getting ready?"

"Huh?"

His voice went up an octave. "Aren't you going out on your date?"

Words that jolted me back to reality. "Oh, my goodness . . . I forgot all about it!"

Parker glared at me. "*Geesh*, Mom. You could show a little enthusiasm. I think Mr. Yarborough is looking forward to this."

"So am I. I just got a little distracted, that's all."

He pointed to the clock. "Fine, Mom. But you'd better get a move on. You're going to be late."

My heart started to pound when I saw what time it was. Exactly how long had I been reading Randall's file?

I *thunked* a hand to my chest. "I'm afraid I didn't get any dinner made for you. So I'll order a pizza. I don't know when I'll be home."

Parker shook his head and sighed. "Seriously, Mom, I've ordered pizza before. I can take care of myself. It's not like you're leaving for a week or something."

"Well, now that you mention it, I wanted to let you know that I will be going out after I get home from dinner."

His eyebrows shot up his forehead. "You mean . . . you have a date *after* your date?"

"No, no, nothing like that," I said, waving him off. "I've just got something I need to investigate."

"Like what?"

"It's nothing important. But I might be home a little late."

"How late?"

"I don't know. Sometime after midnight. At the latest."

"Wait a minute . . . Like what time are we talking about here? One? Two? And what are you going to be doing out there?"

For a moment, I was starting to wonder who was the child and who was the adult in this exchange.

"I simply need to check something out," I told him. "Something at a car lot."

Parker's mouth dropped open. "Would you like to explain to me what you're going to be doing? All alone, in the middle of the night?"

"It's a long story, Parker. But I won't be completely alone. I'll be taking Mr. Poe's SUV, and he'll be monitoring my movements from his home computer. So I'll be fine."

Parker planted his hands firmly on his hips. "I don't think so! You're not going out there all by yourself. I'm coming with you. And while you're at it, I think I deserve a *waaay* better explanation than the one you're giving me."

"Parker, you're not coming with me. And I don't have to explain what I'm doing, because I'm your mother and the grown-up in this scenario."

"Well, you're not acting like one. And you gotta admit, it sounds really weird."

"I'm sorry, kiddo, but I don't have time for this right now. I'll tell you all about it later."

When he was about forty or so.

He folded his arms across his chest. "Nice try. But here's the deal, either I'm going with you, or I'm going to follow you. And you can't stop me."

"No, but I can ground you."

He shook his head. "Not if I tail you, and you don't see me. And then I get back home before you do."

I sighed and stared at my second born. My very, very stubborn second born. Clearly a quality he got from his father. While Parker rarely defied me, he could certainly dig his heels in and refuse to budge on some occasions. This, apparently, was one such occasion.

And that's when it dawned on me—having Parker with me later tonight might not be such a bad idea. After all, he could act as a lookout. Plus, if someone should stop and ask what I was up to, I could simply say that I had just picked Parker up from a party. But more importantly, it would prevent him from sneaking out and doggedly following me. Like he was threatening to do.

"Fine, Parker," I conceded. "You can come. But only if you promise to follow my orders and stay in the car."

"Cool!"

"And don't broadcast this all over town. In fact, I also need you to promise that you're not going to tell anyone."

"Why not?"

"Because, Parker, I'm going to be . . . well . . . like I said before, I'm going to be investigating."

He crinkled his brows. "Investigating? As in, solving a mystery?"

"Yes. But I will explain it to you later. In the meantime, I don't want you to tell a single soul what I've just told you. No texting, no emails, nothing. Not to your friends or your teachers. Including Mr. Yarborough. *Especially* Mr. Yarborough."

Parker closed his mouth and made the motion of turning a key and tossing it away. "It's in the vault, Mom. I won't tell a soul."

"Okay. Now, if you'll excuse me, I'd better hurry up and get ready to go."

Whereby he flashed me a gigantic grin. And somehow I knew I'd just lost the battle, and he had very successfully maneuvered his way into going along with me tonight. But like they say, as long as I won the war, I was okay.

At least I thought I was anyway.

The kitties followed me as I raced to my bathroom, where I took a quick shower, fixed my hair and makeup, and put on my blue dress. Agatha positioned herself on the counter while Ellery sat right next to my shoes. They continued to stare and purr as I put the finishing touches on my outfit. As near as I could tell, they approved of the final product.

By the time I emerged from my room, I found Nick and Parker sitting in the living room, drinking colas. All at once, I became acutely aware that Parker was far happier about this date than I was. Maybe he was seeking a father figure in his life, and his favorite teacher could certainly fit the bill.

Though I also wondered if Parker was hoping to turn his "father figure" into his stepfather. Something that was a real long shot, as far as I was concerned.

But if nothing else, I did appreciate that Nick had the good manners to stand when I walked in the room. "You look lovely," he told me.

And well, I had to admit, he didn't look so bad himself. In fact, I suddenly realized that Nick truly fit the description of tall, dark, and handsome, which made his vivid blue eyes almost piercing in comparison.

Right away I felt a fluttering inside my stomach. It had been a long time since I'd felt that kind of fluttering. Was I feeling the first twinges of a serious attraction? Or was I just really, really hungry? To be honest, I wasn't entirely sure.

But first things first.

I turned to my grinning son. "Is your pizza on the way?"

"Sì, sì, Mamma Mia," he told me, obviously pleased with himself.

"And you're going to stay in, right? And keep the doors locked and not answer the door for anyone?"

This time he saluted me. "Aye, aye. Me and the felines are going to watch *Dr. Who*." Right on cue, the two kitties jumped up and joined him.

"Sounds like a good evening," I said, scratching behind Ellery's ears. "I've got my phone, so you can reach me if there's an emergency."

He rolled his eyes. "Yes, Mom. Now go already! You're embarrassing me."

I felt Nick's hand slide across my back. "I won't keep her out too late," he said with a laugh.

"I know, because she's going to . . ." Parker started to say and then quickly clamped his jaw shut.

Which meant he had almost spilled the beans about our escapade later tonight. Something that made me question my decision to let him go with me.

Especially when Nick started to quiz me as soon as we walked out the door. "So, am I to guess that you and Parker have an escape plan in case this date doesn't go well? Will he be calling in the middle of dinner to say he's had some kind of major emergency? Maybe a burst appendix or an accident involving a small appliance?" He laughed, though it sounded somewhat forced.

And for a second, I was just a little floored. "I guess I didn't realize I was supposed to have an 'escape plan.' I'm afraid I've been out of the dating world for a long time. Have you dated much since . . ."

The words hung in the air, and more than anything, I wished I could take them back.

"Since my divorce?" he supplied as he opened the passenger side door for me.

He let me in and shut the door. As I watched him walk around the front of the car to the driver's side, I couldn't help but admire the grace and smoothness of his movements. And I couldn't help but notice the width of his shoulders beneath his navy sports jacket.

But I also couldn't help but notice how plain his car was as he got in. Sure, it was nice enough, and clean, and probably pretty new, but it just didn't have any "personality" to it. Not like the Continental that Charlie had driven on our first date.

Though, honestly, that was hardly a reason to think any less of *this* first date.

Nick pressed the starter button and put the car in drive. "I've dated a few times. Nothing serious. Just enough to get my feet wet. Parker says you haven't gone out at all. In fact, I get the impression he's been pretty worried about you."

"That sounds like him. Much as I am so thankful not to have a typical teenager under my roof, sometimes I'm concerned that Parker may be too grown-up already. I want him to enjoy his years as a kid. They go by so fast. But ever since he lost his father—my late husband—he's matured very quickly."

Nick chuckled. "He's a great kid. But don't worry, I've seen him acting like a regular teen many times."

"That's good to know."

And from there we continued to talk freely, though mostly about Parker, while Nick drove us to the restaurant.

When we arrived at Cattivo Gusto's Italian Restaurant, the curvaceous, dark-haired greeter gushed over Nick like a Labrador retriever who had just spotted her favorite chew toy. A Labrador retriever who also happened to be in heat, from what I could tell, as she took his arm and led us—or more accurately, *him*—to a booth. I followed mutely behind as the two of them talked on and on about some party they'd both attended last weekend. Giving me the impression that Nick may have dated a lot more than he'd let on.

Though I had to say, what Nick did last Saturday night was really none of my business. This was the first time I'd gone out with him and that hardly implied some sort of commitment. And of course, he probably had tons of friends that I knew nothing about. Mostly because I barely knew him at all.

So why did I have the inklings of the green-eyed monster making an appearance? And so soon into our date?

Maybe because jealousy wasn't really what I was feeling at all. Good manners would have dictated that Nick introduce me to this other woman and include me in the conversation. Rather than acting like I wasn't there.

Much like the greeter completely ignored me when she didn't even bother to give me a menu. Not until I asked her for one as she was walking away.

But if nothing else, at least Nick turned his attention to me once we were seated, at which point he stared at me without blinking. And he kept on staring, in a way that started to make my skin crawl.

"So, here I am," he finally murmured in a low, rumbling voice, "out to dinner with famous mystery writer, Maddie

Montgomery." He paused and licked his lips. "What's it like to be such a successful author, one who is so breathtakingly and stunningly beautiful, as well as a true celebrity on top of everything else?"

Okay, I have to admit, I like a compliment as much as the next woman, and normally I appreciate being called "beautiful." But for some reason, the delivery of his line left me feeling oddly uncomfortable. It struck me as being less like a compliment and more like phony flattery. Not to mention, over-the-top, at that.

So I decided to steer things in a different direction. "I'm sure you know how much work it takes to become a successful author," I told him. "What made you want to start writing?"

This brought a smile to his face. "I was always such a sci-fi nerd, and when I wasn't reading sci-fi, I had this ongoing storyline in my head. One day I decided to write it down. Then after I published it on my own, I found I had an audience for it."

And from there the conversation took off. While the waiter served us a very nice cabernet, we talked about what it was like to write late into the night, and what it was like to get reviews from readers. Eventually, I started to relax and let down a little. By the time we put in our orders, I even found I was enjoying myself.

That is, until *he* decided to steer the conversation in yet another direction after our food arrived.

"It's so nice to be with a woman who appreciates my passion for writing," he gushed. "My ex-wife hated it."

"Oh? I'm sorry to hear that. My husband was always very supportive of . . ."

Without letting me finish, he cut me off with, "Yeah, she said I didn't have time for her and the kids. But I think my writing is good for them. Kids should see their parents pursuing their dreams."

Funny, but this was the first I'd heard Nick even mention that he had kids. It seemed like a subject that should have come up long before.

"I get them on weekends," he went on. "But we don't have a very good time. I think my ex has turned them against me."

"How unfortunate. Divorce can really be hard on children, especially when . . ."

"Tell me about it. The divorce was never my idea. It was all my ex's fault."

"That's a shame, but you know . . ."

"Yeah, she is some piece of work. Do you know what she did on our last anniversary? She took the kids to a ball game. Didn't so much as ask me to go. That's the kind of woman she is."

And on it went. He had picked his favorite topic and he was sticking to it. If I were to title this portion of the dinner, I would have called it: *What My Ex Did and When, in Detail, and How I Will Eternally Hate Her for It*. While I did my absolute best to change the subject about a thousand times—choosing everything from politics to the whole "meaning of life" paradigm—I soon found that Nick Yarborough had a one-track mind. Something that got worse with every glass of wine he downed. And after a few hours of that, I was more than ready to take a flying leap from this particular train of thought.

Thankfully, I was saved by a bell. Or rather, a *belle*. A Southern belle. Though certainly not one who bothered to practice Southern manners. Not when she waltzed over to our booth and held up a hand to me like a crossing guard signaling cars to stop.

"Hold on there, honey," the redheaded woman commanded.

Then she made eye contact with Nick and let out a little squeal. "Nick, sweetheart, how are you?" She leaned down and kissed him on the cheek, mere centimeters from his lips.

He smiled brightly. "I'm good, Amanda. How about you?"

"I've missed you, Nick, ever so much," she drawled.

He focused his blue-eyed gaze directly into hers. "I've missed you, too. I meant to call, but you know how busy it can be at school."

"You work so hard. Like I told you when we were out to dinner a couple of nights ago," she said, emphasizing the "out to dinner" part and giving me the side-eye, "I so admire what you do."

Nick beamed at her. "You're too kind, Amanda. I had a great time the other night, too. We'll have to do it again sometime."

"Sounds good to me," she added, slipping her arm around his back and running her fingers through his hair. "You and me and a bottle of something good. Yes, let's do it soon."

From what I could tell, they were practically doing it *now*. And once again, apparently, I didn't even warrant an introduction. While I'd already realized that I didn't want a relationship to develop between Nick and me, I really hated being treated like I was invisible.

"Excuse me," I said to them both, before I held out my hand to shake the other woman's. "I'm Maddie. I'm afraid we haven't been properly introduced. Are you a friend of Nick's?"

The other woman gave me one of those half-hearted fingertip handshakes, and yet neither she nor Nick spoke to me as they cuddled ever closer. Despite myself, I couldn't help but laugh. Even *I'd* never written a date scene quite so ludicrous as this one. And believe me, I'd put Blaze through some pretty bizarre dates over the years, before I brought Detective Angus Steele into the picture.

I finished my wine and excused myself to go to the ladies room. I glanced back just in time to see "Amanda" slide into my seat. Normally, such intrusive behavior from another woman would have annoyed me beyond compare. But tonight it was just too comical for words.

I returned about five minutes later to find them both with a fresh glass of wine in their hands. Nick barely glanced up while Amanda pretended I wasn't there. Yet the anger that blazed from her eyes when she finally did face me said that she was *well aware* of my presence. Either way, she didn't budge, and she wasn't about to let me return to my seat.

Which left me with a couple of choices. There was Option A, where I would ask, insist, or drag Amanda out of my spot. And then there was Option B, whereby I would scoot right in next to Nick on his side of the booth. But frankly, I wasn't crazy about either option.

So I quickly came up with Option C.

I waved to catch Nick's attention. "Thank you for a nice dinner, Nick. I'm going to call a cab."

He reacted as though my words had pulled him out of a trance. "Oh . . . what? You're leaving?"

"Yes, I am. I've aspired to be many things in life, but a third wheel has never been one of them."

"Well, okay. I could drive you home after I'm finished talking to Amanda," he said, completely oblivious to the death glare she was giving me. "Though I thought we might go have a drink somewhere after this. I would invite you back to my place so we could let nature take its course, but I'm living in a lousy apartment."

And that's when I'd had just about as much as I could stand. Sure, I knew dating was going to be a challenge after losing a husband whom I loved and respected. Especially since Charlie never would've treated me with such disregard. Maybe his being in the military had played a big role in that. Because even though he was technically the one who had signed up to serve our country, we both served in a way. And believe me, we went through a lot together. Plus, we knew people who were killed or injured in the line of duty, and we knew how fragile life could be. So we were well aware that our time on earth together was limited. And precious. As a result, we probably appreciated each other more.

So one thing was painfully clear in my mind at this very moment—I deserved much more respect than my so-called date was giving me.

"No worries," I told him through clenched teeth. "I'll just call Parker to come get me."

Nick's eyebrows practically shot to the top of his head. "Not Parker! What would he think of me if I didn't bring his mother home?"

"Probably the same thing that I'm thinking right now."

And with that, I walked out.

Unfortunately, I soon found him following and running to catch up with me. "Maddie, please, I'm sorry. Let me give you a ride home."

"No, Nick, really it's fine." I pulled my phone from my purse.

"Please don't call Parker." His voice took on the whine of a five-year-old.

Then, despite my better judgment, I finally gave in and got in his car. After all, I didn't want to put Parker in the middle of this mess. Especially since I wondered how this man could be such a great teacher to my son and such a lousy man to go out with. Besides, I didn't have time to wait around for another ride, since I needed to get over to Vinnie's car lot and watch for Dillon to return from New Orleans.

"Look, Maddie," Nick started to say once we were headed back to my house. "I apologize if I was being rude back there. I probably should have asked Amanda to leave. It's just that I work with her sister, and Amanda's been going through a rough patch lately. I didn't want to upset her."

*Though I guess it was okay to upset me.*

Thankfully, nighttime had set in, and he couldn't see my gigantic eye roll in the darkness. "We all have our priorities," I told him. "Frankly, I think you and Amanda make a very nice couple."

"Oh, no. She's not my type."

"Really? I think you're perfect for each other."

"Whoa . . . you're giving me dating advice? You? The woman who hasn't gone out with anyone since her husband died?"

Much as I wanted to let him have it, I decided this guy wasn't worth getting worked up about. So I made the choice to hold my tongue.

He, on the other hand, did not. "Maddie, do you know what your problem is? You've idealized your late husband. It's not uncommon for widows to do that. But you need to get into reality and understand that modern men aren't like the mythical man you've built up in your mind."

And while he started to ramble on and on and on, I essentially tuned him out. I kept my eyes on the road and my hand on the door. Then I climbed out the very second we stopped in front of my house. I slammed the car door behind me, just as I saw him reach into the back seat and grab an open box full of papers. A collection of papers that I instantly recognized as a book manuscript, judging from the title page on top.

"Say, Maddie, could you do me a favor? Would you mind reading my newest book and tell me what you think?"

"No, I'm not really a sci-fi reader. I wouldn't be a good judge of your storyline."

Once again, he was persistent. "Please," he said as he joined me on the walkway. "Your endorsement could really be a big boost for my career."

"Nick, I'm sure your work is very creative. But the answer is no. In fact, aside from the occasional parent-teacher meeting, you and I will have nothing to do with each other." I glanced toward my front door, and I was so grateful that Parker had thoughtfully left the front light on for me.

"Okay, you're obviously mad," Nick went on. "Mind if I come in so we can talk about it? Don't forget how much help I gave you the other night with independent publishing."

"I've got errands to run," I told him as I reached the front door in record time.

"Now?"

I turned to wave goodbye. "Research. For my new book."

"Okay, then."

And before I could open the door, he slid the box with his manuscript into the crook of my arm and wrapped his arms around me like an octopus attacking its prey. Then he pushed me back into the door and planted his lips solidly onto mine. I tried to shove back against him, but he'd caught me off guard and off-balance, literally, so I couldn't get a firm foothold to push him back.

I tried to scream but nothing came out—probably because he'd put a lip-lock on me and pinned me to the door in a move worthy of a worldwide wrestling champ. With my eyes wide open, I glanced down the street, searching for help. That's when I saw June, Tiffany, Emily, and Gia, standing under a streetlamp in front of June's house.

Staring.

# Chapter Nineteen

More than anything in the world, I wanted to scream while Nick Yarborough had me pinned against my front door, with his lips shoved against mine. A painful position, to say the least. And one that prevented me from getting the attention of June and gang, in hopes they might come to my rescue. Yet judging from the huge grins on their faces, I knew they didn't even realize I was in trouble. In fact, from where they stood, my predicament probably didn't appear to be much of a predicament at all. Instead, it probably just looked like I was participating in a very passionate goodnight kiss.

And when they all turned and strolled up June's front walkway, it was clear that I couldn't look to them for help. Meaning, I was on my own to fight off this man who was essentially forcing himself on me.

Anger rose inside of me and quickly reached a boiling point, making me fighting mad. Thankfully, it gave me just the adrenaline boost I needed, and I used my butt to push off the front door and get my balance. In a split second, I raised my leg and planted my knee firmly between Nick's legs.

Hard.

He instantly backed off and bent over, and I knew I'd made a direct hit. Then with every ounce of strength I had, I sideswiped his leg and shoved him to the ground.

"Where do you get off attacking me like that, Nick?" I screamed at him. "You're lucky I'm not armed."

In the distance, I saw a drone buzzing toward my house at full speed.

Evinrude.

"Geez, Maddie, lighten up a little. Didn't you realize I would kiss you goodnight? You *really* haven't been on a date in a long time. Most women like it when I kiss them. You didn't have to get violent." Still cringing in pain, he pulled himself to his feet.

"And you think you were any less violent? There's a huge difference between kissing someone goodnight and out-and-out forcing yourself on them. Besides, I made it perfectly clear that I didn't want to see you anymore. You had no business trying to kiss me at all."

"You'll never get another date with that kind of attitude."

"And *you* didn't *stop* dating long enough to go out on *our* date. Good night, Nick."

With that, I smacked him in the stomach with the box holding his manuscript.

"Wait a minute," he said. "Aren't you going to read my book? After all the help I gave you? To get your *own* Indie publishing career off the ground?"

By now Evinrude was hovering about five feet away. His little lights were blinking furiously.

I put my hands on my hips. "I've got news for you, Nick. My publishing career *has* been off the ground for decades. And it's going to stay there. And I would've figured out independent publishing without you."

"The least you could do is return the favor and review my book. And give me a quote for my webpage. Please?"

"Nick, I'm sure your book is in a world of its own. Much like your mindset when you thought it was acceptable to shove me around and manhandle me just now. So let me be clear—you and I will have no further personal dealings. You may be my son's teacher, but that's as far as any relationship between us goes. Parker really looks up to you, though I'm guessing you must show a very different side of yourself on the job. And just so you know, there'd better not be any problems with the way you treat my son. Just because *I* rejected you doesn't mean you can take it out on *him*."

"I don't like what you're implying! I'm always perfectly professional at school. Don't you dare try to smear my good name. Not that you'd get away with it. If you tell anyone what happened here, no one will believe you." He smirked and stood completely upright, cradling his manuscript box like it was a baby.

I pointed to Evinrude. "The drone that's been filming this entire thing will believe me. And the camera right above my front door will believe me. So, mark my words, if you ever take any of this out on my son—in any way, shape, or form—the videos of you attacking me will be all over the Internet. Including the school's webpage. Then you'd better hope you sell lots and lots of books, because you'll be out of a teaching job. Do you understand me?"

"Yeah, yeah, yeah. I get it. Goodbye, Maddie. Thanks for nothing." He turned and started to limp down the walkway.

That's when Evinrude decided to chase him, buzzing dangerously close to Nick's head.

"Go get him, Evinrude," I said.

Nick tried to swat at the drone once or twice, before he finally just leaned over to avoid the dive-bombing attacks. "Call off your drone!" he yelled back to me.

I shrugged. "There's nothing I can do. It's programmed to protect me, and you've just made it really good and mad."

He barely managed to jump inside his car when the drone perched on his hood, staring at him. Finally, Nick drove off, and Evinrude took to the sky once more.

My phone rang, and I immediately knew who was calling, despite the "Unknown Caller" message on my screen. "Hello, Spencer," I answered.

"Are you all right, Mrs. Montgomery? If I were a younger man, I would have run right over and incapacitated that brute myself."

"And I'm sure it wouldn't have been pretty," I told him. "But yes, I'm fine. Thankfully, I was able to handle the situation."

"You performed admirably, Mrs. Montgomery. Nevertheless, it never hurts to have back up. And my drone can be intimidating at times."

"He certainly can," I added with a laugh. "Except to those of us who know him. Thanks for sending him over. It was pretty funny to see Nick being chased like that."

"I am afraid I fail to find the humor. And in light of this ruffian's recent assault, perhaps you no longer feel up for a stakeout at Mr. Delvecchio's car lot."

"Oh no, Spencer, I'm still going. I wouldn't let a jerk like Nick Yarborough put the kibosh on my plans for tonight."

"Bully for you, Mrs. Montgomery. Shall I deliver my SUV to you soon?"

"Absolutely. Just let me change clothes and grab Parker."

That's when the phone went silent for a few seconds. "Your son is going with you?"

"It's a long story, but yes, he is. Though he'll be staying in the car the whole time." I opened the front door and stepped inside.

"I trust your judgment, Mrs. Montgomery. And Parker is an outstanding young man already."

"That he is." I reached down to pet Ellery and Agatha who had raced in to greet me.

"If you like, I can stay in communication with him as the evening unfolds."

"I think he'd appreciate that. I'll let him know."

"Sounds good, Mrs. Montgomery. I shall see you both in a matter of minutes."

I clicked off the phone just as a very sleepy Parker wandered in from the family room. "Hey, Mom, how was the dinner? Do you have another date? Any plans to meet the 'rents? Or, in your case, the kids?"

His eyes were full of mischief until he saw me. "Mom, are you okay? What happened? Your lip is bleeding . . . Were you in an accident?"

I touched my hand to my mouth. And sure enough, Nick had actually split my lip open.

"Parker, I'm sorry to tell you this, but things didn't go so well between your teacher and me."

"Mom, did he *hit* you?"

"Not exactly."

"Then what did he do?" His dark eyebrows furrowed into an angry line across his forehead, and he stomped toward the front door, glaring.

"Hold on a second, kiddo. I already took care of it. And Mr. Yarborough is gone. But let's talk about it in the car. I'm going to change, and then Mr. Poe will be bringing his SUV by for us."

"Okay, Mom," he said quietly. "But we *definitely* need to talk about this."

"That's fine. We will."

Though to be honest, I wasn't really sure how much I should tell him. While it was true that this could be considered one of those "teaching moments" about how men should treat women, I didn't exactly think Parker had a problem in that arena. Not when he'd been raised watching Charlie treat me like a queen. Even so, there was the added complication that Parker would still have to see Nick several times a week until graduation. And while I wanted to believe that Nick would be on his best behavior—considering I had something to hold over him—I still wasn't sure I could trust the man. That meant Parker needed to be in the loop, so he could report any problems directly to me, and let me take care of it.

The drawback, of course, was that Parker would probably feel awkward and uncomfortable around his teacher when he went to school.

Unfortunately, my bleeding lip had already told my son plenty, and like it or not, withholding information from him wasn't exactly an option at this point.

I felt anger rise inside me once more, because Nick Yarborough had done an admirable job of complicating Parker's life, as well as my own. It was hard to believe that the man I went out with had been the same man who had been on his very best behavior at my dinner table. He was certainly a chameleon. Not to mention, a womanizer, especially the more he drank. All of which, no doubt, were the real reasons for his divorce.

Agatha and Ellery followed me as I headed to my bedroom and into my closet. As usual, they must have picked up on the fact that I was upset. And they had a wonderful way of consoling me whenever something was wrong.

I bent down to stroke their soft fur. "You kitties are pretty good when it comes to stealth. Any advice on what I should wear tonight?"

Agatha stretched her long, black legs, and I took the hint, going straight for the black leggings and a black tunic.

Once I was appropriately attired, I returned to the kitchen. I found Parker there, reviewing the front door video from the moments when my "date" had come to a rather ugly ending.

Oddly enough, Parker had a very satisfied look on his face. "Mom, you really clocked him. That was pretty cool."

I smiled at my son. "Yes, I did. And maybe that should be enough for you to stop worrying about me when you go off to college."

He tilted his head from side to side. "Well, okay . . . yeah, I guess . . . maybe you can take care of yourself."

"And I will."

"Promise?"

"I promise."

He shook his head and frowned. "But I won't get to go to college if I don't even graduate from high school. And well, things are going to be pretty weird now in Mr. Yarborough's class."

I sighed. "I know. And if he gives you any problems, or tries to cut your grades or anything, just let me know. I threatened to release this video to the school if he does."

"Okay, Mom."

"And Parker, don't let him drag you into the middle of this. I know you saw him as a father figure. But he's not your father, and you have no obligation to him. If he wants to discuss it, just tell him no, that you're not comfortable with it."

"Mind if I nail him like you did?"

I laughed. "You'd probably better not. No need to end up in jail over this."

"This all sucks, Mom. I mean, I always thought he was a nice guy."

"So did I. And yes, it does suck. It hurts when we find out people aren't who we think they are."

He nodded. "Good thing you didn't marry the guy."

For some reason, this made me laugh. "Good thing," I agreed, just as a knock came at the door.

For a second or two, I was afraid that Nick had returned. But then I realized it was Spencer, dropping off his huge, black SUV. He gave us a few quick instructions on how to work some of the equipment, and then Parker and I were off. Parker, of course, immediately pulled the night-vision binoculars from the glove box.

"These are so cool," he said with excitement in his voice. "Dad let me try these once. They're pretty awesome. Maybe I should join the military."

"If you like. But I want you to go to college first."

"No worries," he told me as he started fiddling with the dashboard computer. "Wow, Mom, Mr. Poe has some pretty cool gadgets."

"I know," I agreed.

But what I didn't know was *why*.

I gave the SUV some gas, and it handled so smoothly that it felt like the vehicle was practically driving itself. Which was both odd and amazing, not to mention, a little disconcerting, considering it was the size of a small boat. We reached the vicinity of Vinnie's car lot before long, and just to make sure we were alone, I did a quick drive around the perimeter, outside the huge metal fence. When I didn't see any signs of anyone else around, I drove onto the side street where Dillon had been told to leave the car he was transporting back from New Orleans. Another car was already parked there against the curb, one that was older and had its share of dents, making me guess it probably belonged to Dillon.

So I pulled against the curb on the same side of the street but stayed a decent distance behind the other car. And just like Spencer had advised me, I avoided any streetlights and open areas. Instead, I parked under the canopy of a huge elm tree, squarely in the shadows.

That's when I checked the clock. 11:11. Perfect timing. We were in position to watch for Dillon, and thankfully, I was wide-awake, so there was no danger of nodding off and missing his return.

Parker seemed pretty jazzed about the whole situation. "Okay, Mom. Spill it. Obviously we're on a stakeout here. And

I'm guessing it has something to do with that car up ahead. So what gives?"

I smiled. "All right, Parker, if you want me to fill you in, I need your assurance again that you can keep quiet about all this. Meaning, it's really important that you keep your lip zipped."

"Sure, Mom, no problem."

"That means you can't go around telling all your friends or your teachers. Or the neighbors. *Especially* the neighbors. Do you promise?"

He gave me an exaggerated nod. "Promise."

"Okay, then. Here's the scoop. You know that Randall, Mr. Rathburn, died recently."

"Uh-huh."

"Well, Mr. Poe thinks he was the victim of foul play."

Parker's eyes went wide. "You mean . . . you mean . . . he thinks Mr. Rathburn was murdered?"

"Yup, that's right. And since I started looking into it, I have to agree with him. I believe Mr. Rathburn was murdered, too."

"Whoa . . . that's so weird. But why are *you* investigating it? Why isn't Mr. Poe doing that?"

"Well, it's a bit complicated. But since I'm a mystery writer, Mr. Poe thinks I know a lot when it comes to investigating a murder."

"Okay, I guess that's true. But shouldn't he just tell the police?"

I shook my head. "He already did. And the police didn't believe him. They've pretty much decided that Mr. Rathburn's death is an accident."

"Oh. Well, that's pretty cool that you're going to catch the bad guy."

"Or girl," I added.

Parker grinned. "My mom the detective."

I chuckled. "I appreciate the vote of confidence, kiddo. But remember, I haven't solved anything *yet*."

"Maybe not, but I'll bet you're going to crack this case wide open, Mom."

He had barely spoken the words when a car turned onto the street with its headlights pointed right at us.

"Duck!" I hollered to my son.

In a split second, we both dropped down in our seats before the car drove any closer. I peeked just above the dashboard to see the vehicle make a lumbering U-turn and then park against the curb, right behind the car that was already parked up ahead.

And there was no doubt about who had just pulled up—it was Dillon, all right. Though he didn't exactly make a quick leap out of the car. Instead, he seemed to be taking his time. Too much time, as far as I was concerned. In fact, the whole street was dead silent as we sat there and waited.

That's when my heart started to pound. Had the arrangements between Vinnie and Dillon changed? Was somebody going to meet Dillon here instead?

Thankfully, he finally got out of the car, locked it up, and headed for his own vehicle. A few minutes later, he drove away.

I sighed with relief.

"Now what?" Parker asked in a stage whisper.

"Now I need to find out what's in the trunk."

"What if it's locked?"

I held up two metal picks. "That's why I brought these."

His eyes went even wider than before. "Awesome, Mom! I didn't know you could do all this stuff."

For that matter, I wasn't entirely sure that I *could* do it.

"Okay," I told him. "I want you to stay here. Do not leave this car under any circumstances."

"I know, I get it. I'm the lookout." He held up his phone and then pointed to the computer on the dashboard. "I'll be texting back and forth with Mr. Poe. Just promise me you'll wear protection."

I crinkled my brow. "Protection . . .?"

Where exactly did my son think I was going?

He held up a pair of thin latex gloves. "Well, duh. So you don't leave any fingerprints."

"Oh, right. Gloves. Good call."

With that, I took the gloves and slipped them on my hands. Then I grabbed my phone and opened the door. Thankfully, the interior lights didn't go on, and instead, dull red lights glowed along the running board. Just enough so that I could see to safely step into the street, yet not enough to alert anyone of my presence.

"Break a leg, Mom."

"That's for a play, kiddo."

"Okay, then step up to the plate . . ."

"And get the job done. I know."

"I'll text you if anyone is coming." He put the night-vision binoculars to his eyes and glanced around.

"Roger that," I replied, wondering why such a phrase had popped out of my mouth.

Then without another word, I gently shut the door and moved to the front of the SUV. And I sort of tiptoed up to the car that Dillon had just parked, until I realized I was moving like a cartoon cat burglar. Again, I had no idea why. Clearly, I did not have the drill down pat, but then again, I hadn't exactly been on a million of these clandestine "missions" in my life. Even so, I chided myself and decided there was no need to emphasize the "amateur" part of amateur sleuth.

So I took a quick glance around before I kneeled down and put my picks into the lock of the trunk. The sounds of the night seemed amplified in my ears, and the scent of azaleas drifted in on a little breeze. My heart began to pound again, and I was amazed by how incredibly exposed I felt right at that moment.

Funny, but I'd written scenes like this one about a thousand times, when Blaze was out doing some high-stakes snooping. I'd always given her a major adrenaline rush, and of course, she enjoyed the secretive nature of her investigations. But now that *I* was the one outside in the middle of the night doing something I probably shouldn't have been doing, I mostly just felt stone-cold terror. The words "what if I get caught" kept ringing through my brain, though I wasn't sure what I was more afraid of—getting caught by the police or getting caught by Vinnie. After all, what Spencer Poe had said was true—I might inadvertently be investigating a drug run. A dangerous situation all around. But whether Vinnie was transporting drugs or not, the truth was, he was likely involved in some kind of criminal activity, and it probably wouldn't bode well for me if I got caught checking it out.

So I tried to hurry things along, which I quickly realized was a very bad plan. Because, after a few missteps, I learned it took less time when I simply settled down and focused on the job at hand. Especially after I felt the lock give away, and I heard the glorious sound that I wanted to hear—the pop of the trunk as it unlatched and opened a couple of inches. After that, I didn't waste any time pulling up the trunk lid and turning on the flashlight of my phone. At first, I didn't see a single thing in the trunk. Nothing except for dark carpet. But then I spotted it—an odd rectangular protrusion off to the left side, in a place where there shouldn't have been any odd rectangular protrusion. And since it was covered in carpet, it was nicely camouflaged.

Making it the perfect hiding spot.

So I tugged on the top piece of carpet, and I was surprised when it came off without much effort. Underneath was a metal box that looked like it had been welded to the car itself. The box even had a lid, complete with hinges and a recessed handle. As near as I could guess, one of Vinnie's workers must have secured it in place.

Naturally, I didn't waste a single second before I grabbed the handle of that lid and slowly pulled it open. Then I shined the light from my phone inside.

What I saw nearly took my breath away.

And I could hardly believe my eyes.

# Chapter Twenty

There I was, staring at the hidden stash in the trunk of Vinnie's car. And even though I knew I was supposed to be exercising some kind of stealth and subterfuge, I couldn't help but gasp in shock.

Because glimmering and sparkling back up at me in the light of my phone's flashlight was a dazzling pile of loot. And when I say "loot," I do mean loot! It was the kind of plunder you'd expect to see in a pirate's treasure chest. There were necklaces and bracelets and earrings. There were rings and brooches and even a few pairs of cuff links. Everything appeared to be made from real gold or platinum, and set with what looked like real diamonds and emeralds and rubies. And sapphires. Not to mention, plenty of other stones that I couldn't quite place. There were watches—very nice watches, as a matter of fact—and coins and collectibles and on and on and on. All extremely valuable items. And judging from the way those expensive items were in a jumble, and not a single one was in a box or a case, I had a pretty good idea that the entire stash had been stolen.

In fact, the more I looked at it, the more I realized it was the kind of stuff that home invaders were known to snatch.

I immediately thought back to the diamond tennis bracelet that Vinnie had tossed to Gia on the day I went to her house for lunch. At the time, I thought it was a pretty strange way to give her a gift. Especially when such a high-dollar item didn't even come in a case. Of course, she tried to downplay the situation when she dropped the bracelet into her cleavage and acted like nothing had ever happened.

I also couldn't forget that Vinnie had used the line, "Look what fell off the truck." Though in his case, maybe he should have said, "Look what I found in the trunk."

But those were all things I could ponder in detail later on. Because the longer I stood there, the more nervous I got. By now my heart was pounding out a mambo beat, especially with the realization that Vinnie's operation was pretty well organized, and that he might be more than a little miffed if he knew I'd uncovered the truth.

That meant I needed to finish what I was doing and amscray. So I started taking pictures and just kept on taking them. I photographed everything from the loot to the trunk and to the welded-on box.

And as soon as I was sure I had what I needed, I closed the box, slid the carpet back in place, and slammed the trunk shut. Then I made a beeline for the SUV. I didn't even realize I was shaking until I started the car.

Parker stared at me wide-eyed. "Mom, what did you find?"

I responded by handing him my phone. "Take a look. Would you like to send these pictures to Mr. Poe?"

Parker began to scroll through the mass amount of photos I'd taken and let out a low whistle. "Wow, this looks like . . . like . . ."

"Uh-huh," I said while he was still searching for the words. "And considering the way it's being transported, you can bet this stuff is stolen." I rolled off the latex gloves and dropped them into my purse.

Parker continued to gawk at my pictures. "And it's a *lot* of stuff, Mom."

"It sure is," I said as I fastened my seatbelt. "I can't even imagine how much it's all worth."

"Enough to send me to college and buy me a new car," he said with a slight chuckle. "I'm sending the pictures to Mr. Poe right now."

I quickly put the car in gear, not wanting to stay there another minute. But I was careful to drive the speed limit, so I wouldn't draw attention to us. I was also thankful that Spencer had insisted I take his car. Because he'd been right—it was the kind of vehicle that didn't stand out at all, considering there were probably a gazillion others that looked just like it on the road.

Spencer called once we were on our way home. "It appears that Mr. Delvecchio has quite the operation going on—moving stolen goods across state lines and making them much less traceable. All while getting innocent drivers to do his dirty work for him."

"Which is probably what he had in mind for me," I added as I talked on the hands-free system. "When he offered me a driver's job."

"A very likely possibility, Mrs. Montgomery. And he did so under the guise of one neighbor simply helping out another in her time of need."

"So I wouldn't give it a second thought," I told Spencer as we passed the huge "Welcome to Abbott Cove" sign and officially returned to our city. "Plus, he's already got a place to unload all this loot. He either owns some pawnshops, or has some connection to them."

"Making his operation that much more sophisticated," Spencer added. "Victims of home burglaries typically search for their stolen goods at local pawnshops. Mr. Delvecchio has apparently bypassed that problem by moving the merchandise and selling it far from where it was taken."

"So the owners won't have much chance of finding their things. And judging from the value of the items I saw in that trunk, I'm guessing Vinnie is making a killing."

"Quite likely, Mrs. Montgomery. Perhaps Randall uncovered Mr. Delvecchio's operation and used that information to blackmail him."

"And maybe that's how Randall got Vinnie to sell him his favorite car. Then maybe Vinnie rigged the car so Randall would be killed in a bad accident. To silence him."

"All distinct possibilities, Mrs. Montgomery."

Strange, but until this moment, I'd been operating under the theory that Randall had died from an overdose of Digoxin.

But maybe the car wreck actually *had* killed him. And maybe someone had *caused* that car wreck by tampering with his vehicle. And who better to tamper with a vehicle than someone who owned a car lot and knew a lot about cars. Not to mention, someone who had sold Randall the very car he had died in. Namely, Vinnie and his bunch.

I shuddered at the thought as I drove along Abbott Cove Boulevard.

"In any case, Spencer, we're on our way home and we'll be there soon," I said as I saw a red light up ahead and stopped at an intersection.

"I shall watch for your arrival," were his final words before we ended the call.

I tried to force my heart to slow down while I waited for the light to turn green. There weren't a lot of cars out tonight. I guessed people were either tired from the workweek, or a week of school, and were already home in bed. Or maybe they had gone into downtown Houston for things like the symphony or the theatre or fancier restaurants. Either way, it was pretty late for people in a community like ours to be out and about.

Though there was a small lineup of cars on the other side of the intersection. And the red car in front was one that I recognized.

"That looks like June's car," I said to my son. "I wonder what she's doing out at this time of night."

Parker shook his head. "I don't think she's the one driving."

But if *she* wasn't driving, that meant Tiffany or Aiden had taken her car. Something that seemed unusual, given that Tiffany had her own vehicle. As for Aiden, well, I had no idea whether he had a car or not.

I leaned closer to the dashboard. "Mind if we check it out?"

Parker grinned. "Sure, Mom, this 'investigating' stuff is cool. So is having a private eye for a mom. It's like being in a movie or something."

I laughed. "Sorry, kiddo, but I'm not actually a private eye. At this point, I'm only an amateur sleuth."

Much like the kind of sleuth I wrote about in my books. Though I didn't have the great advantage of operating in a fictitious world, where an author was going to write me out of whatever scrapes I got myself in to.

I put my turn signal on and scooted the SUV over to the left-hand turning lane. "Would you keep your eye on June's car while I flip a *U*?"

"Got it, Mom. So if you're an amateur sleuth, what does that make me? Your son the sidekick? Dr. Watson?"

"My son who will be going to college in the fall."

"Hmmm . . . that's months from now," he murmured as I completed the turn. "You could have a whole bunch of cases before I go. And I'll help you crack those cases, which means I'll need a good detective name." His head swiveled as he kept his eyes glued to the red car.

"You've already got a *great* detective name. There are plenty of 'Parkers' in mystery fiction. Not to mention a couple of mystery authors with the last name of Parker."

"Okay, okay, Mom. You told me all this before. And that car just took a left up there."

"They turned into Abbott Cove Park?"

"Yup."

So I followed along behind, keeping a nice distance away. After all, I didn't want whoever was driving June's car to spot me tailing them. Especially after we reached the gravel road that led into a heavily wooded area, a small forest that completely bordered Abbott Lake, which included the very scenic Abbott Cove—the geographic wonder that our small town within a giant city was named for.

"Now that car just took a right," Parker reported. "Onto the road around the lake."

"Still got those night-vision binoculars?" I asked him.

"Way ahead of you, Mom." He grinned and held them up to his eyes.

"Then I'm going to kill the lights and slow down. I can see pretty well, but I want you to warn me if I'm about to drive off the road."

"No problemo. I can see everything like it was daylight. These are so awesome."

"Glad to hear it," I told him as I turned off the headlights, leaving us to drive in complete darkness. "Be sure to keep your eyes peeled for June's car, too."

"Already on the lookout, Mom. Now take the same right that the other car took. In forty feet . . . now thirty . . . now twenty . . . now ten."

"Got it," I said with a nod before I maneuvered the turn smoothly and even managed to avoid a big raccoon.

"The other car's way up ahead," he reported. "Looks like that driver killed their lights, too."

Okay, that wasn't exactly a *normal* thing to do. Not unless they were following someone like we were.

"Let me know if they stop," I told Parker. "So we don't drive past them."

"Aye, aye, Mom. Keep on going. They're coming up on the bend around the shoreline. So in a few seconds, steer slightly to the left."

So I did just that. Soon my eyes had adjusted nicely to the darkness, and I was amazed at how well I could see. The big, bright moon in the sky and the gazillion stars that were out helped a lot, too. And, of course, by keeping my speed down, I didn't kick up any gravel or dust to impede my view.

Though I couldn't say the same for whoever was driving June's car, because they were kicking up so much dust that it was rising in a cloud above the trees. All the while, I wondered what they were up to. Was it possible they were just out for a night drive?

"Hold on," Parker suddenly hollered. "There's another car way up there. And it's parked. Facing our direction. And Mrs. Rathburn's car is slowing down. The driver just hit the brakes."

Something I could easily see myself, considering the way the bright red of the brake lights burst through the darkness. The light also let me see an outline of the other vehicle, which was well hidden beneath some trees. The prospect of this second car made the little hairs on the back of my neck stand on end. By now I had a pretty good idea that this late night drive around the lake was more than just a simple outing. Instead, it seemed like there was a specific purpose for it.

I took my foot off the gas and steered the SUV to the side of the road, letting it roll to a stop. Then I briefly touched my own brakes, just long enough to put the vehicle in park.

"Okay, Mrs. Rathburn's car is pulling over, across from the parked car," Parker told me. "And someone is getting out . . . I think it's . . . yup, it's Aiden."

"What in the world is he up to? At this time of night?" I wondered aloud.

"Well, for one thing, he's pulling his wallet from his pocket. And he's handing some money to the guy in the car. Now the guy in the car just handed something to Aiden. It looks like a little bag of pills."

Despite myself, I gasped. "A drug deal."

Even though I knew things like this happened in the real world all the time, it still never failed to shock me. Especially so close to home.

"Oh, yeah. This Aiden guy is a real loser. I wonder why Tiffany married him."

"That's a very good question."

Though I had plenty of other "good questions" running through my mind at the moment. Things like, how many times had Aiden done this before? And what kind of pills had he just bought? If he had connections to buy illicit drugs, was it possible that he'd secretly given his father-in-law a fatal dose of something? Something that had impaired him while driving, so he would wreck his car? Or maybe some drug that had caused Randall to go into cardiac arrest?

"Aiden is still talking to the guy," Parker went on. "And now he's walking back to his car."

Which was my cue to get us out of there, before either Aiden or his dealer drove our way and noticed that we'd been watching them. So without another word, I put the car in gear and walked it through a turn in the road. Then I gave the car some gas and headed back the way we'd come, driving slowly at first, and then accelerating little by little.

I was about to congratulate myself on my great stealth skills when we neared the bend in the road. And that's when I made a mistake—a very *big* mistake—after a large owl flew right out in front of us, almost hitting the windshield. Without thinking, I slammed on the brakes. Purely by reflex. Worst of all, I held my foot in place until I finally realized it had only been a big bird that had flown past us. And even though my headlights were off, my brake lights were blindingly bright in the darkness. The world around us lit up in a red glow for a good fifteen seconds. For as bright as it was, I might as well have set off a flare. Because it was a fair assumption that my brake lights would have been obvious to the two cars parked way down the road behind us.

And I had a pretty good idea that neither Aiden nor his dealer would be tickled to learn that someone had been spying on them. Like Spencer Poe had mentioned earlier, drug dealers were not people to mess with.

My pulse began to pound as I said a silent prayer and kept on going. For the moment, I decided to stick with my subterfuge and leave my lights off, hoping beyond all hope that we hadn't been spotted. I quickly navigated the bend in the road and then hit the straightaway, driving as fast as I dared without headlights. I knew I'd have to slow down when I made the left-hand turn onto the road that led out of the park. But at least I'd be in the homestretch after that, as I raced for Abbott Cove Boulevard. Once I turned onto that main thoroughfare, I'd find traffic and buildings and hiding places.

Meaning, we'd be safe.

But first we had to get out of the park. And the sooner the better.

"How's the road look?" I asked my son, hoping to increase my speed.

"Better ahead than behind," he told me. "There are two sets of headlights back there now."

Not exactly the news I was hoping for. Apparently, Aiden and his dealer *didn't* see a need for subterfuge anymore, so they'd simply turned on their lights. Which upped the odds that they'd spotted our vehicle and were coming after us, having figured out that we'd just witnessed their criminal transaction. And of course, with their lights on, they could see better and drive faster than we could.

Something I was pretty sure hadn't escaped my son's high-Q brain. He probably knew we were in danger, much like *I* knew we were in danger.

Though Parker *didn't* know that I considered Aiden to be a suspect when it came to Randall's murder. And if Aiden *had* killed his father-in-law, he probably wouldn't hesitate to harm us, either. Especially if he thought we'd just caught him red-handed. Much like his drug dealer might not think twice about "stopping" us—permanently—if he thought we'd gathered incriminating evidence against him. And I was pretty sure the dealer's headlights were the first set behind us, considering Aiden would have had to flip a *U* before driving in our direction.

All of a sudden, sleuthing with my son in the car didn't seem nearly as cute as it had before. And I no longer cared about investigating, since my only goal now was to get Parker out of Abbott Cove Park and to safety. But to do that, I needed to outrun both Aiden and his dealer. So I flipped on my own headlights and put the pedal to the metal, as they say. The SUV responded instantly and steered like a dream, even on the gravel road. It gripped firmly as I reached the turn and took it going way faster than I should have. Rocks and dust went flying, but I kept the car in control and quickly steered it back in a straight line again.

And straight for Abbott Cove Boulevard up ahead.

*Way, way* up ahead.

Parker put the binoculars down and turned to look out the back window. "Mom . . . those cars are really speeding up . . . and it looks like they might catch us."

I glanced in my rearview mirror. And sure enough, my son was right. I hit the gas again, just in time to catch a glimpse of my side-view mirror as it exploded. I ducked and looked over to see a small hole in the metal.

A gunshot.

Whoever was in the car behind us had started shooting.

Now the question was, could we make it to Abbott Cove Boulevard and get away from the two cars that were chasing us?

*And* trying to kill us.

"Hold on," I told Parker. "We're going to take the turn up here pretty fast. Onto the main road."

Parker gulped. "Okay, Mom. Just watch your center of gravity. Don't roll us."

"Got it, kiddo," I said, trying to estimate just how fast I could push the SUV and still get us out of this mess in one piece.

For as many times as I'd written scenes like this in Blaze's books, I could hardly believe I was living this out in real life.

Naturally, Blaze always survived her escapades.

Now I only hoped and prayed that we would, too.

# Chapter Twenty-one

I stepped on the gas again, just as Parker's phone rang.

"That's Mr. Poe," he told me before he answered and put it on speakerphone.

"Mrs. Montgomery? Parker? Are you in trouble?" came Spencer's voice.

"Yes, we are!" I hollered as I heard the whiz of another bullet go by.

I could see the headlights of the first car inching ever closer, and the second vehicle—June's car driven by Aiden—was gaining on us, too. So while I focused on driving, Parker quickly explained the situation to Spencer, giving him just enough detail to paint a clear picture.

Spencer responded in a very solid, calm voice. "Parker, I want you to look at the bottom of the dashboard console. Near the center. Locate a button marked with an *X*. You'll have to lift a small, square plastic cover to reach it."

"Found it," said a suddenly cool and collected Parker.

"Now push the button," Spencer told him.

I barely had a split second to wonder *what* exactly that button was supposed to do. Was it going to eject us both and send us shooting up into the air? Whereby we'd come floating back to earth via parachutes? Or would it be launching missiles that would blow up the cars behind us?

But before I could say a single word, Parker did just as he'd been instructed. I heard kind of a *whoosh* sound at the back of the SUV. Or rather, you might say, I *felt* it. And at the same time, I saw a puff of smoke in my rearview mirror. The next thing I knew, the headlights of the car behind us went spinning off.

Spencer's voice came through the speakerphone once more. "I suggest you turn right onto Abbott Cove Boulevard in ninety feet, Mrs. Montgomery. Then drive directly to the strip mall nearby and park on the side of the building by the Tex-Mex restaurant. You will be hidden in the shadows, but you can still keep an eye on the road."

"Sounds like a plan," I told him.

And a minute later, I reached the T-intersection and braked. As I made the turn, I glanced back and saw that the first car was now sitting halfway in a ditch. In fact, it even appeared to be high-centered on something. I also noticed that the second car, driven by Aiden, was limping along past the first car. Clearly Aiden wasn't about to stop to make sure his dealer was okay.

I took a quick look in the remaining side-view mirror, on the passenger side of the car. "Parker, can you see what's wrong with June's car? Does it have a flat tire?"

Parker used the binoculars again. "Mom, he's got *two* flat tires. Both on the right side of the car. But he's still driving. He's going to bend the wheels."

"Two flat tires? Wow, I wonder how . . ." I started to ask as I headed straight for the strip mall.

But I didn't even finish my question. Probably because I already knew the answer.

Apparently, so did my son. "I think that button released some kind of big tacks, Mom. Ones that pierced the tires on those cars. Kind of like James Bond."

*Exactly* like James Bond, if you asked me. Which made me wonder even more about Spencer. Especially since I noticed that he remained silent on the whole subject.

"According to my screen, I see the two vehicles are no longer in pursuit," Spencer finally said through the phone. "Can you confirm?"

"Yes, sir," Parker replied, his eyes lit up with excitement. "We lost 'em, Mr. Poe. It was pretty cool."

"Excellent," Spencer replied. "My tracking device also tells me that you are well away from the park now."

Parker glanced around. "Yup. My mom is just pulling into the parking lot of the shopping center."

In the distance, I could hear sirens screaming, and as near as I could tell, they were headed our way.

"I would suggest that you stay in place for a few minutes and lay low. Until the . . . umm . . . heat dies down," Spencer added. "I shall remain on the line in case you need further assistance."

"Thank you, Spencer," I hollered over to the phone as I pulled to the side of the Tex-Mex restaurant and put the SUV in park.

"Happy to help," he said.

I glanced at my son who was clearly enjoying our entire escapade. "Wait a minute . . . when did you see James Bond?"

He gave me his goofy grin. "Dad and I used to watch them. When you were out of town at conferences. The old ones are really cool."

I fought the urge to roll my eyes. Funny, but I didn't realize the two had had a "bonding moment" over James Bond. Now I wondered if we had a real, live James Bond in our neighborhood. Or at least, a retired one.

By now the sirens were becoming louder, and seconds later I saw a couple of police cars go flying by on Abbott Cove Boulevard. Headed to the lake road, no doubt. Amazingly, we even caught sight of June's car hobbling along right past the strip mall, going away from the park as the patrol cars raced toward it. Of course, the police probably didn't notice Aiden's two flat tires, since the right side of June's car wouldn't have been visible to them as they whizzed on by. That, and they most likely thought Aiden was only driving slowly because emergency vehicles were approaching.

"I wonder if he's going to drive all the way home on those rims," I sort of muttered.

Parker put the binoculars to his eyes again. "I'll bet he does. Too bad the police don't arrest Aiden like they're arresting that other guy. They've got *him* handcuffed and out of his car already." He pointed in the direction of the lake road, which was in our line of sight, though a long way from our parking spot.

And even without binoculars, I could see the police had surrounded the sedan of the man who'd sold pills to Aiden. I truly hoped the police cars didn't hit any tacks that might be left in the road. Provided, of course, that whatever had come out of the back of Spencer's car actually were tacks. And provided they didn't somehow mysteriously "self-destruct" and go up in a puff of smoke.

Something that would hardly surprise me at this point.

Spencer joined in on the conversation once again. "I believe the threat has been neutralized, Mrs. Montgomery. That drug dealer should not be bothering you any longer, as long as he did not see your faces."

"He didn't see us," I assured him. "Neither did Aiden. I was very careful about that. But I'm really sorry about your mirror. I had no idea there would be guns involved."

"Hardly your fault," he went on. "I am simply relieved that you and young Parker were not hurt. I must say, you kept your cool back there and did some excellent driving. The Colonel would have been proud. Plus, I applaud your decision to investigate the situation in the first place."

"Thanks, Spencer," I told him. "It definitely shines some new light on things. Aiden just climbed to the top of my 'People Who Might Have Murdered Randall' list. Aiden would've had the motive, since he had the strange idea that he and Tiffany would inherit half of Randall's wealth when he died. Apparently, Aiden owes tons of money in school loans, and he shows absolutely no interest in getting a job. Plus, I also learned that Aiden and Tiffany were in town on the day of Randall's accident. Though they kept quiet about that little fact and led everyone to believe they'd only flown back for the funeral."

I could picture Spencer shaking his head on the other end of the phone. "Interesting," he murmured. "Those points certainly make him a sound suspect."

Once again, I thought of June, and I worried that she might not be safe in her own home. If Aiden *had* murdered his father-in-law, his mother-in-law might be next. Especially if Tiffany now stood to inherit everything from her mom.

All of which made it that much more urgent for me to question Tiffany and Aiden, and find out why they had come home early from their honeymoon. *And* find out what they had been doing in the hours right before Randall's death. Of course, June's open house would be the perfect time to do just that. I could pull the two aside and start with a nice, friendly chat before I hit them with the hard stuff.

"It is probably safe for you to return home now," Spencer informed us. "You have both had a very long night. And please do not feel any distress over the mirror. I have spares, and I will simply change it out."

For a second or two, I wondered why Spencer kept spare side-view mirrors on hand. I was also a little surprised that he didn't seem too upset over a gunshot to the mirror. Could it be this wasn't the first time one of his mirrors had been shot out?

But as the saying goes, there are some questions better left unanswered.

In the seat beside me, Parker raised his hand. "Mind if we drive through Abbott's Big Burgers first, Mom? I'm starving. All that 'investigating' made me hungry."

And despite the drama and trauma of the night, I couldn't help but laugh. Never mind that my son had just watched me break into the trunk of a car and uncover a stash of jewels and riches. And never mind that he'd just witnessed a drug deal and been chased and shot at by some bad guy. Not to mention, played with plenty of "spy" gadgetry. He was hungry, and being hungry was his normal. Meaning, he didn't seem too terribly fazed by all that had happened tonight.

I leaned toward his phone. "We'll be back just as soon as I get some food for Parker," I told Spencer.

"Take your time, Mrs. Montgomery," came his reply. "I shall monitor the vehicle's movements from here."

Half an hour later, Parker had inhaled a couple of burgers, Spencer's SUV was sitting snugly inside his garage, and we were back at our house. We had barely stepped in the door when Parker said goodnight and headed straight for his room. And since his eyelids were practically falling shut as he walked,

I guessed he probably conked out the very second his head hit the pillow.

But I couldn't have gone to sleep even if I tried. Instead, I sat on the couch with Ellery and Agatha, and sipped a glass of my favorite sauvignon blanc. I glanced at my Vincent Van Gogh print above the mantel, and oh, how I wished I could be sitting there at that *Café Terrace at Night*, where surely the world was so much more innocent. And peaceful. Because right at that moment, I was feeling anything *but* peaceful.

Not when my brain seemed determined to replay every moment of my entire evening, from my horrendous date with Nick to a bullet blowing out my side-view mirror. It was a lot for one night, and now my mind kept running off on tangents, hard as I tried to organize my thoughts. Especially those that might be related to Randall's murder. If nothing else, from what I'd gathered so far, I knew there were several people who could have benefited from his death. And he'd clearly made an enemy or two. Including the man I was about to visit in the morning.

Hedley Haus.

A man who had ice water running through his veins. And someone who absolutely fit the "cold" part of the term "cold-blooded killer." I shuddered at the thought. Right before I checked all the doors, set the alarm, and headed off to bed.

Only to wake up early thanks to my throbbing lip. Bleary-eyed, I dragged myself out of bed and glanced in the mirror. And there, sticking out like a sore thumb, was my sore *lip*. A very bruised and swollen lip, which included an angry red line where it had been split open.

I wanted to scream, but I figured it would hurt too much if I did. Instead, I purposely recalled the image of Nick limping down my front walkway as he tried to get away from Spencer's drone.

"If you think I look bad," I told my image in the mirror, "you should see the other guy."

At least I hoped Nick had some misery this morning after I'd "clocked him," as Parker had said. If only I could use the same technique when it came to dealing with Hedley Haus. The mere idea of it made me feel strangely powerful as I showered, dressed, and ate a well-buttered English muffin—

very carefully, I might add. Parker was still sound asleep, and I guessed he would be dead to the world for hours. So I left him a quick note to tell him I'd be back before lunchtime.

Then I stepped into the garage and glanced at the Continental, pausing for a few seconds while I seriously considered taking it today. After all, it was the kind of car that could really make a statement when a girl wanted to look big and bad for taking on a jerk like Hedley. Even so, I didn't want the worry of leaving the prized automobile in a parking lot where someone might damage it. So I settled for driving my regular, navy blue SUV, which felt like a real step down after driving Spencer's gadget-loaded vehicle the night before. Partly because my car didn't have the capability of releasing tacks or whatever Spencer's car had shot out.

I grinned to myself, wondering if I should ask for such a feature the next time I traded in my SUV. Especially since I'd seen firsthand just how handy something like that could be.

Unfortunately, this morning I was armed with nothing more than an extra cup of coffee. A definite must for me today, since I needed all my ducks flying in formation to deal with Hedley and his harassment. After all, Randall hadn't had much luck when it came to handling those issues, and I wasn't nearly as versed in HOA legalities as he had been. Nor did I enjoy doing "battle," as June had said of her husband. Regardless, I had no choice but to go in and duke it out—hopefully not quite as literally as the night before when Nick shoved me into my front door.

But I tried not to dwell on it as I drove to Haus Oversight Services. The sun was shining brightly when I entered the building and raced up the stairs to the second-story office. I opened the door to find a woman with cropped, gray hair working at her computer in the outer office. She glanced up when I walked in and gave me a saccharine smile. A very smug, saccharine smile.

"Let me guess," I said, sounding far more sinister than I'd intended to. "You're Carla, right?"

She pointed in the direction of the parking lot. "You just missed him."

Much to my amazement, she didn't seem to need an introduction, though we'd never met before. At least not in person anyway. And she also seemed to know *why* I was there.

"Him?" I repeated. "You mean Hedley?"

She nodded and scowled with an expression that absolutely oozed passive-aggressiveness.

But aggressiveness, nonetheless.

From what I could guess, she and Hedley must have seen me coming. Maybe through his office window. And while I took the stairs up, he must have taken the elevator down, thus successfully avoiding me. But that also meant he didn't have much of a head start, and I could probably still catch the man.

If only I knew what he looked like.

So I took a step closer to Carla, hoping the cut and bruise on my swollen lip would make me appear pretty bad-to-the-bone, like someone who wouldn't back down from a fight.

"Show me a picture of Hedley," I demanded.

Carla shrugged. "I don't have one. And there isn't a single photo of him in the whole office."

"All right, then . . . *tell* me what he looks like."

"Oh, I dunno. He's tall. Thin. Average looking. Dark hair turning gray."

"And what is he driving?" I demanded.

She shrugged again. "I don't know."

"I think you *do* know."

"He's got so many cars . . . I have no idea which one he brought today. By the way, this is supposed to be my day off, so I'm afraid I can't help you. I was just about to leave the office myself."

And that's when I took it up a notch and went into my best imitation of Blaze interrogating an obstinate suspect. "Answer the question *now*, Carla!" I hollered. "No more games. Tell me what kind of car. I don't have all day! *Now, now, now!*"

She jumped up and practically snarled at me. But at least she answered my question. In fact, the words practically exploded from her mouth. "It's a silver Mercedes! Okay? A new one! There, are you happy?"

I lowered my lids and squinted, a gesture I'd written many times for Blaze. "Oh, I assure you, Carla," I said in a low, throaty voice, "I haven't even *begun* to be happy."

She crinkled her brows and cocked her head to one side. "Huh?"

Okay, so it wasn't exactly a great exit line. And fine, it probably didn't make much sense, but it honestly didn't matter. I squinted at her once more before I raced from the office and back down the stairs. I got to the parking lot just as a silver Mercedes was turning out onto the street.

In a matter of microseconds, I was in my car and flying through the parking lot at record speed. I took a right-hand turn from the lot onto Abbott Cove Boulevard and spotted Hedley's car up ahead as he was making a U-turn from the turning lane. So I hit the gas, zoomed in front of a car, and grabbed the inside lane. Then I immediately hit the gas again, wiggled in front of yet another car, and barely managed to slide into the turning lane, just as the light turned red. It was a move that I would never, ever make under normal circumstances, and judging from the honking cars behind me, it was clear the other drivers didn't think much of it, either.

Nonetheless, when the light changed, I made the U-turn and quickly had the Mercedes in my sights. Without a doubt, I knew I could close the gap. That is, until he made a high-speed U-turn himself at the next intersection and was now driving the way I'd just come. He passed cars right and left, weaving in and out of lanes like a cheetah trying to weed out the weakest gazelle in a herd. Then he suddenly zoomed off, leaving everyone in his dust. I could only guess that Carla had phoned him and warned him that I was coming. So like it or not, it was going to be a lot more difficult to catch the guy.

Provided I *could* catch the guy.

Anger was rising in my throat by the time I finally managed to make the second U-turn and follow his route. And even though I gave my SUV plenty of gas and took off much faster than I should have, I couldn't spot the silver Mercedes in the blocks up ahead. No matter how much I craned my neck. But I wasn't about to give up, and I kept my eyes peeled for that little, silver car.

Funny, but until that moment, I hadn't realized just how many silver cars there were out on the road. As far as I was concerned, they all pretty much looked alike, and it wasn't long before I realized I was going to need a major miracle to find

Hedley. And that's when somebody upstairs must have smiled on me. Because several cars in front of mine suddenly turned off Abbott Cove Boulevard, leaving a nice, wide-open gap in the traffic. Shortly after that, I ended up being the first car in line at a red light that was situated at the top of a slight hill, which allowed me to see blocks and blocks ahead. I squinted my eyes and searched again for a silver car, and after a minute or two, I finally spotted one in the distance. And it was taking a right-hand turn into a subdivision.

Instantly, something inside my brain told me it was Hedley. So I zoomed down the street the very second the light changed and took the same right turn that I'd just seen the silver car take. Of course, the speed limit dropped once I drove into the neighborhood full of tree-lined streets and bright green grass, along with azaleas blooming in every possible color. But I continued on, keeping my eyes peeled, as I steered around curved streets and past plenty of well-cared-for homes. Unfortunately, the one thing I didn't see was a silver Mercedes.

That is, until I rounded another bend and my eye was drawn to a yellow "For Sale" sign in the perfectly manicured yard of a two-story, brick home. And there, much to my great joy, was a silver car parked in the driveway.

Hedley's car.

My first instinct was to pull up and block him in, but then I noticed another car driving up from the other direction. This other car stopped and parked directly across from the house that was for sale. So rather than create a ruckus, I decided to play it cool. And I remembered what Spencer had told me the night before about parking his SUV out of sight, so I simply slid my own SUV behind a Mini Cooper that was parked on my side of the street. It left me hidden enough, but still allowed me to see over the white top of the tiny car.

And much like Parker had used Spencer Poe's night-vision binoculars, I grabbed a pair of regular binoculars that I kept in my glove box. I put them up to my eyes just in time to see a woman in a red blazer exit the car and walk toward the house. Judging from the way she held her cell phone in one hand and a leather binder in the other, I guessed she was a real estate agent.

That, and she reminded me of Emily. While her hair was dark brown, she didn't have a single strand out of place, and her makeup was beauty queen perfect.

Once she reached the front door, she merely opened it and strolled on in. Without knocking or ringing the bell. And for that matter, without opening a lockbox and getting a key. Meaning, Hedley must have gotten in ahead of her. But how? Did he know the owners, and had they let him inside? Or was this Hedley's house?

The woman in the red blazer shut the door behind her, and all was quiet after that. Nobody walked out of the house, and nobody else went in.

For a minute or two, I considered going up to the door myself. But I quickly realized that Hedley wouldn't bother answering if he saw me at the front door. So I decided to wait it out. In the meantime, I grabbed my cell phone and looked up the house listing on the Internet. From what I could tell, it was priced well—not too expensive and not bargain basement, either. The pictures showed the home had been given the usual realtor's staging, with nondescript furniture placed just so. It appeared the people who owned it had already moved out.

Which meant Hedley *didn't* own the property. So was he thinking of buying the house? I had a pretty good idea that wasn't the case when I finally saw a tall, thin man emerge about ten minutes later. He appeared to be about my age, with salt and pepper hair. The top button of his pale blue shirt was undone and his tie was pulled loose. From the brief description that Carla had given me, I figured it must be Hedley himself.

I had to admit, I was pretty surprised to see him whistling as he walked, given the way he'd been so terribly nasty to me. And to Randall, too. In fact, from the little I did know about him, this "happiness" seemed pretty uncharacteristic. Though maybe his cheerfulness had something to do with the white envelope that he was holding before him.

A rather fat envelope, one that appeared to be stuffed full of something.

Needless to say, I was absolutely *dying* to know what was in that envelope. But I wasn't kept in suspense for long, because Hedley dipped a hand into the envelope and pulled something out. That's when I caught a flash of green. And then another flash. Until I realized he was counting . . .

"Money," I murmured.

Talk about your suspicious undertones. The scene playing out before me was just bursting at the seams with them.

Much like the envelope that Hedley was carrying.

So what in the world was he up to? And why was he carrying an envelope full of cash?

# Chapter Twenty-two

For a second or two, I sat there absolutely dumbfounded. Mostly because I couldn't imagine any legitimate reason why Hedley would be walking out of a house with an envelope full of cash. Though I think it was a pretty safe bet that some kind of transaction had just taken place.

And given Hedley's history for being despicable, I had a feeling there was something unscrupulous going on.

But what exactly?

I snapped a few pictures with my cell phone and decided to take my chances by going in to get more information—straight from the horse's mouth. Hedley, of course, being the horse in this scenario. I had no doubt that I would be the last person he would expect to see right now, and catching him off guard might even give me the upper hand when it came to confronting him about his most recent, ridiculous violation letter.

So I put my SUV in gear, ready to race over and box his car in before it backed out of the driveway. But just as I was about to pull into the street, the real estate agent came strolling out. Right away, my instincts told me to sit tight, and so I stayed put and watched the agent fasten a lockbox on the front door. As near as I could see, it was the old-fashioned kind where a combination was used instead of a signal from a cell phone.

Which meant that anyone with the combination was free to go in and out of that house. Whenever they wanted to.

In the meantime, Hedley took off in a hurry while the agent traipsed on over to her car. Oddly enough, I noticed she wasn't nearly as put together as she had been when she first arrived. Her hair was still nicely smoothed down, but it seemed to have sort of, well . . . shifted to the left. And her blazer appeared to be a little off-kilter.

Had they just . . . ?

I shuddered at the thought while I waited for her car to drive off. Then I pulled into the street and put my foot on the gas, hoping to catch Hedley's silver Mercedes. All the while, I kept thinking about the envelope full of money that he'd been carrying. And that's when the realization finally hit me—had the attractive real estate agent just *paid* him to . . .

"*Eeeeuuuw!*"

Okay, the idea of someone paying a nasty, condescending jerk like Hedley for a mid-morning tryst was just too disgusting for me to wrap my head around. Worst of all, I now had a mental image that I definitely didn't need at the moment, because frankly, I'd had enough trauma in my life lately, thank you very much. Plus, with that picture in my mind, it was going to be a major challenge to look him in the eye, whenever I did finally talk to him face-to-face. Something I still intended to do, just as soon as I caught up with the man.

And I almost did catch up to him, but I held off again when I saw him pull into the driveway of yet another house with a "For Sale" sign in the yard. This time, there was a second car already parked in front when he went inside—without knocking or ringing the bell. So I parked behind a car in the street and waited for him to come out. Just like I had at the last house. But I didn't have to wait long, since he came strolling out barely a few minutes later, counting yet another envelope full of cash.

"I don't think she got her money's worth," I mumbled, fighting the urge to gag while I watched him drive away.

Once again, I was all set to chase after him when a real estate agent emerged from the house.

An agent whom I recognized.

"Emily . . . ?" I gasped. "*Noooo* . . . not Emily!"

Though she hardly had the disheveled appearance of the previous real estate agent. If anything, Emily looked just as perfectly groomed as she always did, with every hair in place, and her navy suit hanging straight and her diamond jewelry sparkling in the sun. She attached and set a lockbox to the front door so quickly that I wondered if she was practicing for some kind of lockbox Olympics. Whatever the case, it was clear she was in a huge hurry. And I barely managed to duck down in my seat before she zoomed past in her Lexus.

By now I was feeling pretty bewildered as I turned my SUV into the street and took off again to hunt down Hedley. I caught up to him just in time to see a repeat performance of what I'd seen at the last two houses. As before, he entered a house that was for sale, one where another car was parked in the driveway. And once again, Hedley wasn't in the house for long—less than a minute this time—and he walked out counting an envelope full of cash. Then he took off, and seconds later, a female real estate agent left the house and fastened a lockbox to the front door. This last woman appeared to be in her late seventies, and she didn't look the least bit disheveled.

Somehow, I didn't think she was the type to be doing the horizontal hula with Hedley. But then again, who was I to say? Though if she had, and she'd actually paid for the service, she should have demanded a refund.

I shook my head, trying to make sense of it all. To be honest, I figured the odds of Hedley working as a gigolo were pretty slim. Thank goodness for small wonders. Even so, it appeared that several real estate agents had given him envelopes filled with cash. Most likely as some kind of payment.

Was it possible that he was blackmailing them?

And if so, for what?

I pulled my SUV away from the curb and followed him once more. Unfortunately, he turned back onto Abbott Cove Boulevard and took off, weaving in and out of lanes. And that's when I lost him. Completely. I drove around for a little while, hoping to spot his car. But when I couldn't find him anywhere, I finally decided to check the parking lot of his office building.

And sure enough, his Mercedes was back in the lot.

I parked right behind it and glanced in the car windows as I walked past, though I wasn't sure what I was hoping to see. Somehow, I didn't think Hedley would leave envelopes of cash just lying around. In fact, he probably had all that money up in his office and locked away in his safe by now.

If nothing else, at least I managed to climb the stairs and catch him in the hallway, just as he was turning the key to the outer door of his offices. Locking up for the day.

Carla was nowhere in sight.

"Hello, Hedley," I said smugly.

He jumped and turned to face me. Judging from the shock in his eyes, it was clear that he recognized me. Something I found surprising, considering I'd never met him in person, much like I'd never met Carla, either.

"What do you want, Maddie?" he asked with a pained sigh as he pulled the key from the lock.

I quirked an eyebrow at him. "Looks like you've had a busy morning, Hedley."

"You can't prove a thing."

His response nearly bowled me over. Talk about getting right down to business. I was amazed that he didn't even bother to feign innocence and make me work for an admission of wrongdoing. Or something close to it.

Then again, maybe he'd just given me the standard line that he gave everyone. With his obvious lack of moral character, it was possible he had more irons in the fire than I knew about, and maybe this likely blackmail scheme was merely the tip of the iceberg.

And maybe I needed to quit mixing my metaphors.

Nonetheless, I decided not to let *him* know what *I* knew about his "extracurricular" activities. Or at least, what little I did know about them. Not yet anyway. Because I didn't want him to stop doing whatever he'd been doing on my account. Then I'd never have a chance to catch him in the act.

A concept that made me cringe, considering one of the "acts" I suspected him of.

In any case, I countered with, "And you can't prove anything, either, Hedley. That's why I'm here. I demand photographic proof of my so-called trashcan violation."

For a brief second, his eyes flared, as though I'd just hit a nerve. A very big and very *raw* nerve. His fists clenched, but then he caught himself, and his expression became one of pure ice.

"Fine," he said, chomping on the word. "You shall have it before the day is through."

"And since I know you can't provide such a photo, I want you to stop harassing me about a violation that isn't even real."

"As you wish."

"Well, okay then," I replied, feeling oddly deflated. "And by the way, since we've never met before, how do you already seem to know who I am?"

But instead of answering, he reinserted the key into the lock. "I just remembered I forgot something," he muttered.

Then with lightning speed, he turned the key and opened the door just wide enough to slip inside. And without missing a beat, he shoved the door shut behind him and locked it. All in one fluid motion. It was so smooth and so quick that I guessed he must've had a lot of practice making that precise move. Yet in doing so, he also put an end to our conversation, and unless I wanted to stand there all day, I figured it would be futile to wait for him to come out again. Especially since I'd already aired my beef about the violation letter, and from what I could tell, the so-called HOA violation was now DOA. In a manner of speaking.

Which suddenly made me wonder if Randall had once stood in this exact same spot, having had the exact same conversation—or at least, a similar one—with Hedley. And if so, did it play a role in Randall's murder?

I thought of the tacks or whatever sharp objects Parker and I had unknowingly released from Spencer's SUV the night before. They had disabled the car that was chasing us by blowing out the tires and making it spin off the road. Could Hedley have thrown something similar from his own car to cause Randall's accident? Maybe Randall had followed Hedley around, much like I followed him around this morning.

A cold chill passed through me as I walked down the steps and to my car. Hedley was up to something sleazy and probably illegal. But what? I didn't have the answer, but I knew someone who might just be willing to give me more information.

Emily.

And I would be seeing her soon at June's open house. Which meant I was going to have a busy afternoon, between quizzing Emily and more or less interrogating Tiffany and Aiden.

So I got back in my car and drove straight home. I walked into the kitchen to find Parker up and dressed for the day, and grinning like he'd just won the lottery. Much to my amazement, he had also cooked lunch for the two of us. It may not have been the gourmet fare that his sister might have whipped up, but grilled cheese sandwiches and tomato soup were nothing to sneeze at. And more importantly, he was showing the kind of independence that meant he wasn't going to starve to death when he went away to college.

"So what have you been up to this morning, Mom?" he asked as he raced around, plopping the food on the table. "Have you been out pounding the pavement like a regular gumshoe? Did you give some low-down, dirty rat the third degree? Or did you uncover a secret clue that'll crack this case wide open and send the button man up the river to the Graybar Hotel?"

Given the speed with which he talked and moved, I wondered if he'd been sampling my collection of specialty coffees. Not to mention, I couldn't help but wonder why he sounded like he'd just walked out of a Bogart movie.

I grabbed spoons and napkins and added them to our place settings. "Let's just say it was an interesting morning. And it's really nice to come home and find lunch already made. That was very thoughtful of you, Parker." I smiled at him and instantly wished I hadn't, because a sharp pain shot through my lip, making me cringe.

Parker froze and stared at my swollen lip. "Are you okay?"

"Dandy," I assured him.

This made him smile in return, but I could see the wind had gone out of his sails as we sat down and started to eat.

I dipped a spoon into my soup. "What Mr. Yarborough did was very wrong," I told him gently. "But don't forget that I 'clocked him,' like you said. And I've got leverage against him if he ever causes you any trouble."

"I know, and I'll let you know if he does anything weird. You're one tough cookie, Mom." Parker took a mouthful of soup.

Despite my pain and the seriousness of the subject, I couldn't help but laugh. "One tough cookie? It sounds like you've picked up some new expressions today. Where did you learn all this lingo?"

He pointed toward the front of our house. "In our library, Mom. I went through a bunch of the old mystery books in the shelves while you were gone. Trying to get the hang of all this sleuthing stuff."

So that explained it.

"I'm happy to hear you're interested in mystery novels now. Especially since that's what I write . . ." I added with a chuckle, raising my eyebrows for emphasis. "There are worlds of adventure inside those pages."

He devoured half of his sandwich. "Yeah, but there's even more *out here*. So what's next in our investigation?" His grin returned.

I shook my head. "Oh, no. No more investigating for you, kiddo. You were in enough danger last night."

"What? You can't sideline me now, Mom! Not when we're that close to putting the perp in the hoosegow." He held up his thumb and forefinger, inches apart, for emphasis.

I fought the urge to laugh again. One night of investigating, coupled with a little morning reading, and Parker had suddenly turned into Sam Spade. Or Philip Marlowe. Or maybe even Kojak. But any way I looked at it, my son had become a sleuthhound, or so he thought, and knowing him, he wasn't about to let it drop.

"I'll tell you what," I said carefully. "I've got to go to June's open house this afternoon. Maybe you could come with me and keep your ears open."

"Umm . . . wait a minute . . . as your sidekick, shouldn't I be interrogating suspects? Or tracking down clues? Or maybe sniffing around for something suspicious?"

"I'm sure there will be a lot of people there, and you'll probably get more information if you just act like a fly on the wall. You can learn a lot by tuning in to conversations."

He downed another spoonful of soup with a loud *slurp*. "Hmmm . . . So you want me to just stand around and listen? Sounds pretty boring, Mom."

I shook my head. "Oh, no, not at all. The best spies and investigators are people who have mastered the art of being invisible. They have the ability to eavesdrop without anyone even knowing they're there."

Thankfully, it seemed to be enough to appease him. "Okay, Mom. I see where you're going with this. It might look like I'm staring at my cell phone and texting someone, but I'll really be listening for clues. And evidence."

"Exactly," I told him as I finished off the last of my grilled cheese sandwich.

"Cool. I can do that. I guess it's still investigating."

"And it would be a big help," I guaranteed him.

Though to be honest, by the time we were leaving for the open house a half an hour later, I wasn't sure if encouraging him *had* been such a good idea. While I'd gone to my room to change clothes and clean up, Parker had donned a pair of 70s, Vegas-style sunglasses and Charlie's old stingy-brimmed fedora.

Even more surprising was when Parker unwrapped a Tootsie Pop and pointed it at me right after we stepped outside. "Who loves ya, baby? You're beautiful."

Evidently, I had been right about the Kojak reference.

I fought the urge to roll my eyes as I locked the door behind us. "Where did you find a Tootsie Pop?"

"In the back of my desk drawer."

"How old is it?"

He shrugged and stuck the Tootsie Pop in his mouth. "I dunno. But it tastes just fine."

I tried not to think about it while we walked down the driveway. "When did you ever see Kojak? Those shows were from the seventies."

"I watched reruns with Dad. They were pretty good."

I should have known.

And while Parker filled me in on some of his favorite episodes, we ambled over to June's house, and up her front walk and past the rose gardens.

But I interrupted him right before we arrived at the front door. "Okay, kiddo. Here we go. Now remember . . ."

"I know, I know, Mom. Fly on the wall. Buzz, buzz."

"There's a fly in here?" Emily's eyes flared in panic as she opened the door and greeted us.

I shook my head. "No, we were just talking about something that happened earlier."

She let out a ragged breath and passed me a marketing flyer detailing June's home. "Well, thank goodness for that, because this house is spotless and perfect. And when I say perfect, I mean *perfect*. Four bedrooms and three-and-a-half baths. Heated pool in the oversized backyard. And everything is in mint condition."

I smiled and stepped into the front entryway. "Randall and June never skimped when it came to the upkeep of their home."

She nodded. "They most definitely did not. This place is better now than it was when they moved in. So go on in, and you'll find hors d'oeuvres and punch in the kitchen."

"Thanks, Emily."

"Nice hat, Parker," she added as a young couple strolled up.

Parker responded by pointing his lollipop at her, and I could tell he was about to repeat his Kojak line. But I quickly steered him toward the hallway.

And since Emily was busy at the moment, I decided to ask her about Hedley after things slowed down. Instead, I followed Parker into the kitchen and family room area, where everyone was gathered. Right away, I spotted Gia, June, and Tiffany all chatting away in a fairly animated conversation. And since Tiffany seemed to be engaged for once, I figured it was a bad time to interrupt and drag her away. Not if I hoped to wrangle any information out of her.

So I helped myself to some punch, and turned just in time to see Betty Kraukpott parading around. She was in full attention-getting mode while she took pictures of June's house, pulling first one camera forward and then another, as she continued to swap them out from the collection she had slung across her body. She didn't even see Spencer Poe who was standing next to the fireplace, and she almost tripped right over him. Because evidently, *he* had mastered the art of being invisible, much like I'd suggested to Parker.

Spencer gave me a "knowing" nod, and I responded with a smile and a knowing nod of my own. And as the open house went into full swing, I caught glimpses of my son as he slyly wandered from cluster to cluster of people, doing an excellent job of blending into the background. Even with his hat and his Tootsie Pop. I chuckled when I realized how much he was enjoying his new "detective" role.

In the meantime, I managed to say a quick hello to most of my neighbors and did my best to stay out of the way of any potential home buyers. I had to admit, Emily had done a great job of bringing in a nice crowd. Either the people walking around were merely a bunch of lookie-loos, or June really did have a good shot at selling her house. I still found it hard to believe that she was planning to move. Especially since Randall's funeral had been mere days ago, and as they say, the body was barely even cold yet. Though in Randall's case, it probably didn't count since June had him cremated.

But that didn't stop her from giggling as she chatted away with perfect strangers and showed them around the place. Today her hair was an even brighter, more vivid red, with purplish lowlights. She was wearing a sequined evening gown and enough jewelry to be a one-woman disco ball. To tell you the truth, if I thought she'd been acting wild and bizarre the last few times I'd seen her, well, it was nothing compared to how she was acting today. I couldn't tell if she was simply blossoming into a new person, now that she was a widow, or if this was the most unique form of grieving I had ever seen in my life.

She made her way over to give me a quick hug.

"How's it going, June?" I asked her.

She giggled again. "Fabulous, darlin'. Except that dirtbag my daughter married has been a real pain in my backside."

"I'm sorry to hear that," I told her.

Of course, I immediately wondered if she was referring to Aiden driving her car the night before, since it would've been in bad shape when he brought it home.

*If* he brought it home.

"He won't take a shower," she went on. "And he won't stop playing those stupid video games, not even while I'm hosting this open house. Plus, if you can believe it, he said he won't move out after I sell the place. He said something about being a squatter, and how squatters are supposed to have rights. That boy never gets these things right. I should probably just shoot him and have him carted out of here." For a second, her eyes flared with anger, but the emotion quickly passed from her face, like rain being pushed away by a windshield wiper.

Then she giggled again and moved on to another guest.

Which meant that I should be doing the same—minus the giggling part—since I had several people I wanted to talk to. So I refilled my glass with punch and then filled a second one. Carefully balancing both glasses, I made my way to the front door and waited while Emily finished her sales pitch to another young couple.

She had changed clothes since I'd seen her leaving an empty house this morning, not far behind Hedley. Now she was wearing a black, couture suit, and the diamonds hanging from her wrists and earlobes easily rivaled June's.

She turned to me the second the couple had moved on and headed upstairs to tour the house. "Maddie! There you are!"

I gave her my sweetest smile and handed her a glass of punch. "You're doing a great job, Emily."

She stared at my mouth and her eyebrows shot up. "What happened to your lip?" Yet before I could say a word, she answered her own question with, "Oh, I'll bet Nick did that. He can be a bit rough. That means he must really like you."

I stared at her cross-eyed. "Emily, someday you and I need to have a talk about this. But not today, since you're so busy. Though I do have a question for you."

To which she responded by letting out such a loud squeal that I nearly spilled my punch.

"I knew you'd come around, Maddie! I just knew it. We'll get the papers signed and get your house on the market right away! And I'll find a new house for you. Something quite a bit smaller but with a great kitchen . . ."

I held up my hand to stop her. "Emily, I'm not selling my house."

"Oh."

"I just wanted to ask you something about June's house. As I understand it, the HOA management company sent a number of violation letters to Randall and June. Don't those need to be cleared up before the house can be sold?"

She waved me off. "Oh that? I took care of it. There won't be any problem."

I feigned surprise. "You did? How? Did you talk to Hedley?"

She laughed and took a sip of her punch. "Uh-huh, I got things straightened out with him. So no worries, Maddie. It's all taken care of."

Which meant I now understood why Emily had handed Hedley an envelope of cash. Her payment must have insured that he dropped all the HOA violations, and the house was free and clear to be sold. Meaning, he couldn't put some kind of a lien on the property.

I was about to ask more when the young couple whom Emily had just been talking to came rushing down the stairs. The man waved to get Emily's attention while the woman covered her mouth with a hand. Tears formed in her eyes.

"Umm . . ." the man started to say. "Have you been upstairs lately? To that game room?"

Emily shook her head. "Not to worry," she assured him. "I promise you that young man won't be a problem. He wasn't feeling well so he stayed in the game room. But please ignore him."

"Well . . . I, umm . . . I think . . ." the man stammered, as though he was having a hard time getting his mouth to work properly.

But the woman jumped in before he could find the words. "He's dead!" she hollered.

# Chapter Twenty-three

"Dead?" Emily and I both repeated loudly, our words echoing to the top of the wide-open, two-story entryway.

The young woman on the stairs nodded and pointed to the second floor. Then she began to openly sob.

"I can't believe this!" Emily moaned as the blood drained from her face. For a moment, I thought she was going to faint.

I reached out and took her elbow. "Take some deep breaths, Emily."

"Oh, my goodness, I knew he wasn't looking good, and I was just about to go check on him and call an ambulance if he got any worse, but I never dreamed this would happen," she blathered on as I deposited her on a chair. "This is a disaster! A complete and utter disaster. I'll never sell this house if somebody died here!"

"Maybe we should check it out first," I suggested. "It might not be too late to call that ambulance."

Without wasting another second, I left her and raced up the stairs. Naturally, I was already thinking of Aiden's secret shopping excursion the night before, when he'd bought a little bag of pills from some drug dealer. Maybe Aiden had accidentally overdosed on those very pills. Especially if they were laced with something a lot stronger and a lot more dangerous than he knew about.

*That, or someone might have murdered him*, said a little voice inside my head. Provided, of course, that he was actually dead.

But there was only one way to find out.

So I flew to the second floor like I'd practically sprouted wings, and I made a beeline to the game room. A video was still playing on the humongous, big-screen TV, and Aiden still had his hands on a game console. An empty, crushed cola can was on the floor beside his chair, along with an empty chip bag. He was leaning back in a recliner and his eyes were shut. He sat motionless, and frankly, he simply looked like he was sleeping.

Which was exactly what he might have been doing.

I nudged his shoulder. "Aiden. Wake up."

When his head lolled to the side, I placed my fingers on his wrist, trying to find a pulse.

By now a group of people had gathered at the wide entrance to the room. Oddly enough, they'd simply stopped there and crowded together, as though they didn't dare set foot inside a room where someone might have left this world and moved on to the afterlife. Instead, they all stood staring and watching me as I tried to find signs of life within Aiden's body. When I couldn't find a pulse in his wrist, I moved on to his neck. Yet no matter where I put my fingers or how hard I pushed, I couldn't detect any blood flow through his veins. And his skin was a little colder than it should have been.

"Does anyone have a mirror?" I asked the group.

Amazingly, someone produced a compact mirror, and I immediately stuck it under Aiden's nose, hoping to see some condensation to prove that he was breathing. But once again, there was nothing.

"He's dead," I finally declared to the cluster of people at the edge of the room. "Someone call nine-one-one."

And the next thing I knew, everyone had a phone out and thrust against an ear. They all started speaking at once, using a wide variety of descriptions to explain the situation to what I could only guess was a wide variety of dispatchers.

In the meantime, I just stood there in shock. I could hardly believe that Aiden was dead. Judging from his skin temperature and the pallor of his face, I knew the window of opportunity for CPR had passed. To make matters worse, I couldn't shake the idea that he had been murdered. With that in mind, I waited until all the 911 calls were finished, and then I shooed everyone down the stairs. If foul play had been involved, I knew the police would want to gather evidence in the game room, and it wasn't a good idea to contaminate the scene. Any more than it already was.

I followed along behind the crowd going downstairs, surprised by how wobbly my legs had suddenly become. I held onto the railing as I stepped onto the first floor, where I found Emily practically crumpled on the chair where I'd left her.

"It's a disaster," she murmured over and over. "All that work for nothing. I'll never sell this place . . ."

Though it wasn't Emily's sorry state that captured my attention the most. Instead, it was the man standing next to her, massaging her shoulders.

Nick Yarborough.

What in the world was he doing here?

The second he saw me, he dropped his hands and took a gigantic sidestep away from Emily. The movement broke her trance, and she glanced first at Nick and then at me, frowning.

Nick gave me an awkward smile. "Hello, Maddie, so nice to see you again."

I glared at him. "Forgive me, Nick, if I don't return the sentiment. After all, I've got you to thank for my bruised and swollen lip."

He tilted his head. "Well, you got in a few good shots yourself."

"What are you doing here, Nick?" I asked, putting my hands on my hips.

He returned his attention to Emily. "Emily and I are going house hunting, since I need a better place to live. In fact, I'm thinking of buying *this* place. Now that someone has died here, it'll be a major bargain. Probably in my price range. So I might just be your neighbor, Maddie."

"There goes the neighborhood," I said under my breath.

I glanced over to see Spencer standing nearby, and I guessed he'd probably heard the entire conversation. He squinted his eyes at Nick for a moment, almost like he was staring at him through the scope of a gun. Then Spencer skillfully disappeared into the huge swarm of people who were all headed straight for the front door. As near as I could tell, he went with them as they flew from the house like bees buzzing from a hive. Apparently, bad news really does travel fast, though not nearly as fast as a crowd who wants to get out of a house where someone has just died.

I leaned against a wall of the front entry as the throng went past. Eventually, Nick even led a very tearful Emily out and to her car, with his arm around her waist and his body practically melded onto hers.

Yet there was one person whom I hadn't seen in the herd of people making a mass exodus out of there—Parker. So when I finally saw an opening, I returned to the kitchen and family room to find him. I also wanted to make sure that June and Tiffany were okay.

But I had barely found my son and sent him home when an ambulance and a lone policeman arrived. While the paramedics went upstairs, the policeman joined June, Tiffany, and me in the kitchen. Much to my amazement, Tiffany didn't shed a single tear over the death of her husband. Instead, she stood there silently, as cold and frozen as a statue, and looking as surly as ever.

June, on the other hand, giggled and carried on like a bride-to-be at a bachelorette party. "My, my, my," she cooed to the tall, dark, and very handsome officer, a man who had clearly spent many, many, *many* hours at the station's gym. "Aren't you just the finest specimen of manhood on the planet?"

That's when the officer turned to me. "Can you tell me who found the deceased?"

I took a deep breath and tried to keep my voice steady. "It was a young couple who were here for the open house. They were looking upstairs and found Aiden dead."

"He was dead, all right," June said, jumping in. "Dead, dead, dead. Dead men tell no tales." Then she giggled and guffawed like she'd just told the joke of the century.

The policeman raised an eyebrow. "Excuse me, ma'am, maybe you could use some coffee."

"Coffee?" June went on. "I don't need no stinkin' coffee! You're all I need and all I want. Looks like you've got some handcuffs. I've never tried handcuffs. They might be fun."

"Ma'am . . ." he said with the patience of a saint. "If you don't mind . . . a man has died here today."

June blinked a few times, like she couldn't get her eyes to focus. "Who? Randall? Well, of course he's dead."

The officer crinkled his brows. "Randall? I thought the deceased's name was Aiden."

June snorted. "Aiden . . . Randall . . . they're all dead. And I would know."

"How's that?" the policeman quizzed her.

"I've been a very naughty girl." She shimmied and shook, and the sequins in her gown caught the light, reflecting laser-like flashes around the room.

I put my arm around June's shoulders and glanced at him. "Maybe I should take her to lie down."

June shrugged me off. "Only if I can take this big fella with me. What's a girl gotta do to get this guy's attention? Murder someone?"

The officer leaned closer to June. "Ma'am, what exactly are you trying to tell me? That two men have been murdered, and you had something to do with it?"

June laughed uproariously. "Of course, of course."

Shock flared in his eyes. "So you're saying you played a role in the murder of a guy named Randall? And the guy upstairs, named Aiden?"

To which June responded with more giggles and a huge grin. "Yes, yes! Take me, Officer! Take me now!" Then she held out her arms, ready to be cuffed.

I waved to get the man's attention. "Hold on here. June hasn't been herself lately. At all. She's been on some different medication since . . ."

But June pushed me out of the way. "Back off, Maddie. This one's mine. Go find your own policeman."

The officer frowned. "So tell me, Ms. . . ."

"*Mrs.* Rathburn," June supplied. "But I'm a widow. So I'm free and available." Her eyes were wild, and she seemed to be having trouble standing up.

"So Mrs. Rathburn, what role did you play in these murders you're telling me about?" the policeman asked.

June thought for a moment and then raised a finger. "I did the dirty deed! And I'd like to do it again!"

"So you're officially confessing to killing two men? You do realize I'll have to take you to jail," he said, sounding incredulous.

"You can take me anywhere," she told him, slurring her words. Her smile showed she was absolutely enraptured.

"As you wish," he said with a shake of his head. "Let's go then."

June batted her lashes at him. "Aren't you going to cuff me?"

"If you like." Then with one quick movement, he pulled the cuffs from his belt and placed them on her wrists.

She squealed with delight, while Tiffany simply remained silent, shooting daggers with her eyes.

"Wait a minute," I said, putting my hand on June's arm. "She's not actually confessing to anything. She's been on a new prescription, and I'm pretty sure she's having some strange side effects . . ."

The officer glared at me. "Thank you for your input, ma'am, but I'll take it from here."

"You don't understand," I told him. "Like I said before, June isn't herself. She doesn't mean what she's saying."

He furrowed his brow at me. "And you are . . .?"

"I'm her neighbor, Maddie Montgomery."

"Maddie Montgomery, the mystery writer?"

"Yes," I said, forcing a smile onto my face.

That's when he practically snarled at me. "I hate mystery writers. And mystery books. They never get the crime scene details right. And the idea of amateurs solving murders? Well, that's just a pain in my hind end, lady. Now get out of my way while I take this woman to jail. She just confessed to a couple of homicides."

Naturally, I wanted to raise more of a fuss. But it was pretty clear this officer wasn't going to believe a thing I said. He'd made his decision and that was that.

Needless to say, it didn't help that June had practically begged him to arrest her. And for a moment, I even wondered if he was right to do so. The June I had known for years wouldn't harm a garden spider, let alone kill her own husband. Or her son-in-law. Yet here she was, practically telling the whole world that she'd committed two terrible crimes. So like it or not, I had to admit, she was a potential suspect. Sure, she was so under the influence of *something* that I didn't think she really knew what she was saying. But didn't people usually spill their guts when they were drunk or high?

Still, even with all that, it was hard to believe that one of my sweetest neighbors could actually be a cold-blooded killer.

I watched the officer lead her out to his patrol car as I headed for home. He put her in the back seat and then talked to someone on his shoulder mic. In the meantime, I noticed the ambulance attendants hadn't come out with Aiden's body yet, probably because the place was about to be sealed off as a crime scene. With fingerprints and evidence bags and the whole works.

I shook my head, realizing what a complicated crime scene it would be, considering the number of people who had been traipsing in and out of there during the open house. In fact, it was going to be one *major* forensic nightmare. Especially when the police tried to track down everyone who had been inside the house this afternoon. I figured they'd start by questioning the neighbors and move on from there.

Of course, an autopsy would tell more of the tale. According to local laws, autopsies were supposed to be performed in the case of a suspicious death. And now that June had more or less confessed to killing her son-in-law, Aiden's death would definitely fall under the "suspicious" category. If nothing else, at least a postmortem would reveal whether Aiden had died from an overdose of some illicit drug or not. Though it wouldn't show whether he'd taken those drugs on his own, or if someone had secretly slipped him something that killed him.

When I had almost reached my driveway, I paused and sighed, and glanced back at June's house again. Yet with all the activity there, it was Gia's place down the street that caught my attention. The house was dark and closed up tight, with the blinds down and shut, like no one was home. But then I saw a crack in one of the front blinds, letting me know that someone was there after all. And whoever was peeking out continued to do so for a few seconds before the crack disappeared. With Vinnie's sideline business, I had a hunch the sight of a police car in the neighborhood probably sent his anxiety levels through the roof.

Though to be honest, I was feeling pretty on edge myself, watching as June was about to be carted away.

Because, deep down, I couldn't help but wonder if someone else was getting away with murder.

Someone who was still out there and might just want to murder again.

# Chapter Twenty-four

I wandered to the edge of my driveway, with my thoughts racing at about the speed of light. Or at least, that's how it felt anyway. Mostly because I'd just witnessed June more or less make the claim that she'd killed two men. And no matter how many times I replayed that scene in my mind, I truly found it hard to fathom. Much like I found it hard to believe that Aiden was actually dead. It all seemed so strange, considering I'd just seen him the night before, making an illegal transaction at Abbott Cove Park. And while I realized he hadn't exactly been God's gift to society, it was still sad to see a young man die before he had a chance to grow up, change his ways, and make his mark on the world.

Then there was Spencer Poe, who'd managed to blend in with the crowd and leave June's house before the police arrived. Of course, I knew he had his "quirks" when it came to government entities—which apparently included local government as well—but I was still surprised to see him sneak out using such subterfuge. Oddly enough, it would have been helpful to have Spencer around right about now, so I could bounce a few ideas off him. Because "this case," such as it was, was becoming more and more jumbled by the moment.

I shook my head and started up my driveway, but I stopped in my tracks when I spotted something at my front door. I wasn't expecting any packages, so I made a detour up the front walk to check it out. And there, propped against the door, was a large, white catalogue envelope. I picked it up and read the return address: "Haus Oversight Services." My name had been handwritten below as the recipient.

Anger instantly rose in my chest, before I even looked at the contents of the envelope. So what kind of game was Hedley playing now? After watching him in action this morning, and later hearing Emily admit that she "took care of" any outstanding HOA violations on June's house, I had a pretty good idea that Hedley was extorting money from homeowners via phony HOA violations. And if someone wanted those violations to go away—violations that could ultimately lead to a lien on their property—then they'd better pay up. Especially if they were looking to sell their house, free and clear.

So apparently, Vinnie wasn't the only one who had a disreputable sideline business. It looked like Hedley had an underhanded venture going, too, and from what I'd seen this morning, it appeared to be quite lucrative.

I opened the envelope carefully and glanced inside, half expecting to see a snake or a spider pop out. Something I wouldn't put past him, considering it was clear that Hedley had chosen me to be his next victim. After all, as a famous author, he probably thought I had big bundles of cash just lying around the house collecting dust. Money I wouldn't mind passing on to him.

Yet if Hedley wanted people to pay up, how exactly did he communicate those demands? Surely he didn't do it in a letter left on a doorstep. That would leave a paper trail and evidence that could be used in a trial. Which immediately made me wonder if he'd approached Randall for a payment. Oddly enough, other than the threat of a fine, I hadn't seen anything about it in Randall's HOA file. And Randall seemed to be pretty thorough when it came to keeping records.

No, Hedley must have had a much sneakier way of communicating to his victims.

The memory of him walking out of those houses this morning, counting his money, was enough to make me seethe. And I was practically growling when I pulled the single sheet of paper and a grainy photograph from the envelope. The handwritten words on the paper read "Proof of HOA Violation."

I was so stunned that I just stood on my front doorstep, frozen to the spot. Though I wasn't sure why anything Hedley did at this point should surprise me. Even so, there I was, gasping as I reread the words and stared at the poorly printed photo, trying to make sense of it. The foreground was full of blurry leaves, and whatever I was supposed to see through that haze of foliage was barely visible. In fact, I had to stare at it for several seconds before I realized it was a picture of my front yard and driveway. Taken from quite a height and distance. And in the middle of it all was a little section circled in red, one that showed a teeny, tiny dark speck peeking out from behind some large shrubs.

"Is that . . . a corner of my trashcan?" I wondered out loud.

And sure enough, when I examined it some more, I realized the shrubs in the photo were the very ones that concealed my trashcan from the street. And since those bushes were taller than the receptacle itself, there was only one way the trashcan could be visible.

From above.

Had the picture been taken by a drone?

It didn't seem likely, considering a drone would have been maneuvered into place to get a much better, much clearer shot. And this picture had obviously been taken through some trees. So where did it come from?

Still holding the photo before me, I walked over to my shrubs and tilted the picture up and down, trying to match the exact angle. Finally, when I thought I had it right, I looked up from where I stood. And there, way across the street and through the tree-filled island of our cul-de-sac, I saw the window that was in the direct line of sight.

A second-story window.

At Betty Kraukpott's house.

That meant Betty must have taken the picture, using a *major* telephoto lens. That also meant she was in cahoots with Hedley somehow. And now I had a pretty good idea what she'd *really* been up to on the day she'd been out walking around the neighborhoods with a camera. The camera she broke as a result of Randall's car wreck, when she was the first on the scene right before he died. She'd probably been out taking pictures for Hedley.

Yet much to my amazement, when I saw her at the mailbox yesterday, she pretended like she'd never even heard of things like HOA violation letters. When, all the while, she was secretly playing a role in the whole process.

"Of all the rotten, low-down, nasty things for a neighbor to do," I muttered.

I stared at her front walk and doorway that sported enough mold and grime and overgrowth to have its own ecosystem. I could hardly believe that she had the audacity to conspire with Hedley to create some trumped-up HOA violation against me. And probably plenty of other people.

At that very moment, I suddenly developed the fury of a fire-breathing dragon. I marched right over to her property and up the moldy walkway and past the densely packed gardens and pounded on her filthy front door.

"Maddie, I'm busy!" Her muffled voice sounded so close to the door that she must have been standing right next to it.

Like she was expecting me.

I pounded again. "Open up, Betty! I know exactly what you've been up to. Open up or I'll tell everyone in the whole neighborhood about your 'extracurricular' activities."

And the next thing I knew, she appeared at one of the floor-to-ceiling windows in her dining room and pulled a curtain aside to see me better. "Maddie, you don't understand. I can't help it. I needed the money. My blogs aren't doing so well and I can't get advertisers on board. And Hedley pays me really well."

I pushed the so-called photographic proof of my trashcan violation up against the dirty glass of the window. "How can you do something like this, Betty? To your own neighbor!"

She gave me a wan smile. "You don't know what it's like, Maddie. You've never had to work like I have."

By now steam was practically shooting out of my ears like a cartoon character. "Seriously? How do you think I wrote all those books? By sitting on my couch eating bonbons? No, I've worked hard since the day I started writing my first book. And I've been working hard ever since."

She rolled her eyes. "Okay, I can tell you're kind of mad."

"Kind of? 'Kind of' doesn't even begin to cover it, Betty. Let me ask you, did you take the same kind of concocted pictures of June and Randall's house?"

"Well . . . yes. Some. If I use the right telephoto lens, I can get a shot of their place from one of my bathroom windows. Upstairs. But you have to understand . . . Randall was mad at me a lot. And he wasn't very nice to me when he was mad."

I shook my head in disbelief. "So you think this is okay because Randall was mad at you? Are you kidding me? When *wasn't* Randall nice to you?"

"Ever since . . ."

"Yes?"

She crossed her arms. "He got sick one time and he had to go to the hospital. He blamed me for it. He said I gave him food poisoning."

"Did you?"

"Well . . . maybe . . . Okay, probably."

"And you used that to justify what you did?"

She gave me a snarky smile. "I don't see what the big deal is."

"Extortion is a pretty big deal. It's a felony, if I'm not mistaken."

"Extortion?" she gasped. "I don't know anything about any extortion. I just got paid to take pictures, that's all."

"But you were in on Hedley's scheme, weren't you? Blackmailing homeowners into paying out tons of money."

"I wasn't blackmailing anyone. Hedley just paid me for the pictures. And well, he knew how creative I was, and I could figure out how to get pictures that other people couldn't."

"So you happily went after Randall. And me. And you're telling me that you didn't know anything about this extortion scheme?"

"No, Maddie. This is the first I've heard of it. I just wanted to make some money . . . and get even with Randall."

"And me?"

She hesitated for a moment. "Umm . . . maybe . . . I guess. You were pretty snotty to me when I asked you to collaborate on a cooking blog."

"Well, if you thought I was snotty then, let me give you a heads up. If you ever do something like this to me again, you'll be hearing from my lawyer. Both you and Hedley. And by the way, try cleaning up your own yard first before you go around gathering phony evidence against your neighbors." With those words, I turned on my heel and stomped away.

And I do mean stomp. Funny how angry I got every time I had to deal with anyone associated with Mr. Hedley Haus. From his file, I was pretty sure that Randall must have felt the same way, given that he'd been locked in a perpetual battle with Haus Oversight Services. So did Randall figure out that Betty had taken the "photographic proof" that he'd requested? Maybe he'd marched home from her house exactly like I was doing now.

And maybe he'd threatened to tell the whole neighborhood what she'd been up to, much like I just did.

Behind me, I heard Betty's front door open. "Maddie, come back," she hollered. "I'm sorry. I won't take any more pictures for Hedley."

But I'd had enough. And I had no intention of dealing with Betty any more today. Especially not when I was so hopping mad that I was barely in control of myself.

As I neared the edge of my yard, I noticed that more police cars had arrived at June's house. It appeared a forensics team was now on the scene, and both the "Open House" and "For Sale" signs had been pulled from the front yard. I guess that meant her house was officially off the market. Strange how life could turn on a dime sometimes.

I marched up the driveway and into my house, still fighting to put my fury aside. It didn't help that my lip seemed to be throbbing even more after my encounter with Betty. Though the heartwarming sight of Parker tossing cat treats to Agatha and Ellery in the kitchen certainly made me feel better.

His eyes went wide when he saw me. "Wow, Mom, are you okay? You look like you're about to explode."

"That's exactly how I feel right now," I said with a sigh. "Like I'm about to explode. So I think I'll just get dinner started. Cooking always calms me down, and tonight, it's going to take a lot of calming."

"Want me to pour you a whiskey?" He flashed me his goofy grin.

Which instantly made me laugh. "Parker, you may not know it, but we don't actually have any whiskey in this house."

He raised an eyebrow. "Really?"

"Really," I said with a smile. "But some sweet tea would be nice."

"Coming right up," he said with a salute. "I'll do the brewing."

"Sounds good. I'll start making the taco fixings. And the homemade guacamole."

"Awesome, Mom."

Of course, the mere mention of the word "guacamole" set Parker's stomach rumbling loud enough for me to hear from across the room. Needless to say, I always tripled the recipe for him and his bottomless pit of a stomach. And now, as I scooped the flesh from one half of an avocado, I couldn't help but wonder if Charlie had been the same way when he was that age. Unfortunately, it was a question that would probably remain unanswered.

Parker got right to work making the tea, humming and zooming around as though *his* speed might motivate me to move faster, too. But truth be told, the only thing his less-than-transparent ploy did was make me fight the urge to laugh again. Funny, but even with all the turmoil of the day, I couldn't help but think of how much this kid made me smile, and all of a sudden I became acutely aware of how empty the house was going to be when he went off to college. Not to mention, how much I was going to miss him. Sure, we had our "teenage" moments, but Parker was generally a joy to be around. Maybe because he'd grown up a lot faster than most kids, having lost his father at such an early age. That, and he was a military brat, which meant he'd had to cope with lots of moving around during his younger years. And while it was hard on him, it also taught him to get along with people and make friends in a hurry. Something I believed played a big role in his becoming such a terrific young person, one I was terribly proud of. And I wanted to savor these last few months while he was still at home.

Of course, the only thing he wanted to savor was the food that he piled high on his plate the second I gave him the go-ahead. Then he carefully took the whole works to the table, along with a glass of sweet tea, balancing it all like he was transporting some precious cargo. He plopped down in his seat, hands poised to grab his first taco, but at least he had the good manners to wait for me before he dug in.

I slipped into my own place a few minutes later and drizzled sour cream over my tacos. "What happened to Aiden this afternoon was pretty sad."

"And strange," he added.

"Yup, that, too. Do you want to talk about it?"

Parker shrugged. "Not really, Mom. The guy was a serious loser. He didn't have a game plan for his life except to sponge off his wife. And play video games. I think he probably overdosed on pills."

I dipped a tortilla chip into some guacamole. "I'd say it's a real possibility."

Parker wiped his fingers on a napkin after he practically inhaled his first taco. "I think Tiffany figured out what a loser he was, too."

"Oh? Why do you say that?"

"She seemed pretty miffed at him today. And I heard some things while I was busy being 'a fly on the wall' at the open house. You're right, Mom, being invisible is kind of hard to do, but it really works. If you keep quiet and just keep looking at your phone, people don't even know you're there."

I smiled at my son. "Sounds like you made a good spy."

He grinned and took a chomp out of his next taco. "Uh-huh."

I added a little salt to the guacamole and tried it out on another chip. "So what did Tiffany say?"

"Well, first she was telling a friend of hers about her honeymoon. She said she and Aiden got kicked off their cruise ship."

I nearly dropped my chip. "Wow, I didn't think anyone *ever* got kicked off a cruise ship. They must have done something pretty bad."

"I guess they were taking selfies. And they got into trouble."

"Hmmm . . . for taking selfies? That doesn't sound so bad."

"Except they climbed up onto the railing to take them. They were holding onto some kind of steel beam or something and leaning over the side of the ship. Up on the ninth deck. And they got caught. I guess the cruise ship people were really upset because they did something so dangerous."

I took a sip of my tea. "I'll bet!"

"They got taken off the ship in Aruba and had to fly home on their own."

Once again, I was reminded that the pair *had* been in town on the day that Randall died. And now I knew the real reason why they'd cut their honeymoon short.

"Funny, they didn't mention that to anyone," I commented.

"Yup, and Tiffany told her friend to keep it a secret. She said she didn't want anyone to know." Parker spooned a big pile of guacamole onto his plate. "Oh, and there's one other thing, Mom."

"What's that?"

"Tiffany also said she wished she'd never married Aiden. She told her friend she made a big mistake."

And that's when I nearly choked on my taco.

# Chapter Twenty-five

That night, while I did the dishes, I couldn't help but think about the conversation that Parker had overheard at June's open house. And once again, I wondered why Tiffany and Aiden had lied about being in town on the day that Randall died. Was it out of embarrassment for being kicked off a cruise ship? Somehow they didn't seem like the types to be embarrassed about much of anything.

On top of it all, it hadn't taken Tiffany long before she realized she didn't want to be married to Aiden. Like so many young women, Tiffany had been completely caught up in the excitement of the big, glitzy wedding and probably hadn't given much thought to the marriage itself. Then, after being saddled with a husband who showed no signs of getting a job—not to mention, spent his days and nights playing video games—I had a hunch she quickly comprehended that her Prince Charming was nothing but an East Texas Toad. Meaning, her happily ever after was not happening. Not with Aiden anyway.

That made me wonder if I should move Tiffany to the top of my suspect list. Maybe she and Aiden had killed her father, believing they'd inherit a lot of money, along with a big house. But when that didn't work out, and when Tiffany finally figured out that Aiden was a "serious loser"—as Parker had put it—maybe she'd done an about-face and gotten rid of him, too.

Naturally, I also wondered if she knew about Aiden's drug habit. Somehow it seemed weird that she wouldn't. And maybe she used that drug habit to slip him a little extra of whatever he'd already been taking.

Still, the idea seemed a little implausible to me. After all, since I lived just a few doors down, I'd watched her navigate her teen years and move into adulthood. And I found it hard to believe that she had the kind of forethought and cold-blooded calculation needed to pull off the murders of the two most important men in her life. But maybe I didn't know her as well as I thought I did. For that matter, how well did we *really* know any of the people who lived in our neighborhood? News crews were notorious for interviewing neighbors who had no idea that the person living next door to them was really a sociopathic serial killer who'd been burying bodies in the backyard for over a decade.

A cold chill tingled down my spine, and I glanced out the kitchen window to the street beyond my driveway. And there, in the middle of the cul-de-sac, was Tiffany. She was pulling a black suitcase behind her as she headed toward Betty Kraukpott's house. I guessed she was planning to spend the night there, since the police and forensic people had most likely sealed off June's house, leaving Tiffany without a place to stay.

Despite myself, I couldn't help but feel sorry for her. Tiffany was now without a husband and a father, and her mother was probably spending the night in jail. Something I never, *ever* could have imagined would happen, not in a million years.

That's when it suddenly hit me—did June confess to killing Aiden just to protect her own daughter? The thought of it caught me off guard. Sure, June had seemed *extra* loopy this afternoon during her open house. But was it simply an act? I knew *I* would do almost anything to protect my own son or daughter, no matter what they did. Then again, I couldn't imagine either one of them doing something as horribly heinous as committing murder.

"I would protect you two as well," I said to Ellery and Agatha as I put plates of canned food before them on the floor. "No matter what."

I received grateful glances and quick meows before they both dug in.

Then, with Parker up in his room working on something, I decided to go to my office to work for a while, too. I checked my in-box the second I sat at my computer, and I was pleased to find emails from the freelance editors and cover designers that I'd contacted. They had all recognized my name and were dying to work on my books—meaning, it would be good for their careers, too, to list a best-selling author as a client. So I responded by asking for samples of their work, and provided I was happy with what I received, I would choose an editor and cover artist from there.

Much to my amazement, I was officially one step closer to publishing my next book independently. I never dreamed I'd be moving along this path so quickly. Though deep down I was still a little terrified, I also enjoyed the idea of choosing the title for my book, as well as the cover. Something that wasn't an option for an author in the traditional publishing industry.

And while all that was lovely, I knew I would never get this new book published if I didn't finish the rewrites on my manuscript. So I opened the file and was about to get started when Parker appeared in the doorway with a huge grin on his face.

"I've got it all set up, Mom. Your blog. Now you just need to make a video to upload for your first posting."

I blinked a couple of times and then stared at my son. "Wow . . . you got that set up already? That was fast."

He picked up Agatha, who had been hovering around his feet. "It was easy, Mom. And as soon as you have a cover for your book, I can put it on pre-order. Then your video will help you get orders in advance. Do you have any idea what you'd like to say or do for your first video?"

"Well . . . let me think . . ." I glanced back at my computer, and at my manuscript file that I had open on the screen. "Maybe I could bake a chocolate soufflé and some cookies, just like Blaze does in this new book. You've been begging me for cookies. And I think you deserve a reward for all your help with getting me set up as an Indie author."

"Cookies . . ." my son repeated, practically drooling. "Chocolate chip?"

For a second or two, I sat there flabbergasted. Here I'd just filled this child full of Mexican food, and he was already dying for cookies.

"Chocolate chip it is," I said with a laugh. "I do believe I've got enough butter and chocolate chips to complete the ingredients list."

He nodded, though his eyes were a little glazed over. "Then I'll get the camera set up tomorrow so we can film it. Maybe first thing in the morning."

"How about after church?" I added. "And a decent lunch. I'll take you out, wherever you'd like to go. Your choice. You can decide tomorrow."

"Cool . . . sounds good, Mom. I think I'll head to bed now. I'm still tired from last night."

"Sleep tight," I told him before he took off.

I was just turning back to my computer when the lockbox I'd found in Charlie's storage unit caught my eye. Figuring out who murdered Randall and Aiden wasn't the only mystery I had yet to solve. I still needed to locate the key to the box so I could find out what was inside. And I couldn't help but wonder what was so important that Charlie wanted to keep it locked up.

Then again, truth be told, the box most likely contained a bunch of business papers and bank account information. Probably nothing all that exciting. And until I found a way to open it—something short of dropping it from a second-story window—there was really no use getting worked up about it.

That's when it dawned on me that a locksmith could probably open it up in a heartbeat. Though it also occurred to me that Charlie might have stored something inside that I wouldn't want a locksmith or anyone else to see. Who knew?

But before I could think about it more, my phone started to play the theme song from Peter Gunn. As always, the lack of an identifiable phone number let me know who was calling.

"Mrs. Montgomery," I heard Spencer's gravelly voice on the other end of the line when I answered. "Quite an eventful afternoon, was it not?"

"Very eventful," I agreed.

Though more than anything, I wanted to ask him why he'd taken off from June's house like he had. But I decided to hold my tongue. After all, I knew how much he hated to leave his own home for fear some government agent might sneak in and bug the place. In fact, I also knew he'd been stretching his comfort zone lately with all that he'd been doing. So I didn't bring it up, and I just filled him in on what I'd learned about Tiffany, as well as my impressions from the open house.

"You have done an exemplary job, Mrs. Montgomery," he complimented me. "And you should know, the police are still at the Rathburn residence, and I expect they will be for quite some time. I am told that Mrs. Rathburn has not been released on bail. Nor has she phoned her lawyer. Apparently, she fell asleep and has yet to wake up. I understand the jailers are simply allowing her to sleep it off."

As usual, I was about to ask him *where* and *how* he'd gotten his information, but once again, I thought better of it.

Even so, I was still shocked to hear about June. "The whole situation is so strange," I commented.

"I concur, Mrs. Montgomery. I understand the police plan to fully interview her in the morning and see if she makes an official confession. When she is a little less . . ."

"Under the influence?" I supplied. "I think her wild behavior was nothing more than a by-product of her medication."

"I agree, Mrs. Montgomery. Which brings me to the reason why I am calling this evening. I was wondering if you would be willing to go down to the jail and talk to her. And see if she will open up to you."

Naturally, I jumped at the chance. Not only did I want to make sure that June was all right, but I was positively dying to get to the bottom of her so-called confession. Had she really meant what she said about killing Randall and Aiden? And would she remember practically throwing herself at that hunky officer, leaving him no choice but to take her in? Plus, I wanted to make sure she had a place to go if she was released, since I was pretty sure she wouldn't be allowed back in her house for a while.

"Of course I'll go visit June in jail," I told Spencer. "Right after church tomorrow. I'll let you know what I find out."

"Thank you, Mrs. Montgomery."

We had barely said our goodbyes when my phone rang again. At first I wondered if Spencer was calling me back, but when I glanced at the number, I saw this call was from Gia.

Goosebumps raced across my arms. To be honest, after what I'd secretly learned about her husband's "other" business, I wasn't exactly dying to talk to her. Not one-on-one anyway. Though I decided it was better to chat with her over the phone than to have her just show up at my door.

So I took the call.

"Maddie! What happened today was so weird, wasn't it?" She spoke in a stage whisper, like she was afraid someone might overhear her.

I could just picture her standing next to her blinds, peeking out every so often. It must have been pure torment for her and Vinnie, having the police parked just a stone's throw away. Or maybe I should say, a "diamond tennis bracelet's" throw away.

"*Weird* is the word," I agreed.

Of course, in my own mind, I wasn't only thinking of the events at June's house this afternoon. No, mostly I was envisioning all those jewels in Vinnie's trunk that had sparkled up at me in the light of my phone's flashlight.

"It's pretty sad," I went on. "That a young man like Aiden should die before he really got going in life."

"Oh, I know," she agreed. "By the way, I was wondering if you could do us a favor."

So much for smooth segues.

"Well . . . I've got my hands full here . . ." I told her, since, on principle, I generally didn't do favors for anyone operating a criminal enterprise.

"I wouldn't ask for your help but we are really, really desperate," she whined, before adding one more, "Really."

"Gia, I'm sorry, but . . ."

Her tone suddenly turned demanding. "Don't you even want to know what we need? I mean, what kind of a friend are you? Where I come from, people usually jump in and help out when someone needs a favor."

"What is it you need me to do?" I finally acquiesced, trying to sound ever so casual. Especially since I already had a pretty good idea what she wanted.

"We need you to transport a car to New Orleans tonight. That's all. I promise. I know you already told Vinnie that you weren't interested in driving for him full time, but we need you to drive just this once. We're desperate. Otherwise I wouldn't ask you. Vinnie's got a buyer who wants to look at this car in the morning, and if we don't have it there, he won't buy it."

I laughed. "Gia, I can't just take off at this time of night. I have Parker to think about."

"You could take him with you."

*Oh, how lovely*, I thought. Now they were even willing to get my son involved in their illegal activities. Obviously, it was no skin off their noses if he landed in jail.

"No, Gia," I said firmly. "I'm afraid I can't. We've got plans first thing in the morning, and right now I've got to get some sleep."

"What a rotten neighbor you are. I suppose if I ever need to borrow a cup of sugar, you'll probably just slam the door in my face." Her voice went up a few decibels. "All I'm asking for is one little favor."

"Gia, if it's so important, why don't *you* drive the car over yourself?"

And that's when she went dead silent.

For a moment, I even thought we'd lost our connection, until she came back with, "Because I'm busy tonight. Seriously, Maddie, couldn't you take this one little trip? To help us out?"

"No, Gia, I'm sorry, but I can't."

"Thanks for nothing, Maddie." Her breathing sounded heavy through the phone. "But don't you worry . . . you'll get yours . . . very, very soon." And with that, she hung up.

All of a sudden, my heart was in my throat.

Had Gia just threatened me?

# Chapter Twenty-six

With my pulse pounding in my ears, I ran downstairs and quickly made sure all my doors were locked. Then I set the alarm. I didn't even realize I was trembling until I returned to my kitchen and leaned against the counter.

I wasn't sure whether Gia's threat was credible or not, but just knowing that she and her husband were already involved in a criminal operation wasn't exactly a point in her favor. I also wondered why she'd been so insistent that I drive a vehicle for them tonight. Was it so they could lay low while there was so much police presence around? Or did they somehow find out about my late-night investigation, where I'd seen the sparkly stash they'd been transporting? Maybe there'd been a hidden camera somewhere that I hadn't noticed. And maybe they wanted me to drive one of their cars tonight because they had an accident all planned out for me. And my son. Randall's car wreck immediately came to mind, and I wondered again if Vinnie—and maybe Gia, too—had played a role in that tragic event. The mere thought of it made my stomach turn flipflops.

Unfortunately, I hadn't calmed down one bit by the time I crawled into bed. And I spent the next few hours jumping at every bump in the night. It didn't help that Ellery and Agatha practically stationed themselves as lookouts at the end of my bed and sat bolt upright a couple of times, staring with wide eyes into the dark hallway.

At three o'clock, I finally got up and checked out the whole house. Thankfully, all was well, and I found Parker snoring away in his bed, completely unaware of any danger. More than anything, I wanted it to stay that way. The mere thought of someone wanting to harm him brought out my inner mama grizzly bear.

Which only added to my insomnia.

So I wandered to the kitchen, made myself a cup of honey milk, and went back to bed. At some point, I must have dozed off, because the next thing I knew, my alarm was buzzing. I hit the snooze button a few times before I forced myself out from under the covers and got ready for church.

By the time I plodded into the kitchen, Parker was already there, looking bright-eyed and bushy-tailed—not an uncommon appearance for someone who'd gotten a full night's sleep. While I, on the other hand, dragged around and barely managed to get breakfast on the table. Though it was hardly my finest meal. At some point, I even heard Parker crunching on eggshells, which he followed with a big swig of orange juice. But at least he had the decency not to say a word about it.

After a third cup of coffee, I finally started to feel better, and I managed to get us to the church before the service started. The same church that had hosted Randall's funeral and Tiffany and Aiden's big wedding. June, of course, wasn't there today, and Tiffany hadn't shown up, either, which wasn't a gigantic surprise, considering her husband had just died the day before.

Now I wondered if Tiffany would hold Aiden's funeral here, too. It still struck me as strange that I hadn't seen her shed a single tear over the death of her father or her husband. And I also wondered whom she turned to for comfort, or for that matter, if she even needed comfort. If she had done the dirty deed herself, well, she probably wasn't deep in despair.

When the church service was over, I dropped Parker off at home and headed to the city jail to visit June. Soon I was sitting across from her at a cold, metal table in a cinder block room. Much to my amazement, the June sitting before me was not the same giggling, wild-eyed woman I'd seen all week.

In fact, tears rolled down her cheeks the minute she saw me. "Maddie, darlin', I don't understand it. I woke up with the most awful headache, and I couldn't make heads nor tails of what's happened since Randall died. It's all so horrible."

"What do you mean?" I asked gently.

"Well, I remember his death and being so overcome with grief that I could barely get out of bed. Kind of like you were when Charlie first died. I was absolutely beside myself. Plus, I remember thinking I had to arrange a funeral, and I didn't even know where to start. And that's about it."

"You don't remember all the disco songs you picked? Or the color scheme? Or the evening gown you wore with your hair dyed to match?"

She looked at me as though I'd sprouted a third eyeball in the middle of my forehead. "I had a color scheme? For a funeral? That sounds more like a wedding."

I nodded without saying a word.

"And what about my hair? When did I get all this purple and red? It's definitely not me. I didn't even recognize myself in the mirror this morning."

I gave her a small smile. "It's not your usual style, that's for sure."

She dabbed at her tears. "And I heard that I've put my house up for sale, and I'm supposed to be moving to a fifty-five-plus community. I can't believe it. I hate those places, with everything being so controlled and all the houses looking like all the others. Besides, I'd never sell my house. Not for a long time anyway. I love that place, and there are so many memories of Randall and Tiffany there . . . that I'd never let it go."

"Do you remember hosting the open house yesterday?"

She glanced at the ceiling. "I can't remember a thing. But I heard I practically threw myself at that officer on some kind of hormonal rampage. And at my age, when I don't even have any hormones raging anymore. I was so embarrassed when I saw the footage of his body cam. I couldn't believe I acted like that."

"I figured it was probably your medication that was making you so . . ."

"Crazy?" She shook her head. "Darlin', I don't know. They gave me one of my pills last night and another one again this morning. Just like I'm supposed to take them. And I haven't felt out of it. But I still have this horrible headache that won't go away."

"Is it possible you accidentally took extra doses this last week? Maybe you forgot you'd taken your medication and ended up taking it again later?"

"No, I'm sure I didn't do that. I have one of those weekly pillbox organizers with everything sectioned out. To keep track of when to take my medications."

"Hmm . . . that's interesting."

June dropped her head into her hands. "Oh, Maddie, it's all so embarrassing. I had to apologize to the police and especially to that poor officer for my awful behavior. I told them I've never acted like this before in my whole life! My lawyer's talking to the police right now, and I think I'll be out shortly. But even so, Aiden is still dead, and they're saying he might have been murdered."

"You don't think . . ."

"That I did it and don't remember? I can't imagine it. I liked Tiffany's husband. Besides, I don't even know how he died," she added with an exaggerated shrug.

"I haven't heard any details, either," I told her.

"How is my poor baby girl, by the way? I haven't been able to talk to Tiffany yet." She dabbed at her tears once more.

"I'm afraid I don't know, June. Last I saw her, she was headed over to Betty's house. I assume she spent the night there. Which brings me to another question—do you need a place to stay? Once you get out?"

She gave me a sweet smile. "That's so thoughtful of you, my dear neighbor. But my Bunco friend, Lois, invited me to stay with her. Until I can get back into my own house."

Then before we could say more, the guard interrupted and told us that time was up. So we said our goodbyes, with no hugs allowed.

I left the building feeling completely bewildered. Something had caused June to act so outlandish. Either she'd taken more of her medication than she admitted to—or realized, for that matter—or she'd developed some kind of neurological problem. Then again, maybe the grief from losing Randall really had overwhelmed her, and not only caused her memory loss, but turned her into a totally different person. Though to be honest, I've never met a grieving widow who acted like June had been acting this week.

Unless "acted" was the key word. Was it possible that June had simply been putting on an Oscar-worthy performance? Was she actually a heartless killer, one who was playing the part of an overmedicated, out of control, grieving widow? And as a result, ensured that no one would ever consider her to be a serious suspect? Last night, I wondered if she might be trying to take the rap to protect her daughter. But what if June had actually been acting bizarro in order to hide her own crimes? Now that the police were about to release her, they probably wouldn't give her a second glance when it came to searching for Randall and Aiden's killer. That is, if the police ever decided that the two had been murdered.

I was still wondering about it all when I drove back home to get my son. I pulled into the driveway to find the garage doors wide open and Parker leaning against the Continental.

"Can we take Dad's car?" he asked after I parked my SUV and joined him.

"Sure. It seems like a nice day for it," I told him.

Seconds later we had our seatbelts on, and I fired up the old automobile, appreciating the purr of the engine as I backed into the street.

"Did you decide where you'd like to go for lunch?" I asked him, thinking he might prefer a nice Mexican restaurant or even a steak house.

But I should have known better.

He flashed me his usual goofy grin. "Abbott's Big Burgers!"

I couldn't help but laugh. "Well, if that's what you want, then that's what you'll get."

I gave the Continental some gas, and we headed straight for Parker's favorite burger place. By the time we motored up to the drive-through window, I could already hear his stomach rumbling. He ordered two triple-burgers and two orders of onion rings and a large chocolate shake. My lunch choice was about a quarter of that and actually involved a few vegetables. Then, with three bags of food sitting between us on the front seat, we drove to our local park and ate our lunch at a picnic table in the bright sunshine.

"Are you ready to make a video for your blog, Mom?" he asked excitedly while he devoured his food.

"Ready as I'll ever be," I told him, trying my absolute best to sound optimistic. I really didn't want to let him down, not with all that he'd been doing to help me set up my independent publishing business.

But truth be told, I wasn't sure if I could even focus enough to make a video today. Ever since I'd visited June in jail, a million thoughts had been careening around inside my cranium, practically bumping into each other. And no matter how hard I tried, I couldn't quit thinking about Randall's murder and Aiden's death, which was most likely a murder, too. Plus, I couldn't stop wondering which of the suspects on my list had committed the crimes. Because I still hadn't been able to put the pieces of the puzzle into place, despite all my investigating. Of course, Blaze would have cracked the case by now, since clearly, she was much better at crime solving than I was. And for a moment, I even wondered what she would say to me at a time like this. I had a hunch she would tell me to listen to my instincts and put all the superfluous stuff behind me. Yet that only added to my confusion, since I couldn't shake the feeling that I'd been looking at things from the wrong perspective, and that somebody out there had done a superb job of hiding their homicidal activities.

None of which helped me figure out the "who" part of whodunit.

To make matters worse, my brain refused to let it go and let me rest. Even after we returned home, and Parker got his camera set up on a tripod while I donned an apron and pulled out the ingredients to make both chocolate chip cookies and a chocolate soufflé.

Once we were both ready to go, he gave me the signal, and I did my best to talk into the camera as I whipped egg whites and mixed and folded the various components for the soufflé. Thankfully, I'd had some training and experience when it came to being on camera, and I relied heavily on that now. Not to mention, I loved to cook so much that I could almost do it with my eyes closed.

But let me assure you, I kept them open as I smiled and looked directly at the camera lens. "As my wonderful readers know, Blaze solves most of her mysteries while mixing up some great culinary delights. And in this new book, she makes a delicious chocolate soufflé that she shares with her longtime love interest, Angus Steele. While I know many people find the secret to making a successful soufflé to be a mystery in itself, I'm here to take the danger out of it."

I saw my son nodding, and I guessed that meant I was doing a good job. Or rather, I was doing a good job of *faking* someone who was doing a good job. And somehow I managed to complete the soufflé preparations and slide the dish carefully into the oven.

"Now that the soufflé is baking," I announced, operating completely on autopilot, "I'll start making the chocolate chip cookie dough. I use a little different recipe than most, since I prefer bittersweet chocolate chips."

And on I went, blending the ingredients together with my stand mixer and making comments to the camera, until I realized that Parker was waving his arms and saying something to me.

"Mom, didn't you hear me? I've been trying to get your attention." He crinkled his brows. "I think you zoned out there for a few minutes."

"Sorry," I told him. "I'm just a little distracted."

He rolled his eyes. "I'll say. Do you know you just doubled up on the brown sugar and salt and eggs in that cookie dough?"

"I did? I had no idea . . ." I stared for a moment at the concoction that I'd been mixing together. "Doubled up," I repeated. "Sugar, salt, and eggs. Three things."

And suddenly the gears in my head started to turn like the bowl that was whizzing around and around on my stand mixer. And my brain cells finally started to work in unison, like a well-oiled machine.

"Wait a minute . . ." I murmured. "I was all wrong."

"No worries, Mom. I can edit this out. No one will ever know you messed up. But you might want to start a whole new batch of cookie dough."

I returned my gaze to the camera. Much like my soon-to-be edited video, things in this case weren't at all what they seemed. And as a mystery writer, a person who had researched and studied crime and criminals, I had missed something that should have been completely obvious to me.

But at least I was no longer in the dark.

Because, right at that moment, I knew exactly who had murdered both Randall and Aiden.

# Chapter Twenty-seven

Once I finally realized the truth, I couldn't believe I hadn't seen it sooner. Especially when it was as clear as the focus on Parker's camera. Not only had I figured out who had committed two murders here in Abbott Cove, but I also had a pretty good idea why.

Now all I needed to do was trap this killer and prove their guilt once and for all. Fortunately, I knew how to do just that, thanks to a scene I'd written in one of Blaze's earlier books. It would be the ideal strategy for putting a murderer behind bars and making our neighborhood safe once more. And the sooner I put my plan into place the better.

Before the culprit had a chance to kill again.

But first I had to get Parker out of the house—and *keep* him out for a while—so *he* wouldn't be the next victim. Thank goodness I had the perfect pretext—I simply sent him to the grocery store for more chocolate chips and butter.

And a *whole* lot of other stuff.

Including some truly obscure items.

His jaw dropped when I handed him the gigantic list. "Seriously, Mom? Custard powder, tapioca pearls, and freeze-dried grapes? And Mering . . ."

"*Mer-rang* powder," I pronounced correctly for him.

"Huh? I've never even heard of half this stuff. And this is a really big list. It'll take me forever to find all these things."

"And don't forget you'll have to go to two different stores to get it all."

"Mom, are you kidding me? You're acting really weird. Did you have an aneurysm or something?"

Normally I would've laughed at his aneurysm comment, because I was pretty sure he had no idea what an aneurysm was. But today, I just let it go.

"I'm fine," I told him as I handed him plenty of cash. "But you'd better get going, so I'll have all the ingredients I need to finish making cookies for you tonight."

"All right," he said, gathering his keys and wallet. "But when I get back, we're going to have a long talk about the way you've been acting."

"Sounds good. And no matter what happens, always remember that I love you," I added just as he was walking out the door.

That's when he stopped and stared at me. "I love you, too, Mom. So what's going on here? Are you dying or something?"

I waved him off. "No, no, no! Now get out of here! I'll see you later."

I managed to keep a smile on my face until he left with a frown on his own. But I dropped the act the second I heard his car drive off. To be honest, I didn't think I'd really convinced him that everything was all right. But it didn't matter, because, by the time he got back, I knew I'd have the evidence I needed to convict a killer. And I'd even have the felon shooed out the door before Parker ever set foot inside the kitchen again.

Then I would contact the police with my proof. Plus I'd give them everything else I'd learned from my investigation, to make sure the killer got hauled off to the "hoosegow," as Parker had put it.

Needless to say, my entire plan wasn't without risk, considering I'd never *actually* done anything like this before. Though I'd certainly written scenes like this plenty of times in Blaze's books. But in that case, as the author, I had complete control of the outcome. Whereas here in the real world, who knew how much control I would have? Especially when I would be going head-to-head with a very clever criminal.

But sometimes a girl just needs to take a giant leap of faith to catch a neighborhood killer. So I took a deep breath and sent a text, using the precise words that I knew would provoke an instantaneous response. Then I set out two goblets filled with red wine—being careful to wipe my own fingerprints off of one glass—and went in search of items I could use for self-defense. Just in case. A pizza cutter, a chef's knife, a rolling pin, a meat fork, cooking spray, and the ridiculously heavy lid to my cast-iron casserole dish. I arranged everything on the counter to look sort of casually placed, though I kept it all within reaching distance.

Of course, I didn't really believe that I would need any of my makeshift weapons. Not when I knew the killer preferred to secretly drug people as opposed to using other, more violent means to murder. And if there was one thing I'd learned from all my research into the criminal mind, once a murderer found a method that worked for them, they stuck to it. Which meant the odds of my needing some kind of self-defense apparatus were slim to none.

Then as soon as I had everything in place, I checked the battery level on Parker's camera, and I scooted it and the tripod next to a floor-to-ceiling column, leaving the whole setup nicely concealed. I had barely set it on "record" when a car pulled up in my driveway, almost to the garage door.

Nick's car.

The very car I had ridden in on the night of our ill-fated date.

I took another deep breath and tried to stay calm. But I quickly gave up on that idea since I soon had enough adrenaline coursing through my veins to make my heart pound out a rumba beat—probably loud enough to be heard on camera. Even so, I at least wanted to give the *impression* that I was relaxed. So I turned and peeked in the oven to check on the soufflé. Then I carefully shut the oven door just as I heard my kitchen door open. Footsteps sounded on the hardwood floor.

"Hello, Maddie. Glad to see you finally came around."

I turned to see Emily standing there, in all her perfectly polished, not-a-hair-out-of-place glory. Her huge smile was almost blindingly bright.

I gave her my most nonchalant look. "Actually, Emily, I've changed my mind. I thought we could chat about it over wine and chocolate soufflé. I've got it baking in the oven and it's almost ready."

"What!" Her smile turned to a scowl so fast I was pretty sure she set some kind of a land speed record. "What do you mean, you've changed your mind?"

"Oh, you know how writers can be. We're a pretty scatterbrained bunch. Anyway, yes, I've changed my mind.

"But you just texted me that you wanted to sell your house," she seethed.

"Yes, I know. I did. Silly me." I laughed and rolled my eyes, doing my best to push her buttons. "For a moment there, I *really* did want to sell my house. But that moment passed in the time it took for you to get over here. Thank God I came to my senses, and I completely decided against it. In fact, I've finally realized that I never, ever, *ever* want to sell my house. Because I'm never, ever, *ever* going to move."

Judging from the way a vein popped out on her forehead, I knew my words were having the exact impact that I'd been hoping for. Because they were making her mad. Murderously mad. Which also meant my plan was working.

She shot daggers at me with her eyes. "But I brought the papers for you to sign. To put this house on the market."

I feigned surprise. "Really? Wow, that was quick! I thought it usually took a while to get those papers put together. If I didn't know better, I'd say you had them all ready to go. Long before I texted you."

"I'm good at my job," she said through clenched teeth.

I shrugged. "I'm sure you are, Emily. But it's my house and I'll decide what to do with it." I took a sip from one of the wine glasses and pushed the other glass toward her. "And I'm not selling. After all, you said it yourself, I *do* have the perfect house."

"Don't play games with me, Maddie. I've had a really bad week. I lost out on a small fortune from a very big house sale, all because that moron, Aiden, up and died on me. Did you know, I already had a buyer lined up for June's house? And the man, some big-time exec, and his family bailed on me the minute they saw the police tape. But since your house is so similar, and in the very same neighborhood, I know they'll jump on it the second it's for sale."

I shook my head and smiled sweetly. "That's a shame, Emily. It looks like you'll have to find another house for them."

"Nothing doing, Maddie. There *are* no other houses like yours. Or June's. So sign the freaking papers. And sign them now!" She *swacked* the papers onto the counter and shoved them toward me, along with a pen, scooting my wine glass out of the way as she did. "I promise you'll make loads of money on the sale." She took a drink from her own wine glass and set it near mine.

"And you would, too, right?"

"Most definitely. I always make a killing. Why else would I sell houses?"

I gave her a smile that absolutely oozed with saccharine. "I'm so happy for you, Emily, but I'm still not selling. Now please excuse me while I check on my soufflé. You're going to love it." Then I turned my back on her, giving her plenty of time to do what I was so sure she would do.

"Parker's gone, right?" she asked quietly.

I opened the oven door and glanced inside. "Ummm . . . yes, he is . . ."

Emily snickered. "So let me guess. This is the moment when I'm supposed to put something in your wine glass, right? Drugs? Poison? Maybe the same thing that's been making June so loopy? And then you shoo me out the door and save the glass for the police? The one with my fingerprints on it?"

Her words chilled me to the bone, even with all the heat blasting out from my oven. I thought I'd been ready for every contingency, but I never dreamed Emily would figure out my plan. This absolutely *never* happened to Blaze.

I gently closed the oven door and turned to face Emily once more. "I have no idea what you're talking about."

That's when she cackled the quintessential villain's laugh. "Oh, please, what do you take me for? I know a setup when I see one. Really, you're using the old 'turn your back on the wine glass' trick?"

"Why would you even think such a thing?" I asked, hoping my voice didn't sound nearly as shaky as I suddenly felt.

"Because you used that ploy in a book you wrote ten years ago," she sneered. "*A Villainous Vintage*? That's where Blaze left a couple of wine glasses on the counter and turned away for a minute, because she knew the killer couldn't resist dropping poison into Blaze's glass. Especially after Blaze made her so mad that the killer was flat-out dying to murder her, too. And once the poison was in the wine glass, Blaze had all the evidence she needed to convict the killer who'd been poisoning people all over town. Do you think I don't know what you're up to?"

My mouth fell open wide. "You *read* my books?"

"Yes, I read your books. And I must say, it's an added bonus for me to sell a house owned by a famous mystery author. I'm going to charge extra for this place."

Okay, I have to admit, I did *not* see that coming. Which meant I needed to come up with a new strategy. And fast.

I stared at her. "Emily, why in the world did you just compare yourself to a killer in one of my books? And why did the thought of putting something in my wine glass even cross your mind?" I asked, setting the hook and getting ready to reel her in.

Or so I thought. For a second or two anyway.

Naturally, my perspective on the situation changed the second she pulled a handgun from her purse and pointed it right at me.

I felt my eyes go wide. "You brought a gun?"

"Of course I brought a gun. To make sure you signed on the dotted line. Ironic, isn't it? Here you are, trying to set me up, and in doing so, you only set up yourself." She flipped off the safety and cocked the gun in one smooth motion.

I gasped at the sight of the pistol, as well as her proper use of the word "ironic." "Hold on a minute, Emily. You've never murdered anyone with a gun before. Everyone knows that a killer always uses the same MO."

This made her laugh again. "You only *assume* that I've never murdered with a gun. For all you know, I might have shot dozens of people."

Again, I did not see that coming.

"Have you? Shot people?" I asked, trying to stall her.

At least until I could figure out what to do next.

She waved the gun in the air. "Not the point, Maddie. No, the real point is that you've completely underestimated me. I know how you operate, and I was always one step ahead of you. And I knew I could trip you up when I came over here. I simply had to change a few things."

"You mean, like changing your usual method of murdering people? From poisoning with drugs to shooting someone with a gun," I sputtered. "But poisoning is still your main Modus Operandi, right? After all, you murdered Randall by putting an extra dose of Digoxin in his coffee, correct?"

"It was so easy. And, I might add, quite ingenious. I found his medication in the medicine cabinet, and I called in a refill for his prescription. Then I told the drugstore that I was picking it up on his behalf. All I needed was his date of birth, and I already had that."

"So you only dosed him once? Or did you dose him more than that?"

All the while I was wary of the minutes that were quickly ticking by. Minutes that meant Parker would be headed home before long. And if Emily was willing to shoot me, she probably wouldn't hesitate to shoot my son.

Though at the moment, she was far too busy bragging about her brilliant killing skills to actually pull the trigger. "It took several doses," she went on. "But perseverance paid off. And I knew an overdose of Digoxin would mimic a heart attack. Which wouldn't be a big surprise to anyone."

"Because everyone knew Randall had a bad heart," I said with a nod as I managed a quick glance at my array of weapons on the counter. While they would all work quite nicely up close, they were absolutely worthless against a gun from a few feet away.

Meaning, never bring a meat fork to a gunfight.

So I just kept on talking and stalling. "And after Randall died, you convinced June to get some medication from her doctor. To take the edge off her grieving. Or so you said. But that's when you started drugging her with something else."

"Absolutely inspired, wasn't it?" Emily flashed me a wicked smile. "June didn't know the difference, because she had no idea what to expect from her new prescription. And the drugs I gave her on top of her own made her positively bonkers. And so very pliable. She was so out of it that I'm not sure she even realized she'd signed the papers to sell her house."

"Because that's all you were really after, wasn't it? You wanted to sell their house and make a ton of money."

She laughed. "Well, of course. And since I already had a client who was looking for a house exactly like theirs, it was supposed to be a quick and easy sale."

"So why bother hosting a big open house? If you already had a buyer?"

"For show. Besides, it never hurts to have a bidding war on a property. Especially when I knew I'd have your house as a backup, since I had no doubt you'd be listing it soon. It all helps me pay for my very lavish lifestyle. And believe me, I do pay my own way. I don't believe in out-and-out robbing people. That would be wrong."

"How nice. A killer with a conscience," I murmured. "And of course, Hedley's fees weren't cheap, either, were they? Funny, but when I saw him counting a bundle of cash as he was leaving an empty house—and then I saw you walk out shortly afterward—I thought *he* was blackmailing you. I thought you were the *victim* in the situation. But you weren't, were you? You were simply paying him to harass homeowners with outrageous HOA violations. Maybe fine them and get them really good and mad. And that's why you thought I'd be putting my house up for sale before long."

Her eyebrows rose a quarter of an inch on her botoxed forehead. "So the great mystery writer has caught on. My, my, my, you've been a busy girl." She chuckled and started to use her gun as a pointer. "Do you know the number one thing that people say when they get slapped with all kinds of ridiculous HOA violations?"

I nodded. "They say they're going to move to a neighborhood without an HOA."

"And once homeowners are really good and mad, I always make sure I'm right there to help them sell their house in a hurry."

I stole a quick glance at the clock, and my heart took off racing, thinking of Parker pulling up in the driveway before long. "But Randall didn't cooperate, did he? Instead, he went to the HOA board and complained, and you were afraid he was about to uncover the whole scheme, weren't you?"

Rage washed over her face. "Randall was a pain. He was like a dog with a bone. He was going to ruin everything. So he had to go."

"The one I can't figure out is Aiden. Why did you kill him? It seems like that worked against you."

She shook her head. "Even the most brilliant among us make mistakes sometimes. I only drugged his cola enough to make him sick, so I could have him hauled away by ambulance. Because he refused to leave the house on his own, and I couldn't think of another way to get him out of there. I still can't believe he died."

"That's because you didn't know he was already abusing drugs. And you essentially overdosed him."

Her eyes flared for a moment. "So that's it. You can imagine my upset. It was so awful for me."

"I'll bet. You kind of shot yourself in the foot there, didn't you?" Needless to say, I instantly regretted using the word "shot," the moment it left my mouth.

Thankfully, she didn't seem to notice.

She polished the top of the gun with the sleeve of her suit. "And after I worked so hard to get that listing, too. But now you will sign these papers, and then we're going for a little car ride. Don't worry, Maddie, I'll leave your body where it will be found right away. So you won't have all that ugly decomposition. And you'll still look nice for your funeral."

"Are you kidding? You'll never get away with it."

"Of course I will. That's why I brought Nick's car. Everyone will see it in your driveway. And plenty of people know that he attacked you. Besides, this is his gun that I took from his apartment. I'm going to leave it close to your body. Then he'll take the fall and no one will suspect me of anything."

"I'm not signing." I took one more glance at my self-defense stash on the counter.

Emily motioned to me with the gun. "Sure you will. Or I'll shoot Parker whenever he shows up."

"You wouldn't . . ."

She gave me a sickly sweet smile. "You know, killing you is going to be a pleasure, Maddie. I've been through so much, and yet, do you know what was the worst part of it all? Nick liked you best. The only man I've really been attracted to in years, and here he was, coming on to you."

Despite myself, I couldn't help but laugh. "If you're here to kill me because you think Nick wanted me, well, I hate to break it to you . . . but there's a *very* long list of women that he's been chasing."

Okay, in all honesty, it probably wasn't the smartest thing in the world for me to say. But when she gasped, I managed to grab the heavy lid of my cast-iron casserole dish and hold it up like a shield, barely a split second before my unfortunate words triggered her to pull the trigger. The bullet hit the lid, making a deafening *ping* sound as it ricocheted off and hit Emily in the shoulder. She screamed and dropped the gun and doubled over.

But before she could go for the gun again, I was beside her, wielding that cast-iron lid like a superhero swinging a sledgehammer. I coldcocked her in the back of the head and dropped her like a sack of potatoes.

"Never forget!" I yelled at her inert form on the floor. "Every good kitchen is loaded with lethal weapons!"

# Chapter Twenty-eight

Mere seconds after I'd flattened Emily, Spencer Poe and my son came bursting through the door.

Spencer was brandishing a firearm that looked a lot like the one James Bond had carried in the movies. "Are you all right, Mrs. Montgomery?"

I smiled and pointed my heavy casserole lid toward a motionless Emily on the floor. "Yes, thank you. I'm fine. *More* than fine. I'm happy to say, I caught the murderer and got proof of her crimes. I think you'll find it all on camera."

Spencer lowered his gun. "I am quite relieved to hear that. If the Colonel were still with us, he never would have forgiven me if anything had happened to you. Though I *am* rather surprised to learn that Ms. Lockheed is our murderer."

He reached down to check that Emily was still breathing. Her moan let me know that she was.

"Emily had us fooled, all right," I told Spencer as I heaved the heavy lid to the counter. "I figured it out when I was making cookies for Parker, and I accidentally doubled up on three of the ingredients. And that's when it hit me—three other instances of doubling up. The first with Randall's Digoxin, the second with whatever illegal pills that Aiden was on, and the third with June's new prescription. In essence, the three of them had unknowingly been dosed with something on top of what they were already taking. That just didn't sound like a mere coincidence to me. Instead, it sounded like someone really knew what they were doing when it came to secretly drugging people. In fact, it sounded like somebody's regular MO. I suspected Tiffany at first, but I just didn't think she'd kill both her father and her husband. And then drug her own mom. Especially since she'd complained that she didn't like her mom 'being all weird and drugged up.'"

I paused for a breath before I continued. "But then it finally dawned on me—Emily had access to them all. On a regular basis. And she could have drugged each one. But the clincher came when I realized that I'd been looking at Emily's encounter with Hedley all wrong. He wasn't blackmailing *her*. *She* was paying *him* to harass homeowners. As part of a scheme to convince people to sell their high-dollar homes. She made tons of money from each sale, and then made even more money when she found a new house for those homeowners who'd been harassed. It was extremely lucrative for her."

Spencer nodded. "Excellent work, Mrs. Montgomery. I shall be anxious to hear the details later, after the police have finished with their part. Thanks to you, we can trust they will view Randall's death as a homicide now. I was right to choose you to investigate, and I am impressed by the way you saw through Ms. Lockheed's ruse. It appears she was rather skilled at deception."

"Yes, she was," I added. "And the more I thought about it, the more I realized that Emily was always there when we had a neighborhood event. Even though she didn't *live* in our neighborhood. She pretended to be everyone's friend when she was really just trying to drive us to sell our houses. And make money from us."

"And no doubt, Randall was not cooperative."

"He fought it with everything he had," I added while Spencer dialed 911.

The whole time, Parker just stood there, staring at me with wide eyes. "Mom . . . you are so awesome. You're like all the famous detectives rolled into one. But why did you send me away?"

I shook my head. "Sorry, kiddo. I couldn't have you in danger, too."

He crinkled his brows at me. "But I missed all the action!"

"Well, you can see the whole thing on video," I told him.

Then I glanced from Parker to Spencer. "By the way, how did you two just happen to show up right at this moment?"

Spencer smiled at my son. "Young Parker came over and alerted me to the possible peril. He thought your behavior was highly erratic and suspected something was amiss. He feared you might be in trouble."

Parker grabbed his camera and started to rewind the video. "Yeah, Mom, things were pretty weird when I walked out. But they got even weirder with the whole 'I love you' thing. By the time I finished shopping at the first grocery store, it was really starting to bug me. I mean, sure, Mom, I know you love me and everything, but we're not all gushy about it."

Which made me laugh. "Well, thank you, gentlemen, for coming to my rescue. But as you can see, I can take care of myself."

Though to be honest, if anyone had asked me about that a few minutes ago, my response might have been a little different.

Parker leaned against the counter to watch the video, and I turned to Spencer. "Funny, but when I woke up this morning, I thought I was in more danger from Gia and Vinnie."

He looked at me like my father used to look at me. "Is there any particular reason you were concerned about the Delvecchios, Mrs. Montgomery?"

That's when I told him about the phone call from Gia the night before. I was about to say more when Parker finished reviewing the video and glanced up at me with a huge grin on his face.

"Mom, you've got some serious superhero skills, the way you swung that lid around. You really KO'd Emily."

Talk about gushy. Or at least, gushing. Funny, but all of a sudden it was all I could take. Because this was one cast-iron slinging, superhero mom who needed to sit down for a moment or two. So I sank into a chair in the adjoining family room until an ambulance and some uniformed police officers arrived. They were followed by a plainclothes detective. A very handsome plainclothes detective, I might add. One who wasn't wearing a wedding ring. Though I barely noticed since I was too busy being mesmerized by his navy blue eyes and dark wavy hair. Not to mention, his broad shoulders that were about chin level to me.

And if I was reading the signals right, he appeared to be a little mesmerized himself.

Was this the beginning of a "beautiful friendship," aka, a romance, with an esteemed member of the Abbott Cove Police Department? Much like Blaze had a relationship with Detective Angus Steele?

Though I had to admit, the whole idea was truly cliché, given that nearly every heroine in nearly every mystery series ever written has a relationship with a police detective.

Then again, who was I to buck tradition? Especially with a man named Remington Reagan? Personally, I took that as a sign from God.

In any case, much like Blaze, I served chocolate soufflé to the dear detective, along with everyone else who was there. With the exception of Emily, of course. Needless to say, I drew the line at feeding someone who had just tried to murder me. Besides, Emily was still pretty groggy as she was being loaded onto an ambulance gurney. It was the only time I'd ever seen her with her hair messed up. I guess I was finally seeing the *real* Emily.

At some point, Spencer touched my arm and said, "Thank you, Mrs. Montgomery. Thank you for catching Randall's killer."

"Anytime," I murmured, feeling very satisfied to know there really was justice in this world.

Spencer pretty much vanished after that.

And naturally, right after Emily was carted away, I said yes to Detective Reagan's offer of dinner later in the week. This time, I figured I might even buy a new dress.

I also handed over the video of Emily's confession and attempted murder of yours truly, though not until my super-smart son had made a few copies for me to put away for safekeeping.

Later, after everyone had left, and Parker and I had barely finished dinner, we heard a commotion out in the street. And there, in front of Gia and Vinnie's house, was a collection of black SUVs and people walking around in navy windbreakers with the letters "FBI" emblazoned on the back. Before long, they even brought Gia and Vinnie out one at a time, handcuffed, and put them into separate vehicles.

I had a hunch their house would be up for sale very soon, and ironically enough, Emily would be out of commission for this one. Both literally and figuratively.

I glanced down the street to see June and Tiffany back at their house again. June had her arm around her daughter, and I prayed they would both recover from losing their respective husbands. Time would tell.

After the excitement in the street had died down, I finally finished baking cookies for Parker, and he seemed overjoyed to get them.

He even took a bunch to school the next day, and he called me during his lunch break. "Mom, it's really weird, but Mr. Yarborough didn't show up for school today. The police are looking for him."

Of course, that meant another visit from Detective Reagan, much to my delight. When he showed up, I served him coffee and cookies in my living room as Agatha and Ellery cuddled up beside him. Something he didn't seem to mind in the least as he questioned me about my one and only unfortunate date with Nick.

I told him everything that had happened and ended with, "I believe he moved on after that. The last I saw him, he was with Emily."

"And Emily was jealous over his attraction to you."

"So she said. Just as she was pointing her gun at me and about to pull the trigger. It makes me wonder if Nick was another one of her victims, though I'm not sure she'd kill the man she loved. Still, you never know, since she was planning to frame him for my murder. It's also possible that one of his other jealous girlfriends bumped him off. Or maybe he simply skipped town to avoid a whole *pack* of angry women." I shrugged and gave him the names and descriptions of the women who had approached Nick the night I had dinner with him.

Afterward, Detective Reagan closed his notebook and fixed his gaze on me. "So, Maddie, are there any *other* men in your life that I need to know about? Before I try courting a woman of your intelligence and beauty? Not to mention, your highly effective self-defense skills?"

I gave him my sweetest smile and answered in my best Southern drawl. "Just a late husband whom I loved dearly, a teenage son whom I *love* dearly, and an almost-elderly neighbor who may or may not be a former CIA agent."

His eyes twinkled. "Doesn't sound like anything I can't handle."

"And how about you? Any Emilys in your life? Or other women I should know about?"

He laughed and shook his head. "Nope, thank God. There is a late wife whom I loved, and two grown daughters that I'm crazy about. But I'm afraid I don't know anyone connected to any spy agencies. At least, none that I'm aware of."

"Tell me," I said, "what will happen to Hedley?"

He slipped his notebook back into his suit jacket. "We're looking at Hedley for accessory to murder. It all depends on what he knew and when he knew it. But you'll be glad to know that he's under investigation and your HOA has dumped him. They're looking for another management company now."

I sighed and stared deep into his eyes. "My, my, Detective Reagan, but you say the sweetest things."

"Please call me Remy."

He left right after we made plans for dinner the next night. But not before he took my hand and put it to his lips.

I could still feel his gentle touch long after he drove away. Seconds later, Evinrude showed up with my mail.

"Thank you, little drone," I said to his winking face. "And thank you, Spencer."

Then I went to my office to work on my manuscript rewrites. I was still working when Parker came home.

He had barely walked in when his eyes turned to Charlie's lockbox. "How come you haven't opened the mini-safe yet?"

I shook my head. "Sorry, kiddo, but I couldn't find the key."

He stared at me incredulously. "Umm . . . Mom . . . I just watched you pick the lock of a car trunk the other night. Can't you pick the lock of that box?"

Well, *duh.* Of course I could.

And so I did.

Then I put the box on my desk and opened the lid slowly, feeling a little nervous about what I might find inside. What I saw took my breath away. Okay, maybe it wasn't filled with gold bars like Parker had originally suggested, but it did hold a handful of gold coins.

Very old gold coins.

"Wow, Mom," Parker breathed over and over. "This is amazing. Where do you think Dad got these?"

I pulled out a folded piece of dingy, yellowed paper, one that looked almost as old as the coins. There I saw what appeared to be poorly drawn landmarks. And some kind of directions. But to what?

"Is that what I think it is?" Parker gasped.

"Well . . . if you think it's a map, then I'd say yes, it *is* what you think it is."

And for a moment, neither one of us could speak.

"Mom, I think Dad was on some kind of a treasure hunt."

I nodded, still dumbfounded. "Parker, I think you're right. And something tells me that we shouldn't breathe a word of this to anyone. Not until we know more."

"You got it, Mom. But I have one question."

"Let me guess. You wonder if we should go in search of this treasure."

"Yup, Mom. I think we should do it for Dad."

"Sounds dandy to me."

Funny, but a week ago, I saw my life as I knew it coming to an end. But now I realized it hadn't ended at all. Instead, I was simply stepping into a whole new chapter. Not only was I mere months away from releasing my first independently published novel, but I'd also gotten enough material from the case I'd just solved to write another new mystery. And I intended to do just that, when I wasn't busy tracking down some treasure via the map my late husband had left. Or possibly solving another murder mystery or two, now that I had my first real case under my belt.

So, all in all, I'd say life was looking pretty good for me, Maddie Montgomery, mystery writer and amateur sleuth.

To top it off, I think Blaze McClane would approve.

THE END

# About the Author

Cindy Vincent is not a native Texan, but as the saying goes, she got there as quick as she could. She is the award-winning author of the Buckley and Bogey Cat Detective Capers, and the Tracy Truworth, Apprentice P.I., 1940s Homefront Mysteries. She is also the creator of the Mysteries by Vincent murder mystery party games and the Daisy Diamond Detective Series games for girls. She lives in Houston, Texas with her husband and an assortment of fantastic felines.

CPSIA information can be obtained
at www.ICGtesting.com
Printed in the USA
BVHW070901050122
625453BV00003B/174